Timi

Dandelion
Book One

Dandelion

Book One

First Edition - August 2016

Copyright © 2016 Timothy R. Jarvis (Timi)

All Rights Reserved

No part of this book may be reproduced in any form, by photocopying or by any electronic or mechanical means, including information storage or retrieval systems, without permission in writing from the copyright owner of this book.

Front cover photo: VegaStar Carpentier
Cover artwork: Timothy R. Jarvis

CONTENT WARNING:
THIS BOOK CONTAINS SCENES WITH SEX, VIOLENCE, SEXUAL VIOLENCE, AND PROFANITY.

www.TimiJarvis.com

In memory of
Carlos Gutierrez-Sáenz,
and, as always, for you.

Prologue

September, in the not too distant future.
Cherry Point U.S. Air Force Base near Havelock, North Carolina

"Hey, Billy-Joe, ain't this just perfect?"

Billy-Joe looked at his girlfriend, Billy-Jean. It still tickled them pink that they were both called Billy-Something.

She had the most gorgeous crystal-blue eyes he had ever seen and long, slightly wavy, strawberry blonde hair. Drop dead gorgeous, he'd thought when they'd met for the first time—and now they'd been together all summer. Unbelievable!

"Sure is, Billy-Jean. It just don't get no better."

An old song by a guy the radio DJ called 'The Boss' was playing on the truck's FM. Kind of sad lyrics, but beautiful in a nostalgic, down-to-earth way.

They'd parked Billy-Joe's truck just outside the perimeter fence of Cherry Point Air Force Base. Billy-Joe had bought the truck with the special employee deal from the car plant where he worked. No way a nineteen-year-old kid would have been able to buy a brand new truck on his salary otherwise.

Billy-Joe had plans. He reckoned that if he worked hard, put in overtime, and never complained about working the late shift, that within a few years he would make floor supervisor. Then he could put down a payment on a house in Havelock and ask Billy-Jean to marry him. Then they would set about raising a family.

"Hey, Billy-Jean. We can call our first son 'Billy the Kid', just like the guy in that western film. How about that!"

"Shush, Billy-Joe, you gonna make me cry!"

Billy-Jean was seventeen. She was still at high school but knew that college was never going to be part of her future. Just not smart enough she'd figured out a long time ago. But she'd found a good man: handsome in a lanky kind of way, with curly brown hair and broad shoulders. He had such beautiful dark brown eyes. Billy-Joe had said that his great-great-great grandparents—he wasn't sure how many greats it was—had come to North Carolina from the south of France. Probably Paris she reckoned, but there again that was the only French place she knew the name of. Anyway, he was in love with her, and that was the most important thing of all. That was all that mattered.

An F-16 jet took off from the base, its engines screaming at full throttle as it roared into the sky.

Billy-Joe and Billy-Jean loved this place. It was here in the back of Billy-Joe's truck that they'd made love for the first time. It had been an evening like this earlier on in the summer. The old guys who sat outside Ben's Liquor Store said it had been the longest, hottest summer in North Carolina for as long as they could remember. Though you couldn't trust those guys—they would make up stories just to kid themselves that they could remember anything at all!

Another F-16 lifted.

"Billy-Joe, we're going to be together forever, aren't we?"

"Sure thing, Billy-Jean. Forever and ever."

"I want to lay on the hood and watch the stars come out."

"Sure, me too," Billy-Joe said, although to be honest, he would have rather climbed into the back of the truck with her. But hey, no point in rushing things.

He grabbed a blanket from behind the driver's seat, jumped out of the truck, and draped it over the hood.

They took their shoes off. No way was he going to let the paint job get ruined. Billy-Joe knew all too well how much work went into getting that high-gloss metallic finish.

Billy-Jean and Billy-Joe lay on the truck's hood holding hands and listening to the FM radio.

The DJ played another song from The Boss.

"He's good isn't he, Billy-Jean?"

"Yeah, maybe my gramps has some of his stuff at home—or we

could grab it off the net. Cool voice."

The F-16's were lifting every few minutes or so. Even some of the big B-27 bombers followed them into the sky. Billy-Jean's dad worked at Cherry Point, so she knew the names of all the different planes.

The moon was going to be almost full that night. They could see its silvery glow behind the hills in the east.

Stars came out. At first one by one, then by the dozen, until they could see the Milky Way stretched right across the whole of the state.

"Hey look!" Billy-Jean said. "A shooting star. Make a wish Billy-Joe. But no telling!"

"Everything I wish for is right here beside me. Best thing that ever happened to me."

"Me too... Look, another one! My turn to wish. Wow! Look! It flew across the whole sky! And there, another one. No, over there!" Billy-Jean pointed to the other side of the sky.

The shooting star she'd seen headed straight towards one of the other ones. It only took a second—then they crashed into each other in a huge fireball that lit up the sky.

"I don't believe it! Cool!" Billy-Joe said.

Maybe for the blink of an eye they saw the missile that struck Cherry Point Air Force Base.

There was a flash of light as the Air Force base, Billy-Jean, Billy-Joe, their truck, and all their dreams and plans were vaporized by the thermonuclear explosion.

NSAMA Tactical Command Center, Colorado, USA

"Dammit people! What's going on?"

Alex Collins, President of the United States of America and Chief of Staff of the North-South American Military Alliance, NSAMA, stormed into the tactical command center deep under the Rocky Mountains. He'd been hustled into the presidential airplane, *Air Force One*, as soon as the first *DEFSAT* satellite had been shot down, and flown at supersonic speed from Washington D.C. to the NSAMA command center.

There were about twenty people in the main control room. Most of them were huddled over computer terminals. Huge screens on the front wall showed maps of the world and of North and South America. Different colored points of light and connecting lines blinked on and off as the maps were continually updated. Screens on either side flashed with numerical readouts.

"Mr. President, sir! The shit's hit the fan, sir!" General McGrath said, turning towards the President. He stood at attention, his back ramrod straight, eyes front. *Hell, if he was going down, he'd go down like a man.*

It had started just three hours earlier. Japanese missiles had simultaneously knocked out most of the *DEFSAT* satellites, effectively rendering their whole laser defense system useless.

Dammit! President Alex Collins thought as he stared at the map of the world in front of him. No one had thought the Japs would side with the Chinese.

For over fifteen years, the Afro-Indian situation had been

getting worse. The war, which had never been officially declared, had been fought on and off for the last five years. At stake were huge oil finds in the deep coastal waters of the Indian Ocean. Everyone wanted control of them: The Africans and Indians, of course, as the oil was closest to their shores, but even the world's superpowers—the Americans, Russians, and Chinese—who were all struggling to keep their energy-guzzling industrial and military complexes supplied with oil. The flow of oil from the Arab nations had been slowing for over a decade. Some analysts even believed that the Arabs had more or less emptied their oil reserves. The price of crude oil kept rising.

The Russians and Chinese had formed an alliance. Originally just an economic agreement covering the worldwide exploitation of oil, within a year its true purpose became clear. In a massive military operation, Russia and China ceded the whole of the Indian Ocean basin. In independent, but obviously coordinated invasions, Russia took control of the western half of the ocean, and China the east. Supported by air attacks and bombardments from warships off the coast, Russian troops quickly gained control of Kenya and Tanzania: the only African states able to muster any resistance at all—futile though it was. China's invasion of India was conversely non-violent. Faced with the threat from its powerful northern neighbor, the Indian government crumbled.

For the USA, this was a nightmare come true. Not just economically—though that was bad enough—a military Sino-Russian allegiance posed a serious threat to their position as the world's mightiest superpower. NSAMA was hastily formed. The USA, Canada, and all the Central and South American countries swore military and political allegiance to each other. Not surprisingly, the only exception was Cuba.

Political and social instability ravaged Africa and India's civilian populations. Civil war broke out in many regions. In Africa, it was tribal; in India, between different castes. Millions died, massacred by their neighbors. In the wake of the violence came sickness and famine. Millions more died.

"Why didn't we monitor the Japs more closely?" Alex Collins said.

No one dared to speak. Not even General McGrath.

It was Pearl Harbor all over again—The Japanese attacking from nowhere.

"Sir! We have confirmed nuclear damage all across the eastern seaboard. Both military and civilian targets…" Lieutenant Susan James faltered. She was trying to keep her voice calm, but everyone could hear her fear. "New York, Washington, Miami… They're all gone, sir!"

Jesus Christ! General McGrath thought. *I need a damn bourbon. Now!*

NSAMA's defenses were controlled by quasi-intelligent computer programs. Complex algorithms started running as soon as the *DEFSAT* satellites had been attacked: calculating responses, predicting consequences, and when incoming Russian and Chinese missiles were detected, retaliating. In deep bunkers across the country, and beneath the world's oceans and seas on nuclear submarines, missiles were automatically armed and launched. The Air Force was scrambled.

Susan James looked up from her computer screen.

"*Sir!* They've launched *everything*. Incoming from Russia, China, the Barents Sea, and the Indian ocean!" The young Lieutenant no longer tried to hide her fear.

The President had codes. Their only purpose was to override the computer launch programs.

No way I'm going to use them now, Alex Collins thought. *Dammit! You attack us—you'll pay!*

"Estimated damage report?"

"Us or them, sir?"

"Just give me a straight answer, Lieutenant!"

"Sir! I'm sorry. It's total."

"What the hell do you mean *total?*"

Susan James came to attention and looked straight into the eyes of the President of the United States of America.

"Sir, primary extinction of biological life is calculated for Russia, China, Africa, India—and the whole of the Americas."

Her gaze never wavered.

President Collins returned it silently. She's young enough to be my daughter, he thought. Christ, how did it get to this? Damn the Japanese. How could they have thought they would get away with a first strike?

"People, I'm sorry. So sorry. God have mercy on us…"

"Sir! Mr. President!" General McGrath's voice rose above the ensuing cackle. "Russian tanks have moved into Western Europe. They're past Berlin already. We have no contingency to nuke Europe." *By God, he needed that drink. No, hell, he needed the whole damn bottle.*

"What do you mean, McGrath?"

"We thought the threat of nuclear war would stop the Russians invading Europe, Alex. We didn't think they'd invade after we'd all gone nuclear." He paused to think it through. "We can't let the damn Russians take Europe. They'll walk straight over them."

"Lieutenant! Advise me," President Collins said, turning to Susan James.

"Sir? Me, sir?"

"Yes, you Lieutenant. What are our options?"

Susan bit her lip. Don't start crying now, she had to tell herself.

McGrath butted in, "Alex, the Europeans have no meaningful conventional defenses. To stop the Russians, we must nuke them."

"What do the *DEFCON* computers say?"

Susan James spoke up, "Sir?"

"What?"

"There is an option."

"There is? Spit it out, Lieutenant."

"The *USS Sedna* is carrying nano-bio missiles. She's in the North Atlantic."

"McGrath! Confirm the *Sedna* is still operational!"

"One moment… Yes. Confirmed. *Sedna* still on-line and battle ready."

"Consequences?"

Susan James spoke up again, "The nano-bio bombing of London, Paris, Madrid, and Berlin would cause total human extinction in Western Europe. But it would only kill humans. It wouldn't affect any other biological life…"

"So what you're saying is that we'd end up killing the total population of Europe, including the Russians, but not the animals, plants, or anything else?"

"Yes, sir."

"McGrath?"

"I agree, Alex. We've either got to nuke them or use the nanos. We can't let the Russians win."

"What about the rest of the world?"

Susan James replied, "Computer simulations show the nuclear fallout from Africa and India will completely wipe out the Middle East, South-East Asia, and Australasia. The rest…" Her voice caught. "The rest is already gone, sir."

So that's it, President Alex Collins thought. That's all that's left? Saving some plants and animals in France! *Jesus!*

"Do it!"

"Do what, Alex?" McGrath asked.

"Use the nano bombs. Anyone want to make a case against them?"

The room was quiet.

"No, sir," Susan James said at last.

"No, sir," General McGrath said, echoing her.

"So be it then."

The mountains above the NSAMA control center had been battered by multiple gigaton nuclear blasts. Radiation at ground zero was orders of magnitude higher than the engineers who had designed the complex at the end of the twentieth century could have estimated. Nuclear bomb technology had come a long way since then. Radiation levels in the control room were already rising. Life expectancy for everyone inside was dropping rapidly from decades to months.

In fact, it was just ninety days before Lieutenant Susan James died. She was the last person in the Americas to do so.

Named after the Inuit goddess of the sea, The *USS Sedna* was one of a new generation of stealth submarines. Undetected by the few Russian RADAR systems still functioning, she sat deep beneath the sea, silently waiting for orders.

When those orders came, it took less than three minutes before seven nano-bio missiles were launched.

Within seconds of clearing the surface, they were detected by enemy RADAR. The submarine's position was compromised, and Russian missiles were launched. Minutes later the *USS Sedna* was utterly and completely destroyed.

The nano-bio missiles flew relentlessly on towards Western Europe.

Traveling at an incredible Mach 30—over 10 kilometers per second—they were simply too fast to be tracked and shot down before reaching their targets. They hit London, Paris, Madrid, Berlin, Munich, Rome, and Athens within a minute of each other. Impact at such high speeds pulverized them completely, releasing the nano-virus into the atmosphere. Apart from minor local damage to buildings, and the initial loss of a small number of lives, nothing happened.

Microbiologists had worked for five years to develop the virus code-named AOV-3. Secret testing had been carried out on death-row convicts. Their next of kin and lawyers were told that their somewhat premature deaths had been caused by illness, prison violence, or suicide. Knowing what kind of criminals they were experimenting on had helped to assuage the scientists' consciences somewhat. Still, it was a horrible way to die.

On contact with human flesh, AOV-3 immediately started to replicate, fed by its only nutrition: human-specific proteins. That was the way it had been designed. Not even chimpanzees were affected by the virus, even though their DNA is 96% identical to that of Homo sapiens. The effect on humans, however, was devastating.

The first sign of infection was a burning sensation on the skin. As the virus replicated, it slowly but surely fed deeper and deeper into the subject's body.

The screams were horrible. The agony unimaginable. On average, it took six minutes for death to occur—sheer pain and shock causing cardiac arrest. Mortality was one hundred percent. It was perfect.

The nano-virus had an inbuilt kill switch. Contact with water would instantly deactivate it. This was a necessary precaution, as a leak could still occur however high the security at the biological warfare testing facility was. If AOV-3 escaped the sealed inner labs, water sprinklers would automatically render it harmless.

After a successful human experiment, the sealed testing room was completely doused with water before the dead body was removed for incineration. Even so, anyone going into the negatively pressurized room always wore a Hazmat Level A suit. Apart from water, the only things known to kill AOV-3 were fire and high levels of radiation.

Borne on the wind, the nano-virus spread rapidly. On contact with humans, it replicated itself exponentially—and spread even faster.

Within just a few hours, everyone in the cities was dead, and within twenty-four hours, human life had been totally wiped out across the whole of Western Europe. The Russians had been stopped.

The enormous rate of replication in such a large human population had caused AOV-3 to evolve.

Biological replication is never perfect. Small, seemingly insignificant mistakes in cell division change an organism's properties and behavior. This kind of mutation is at the core of all evolution. Most mutations have a negative influence and weaken an organism. Some, however, give an organism new beneficial properties.

Having cycled through hundreds of generations, AOV-3 had mutated. No longer able to fuel their reproduction on human proteins, the mutated virus had managed to infect those mammals most closely related to humans: pigs and rats.

In the next few days, AOV-3 slowly moved down the evolutionary chain. First it spread from pigs and rats to other mammals, then to reptiles, birds, and insects. At each step the mutated virus followed evolution backwards—devouring and moving on.

It bridged the genetic border from fauna to flora. Everything that grew was killed.

Yet still it moved on, consuming bacteria and other microorganisms in the soil: deeper and deeper—until at last nothing that had evolved for almost four billion years was left alive.

There were some limits to the virus's proliferation, though—boundaries it was unable to cross: to the west the Atlantic Ocean, to the south the Mediterranean Sea, to the east the nuclear radiation poisoning of Eastern Europe, and to the north the snow line in Scandinavia.

When it could spread no more, the various mutated strains of AOV-3 turned on each other for nourishment. Cannibalism would be its own death.

The process came to a halt just twelve days after the missiles had struck. Europe was left perfectly sterile: free from all forms of life.

Only in lakes, rivers, streams, and canals did aquatic plants still grow, and fish still swim.

The Tale of the Two-Pot Tribe

One

Crete, Greece

This is *it!* Charlie thought as he looked up at the mountain peak above him. He was fifteen years old, black skinned, clear eyed, and gangly in a way only teenagers can be. He had a huge white-toothed smile on his face.

For almost two weeks now, the 7th Fengwidditch Scout Troop had been on its summer camp on the Greek island of Crete. The troop was made up of nineteen boys and girls aged between twelve and sixteen.

Fengwidditch was a small coastal town in North Wales. It had a small fishing fleet but was mostly known as the starting point—or ending point depending on which way you were going—of the Baden Powell Hiking Path. The BP-path, as everyone called it, went north along the coast from Fengwidditch before heading inland over Mount Snowdon's western foothills and back south to the town of Carlway.

Every summer, hundreds of hikers walked the ninety miles between Fengwidditch and Carlway—among them a fair number of Scout troops. The 7th Fengwidditch were always happy to put them up for a night at their Scout hut.

Charlie had been born in Havana, the capital of Cuba, and christened 'Carlos' after his grandfather. He'd been a member of the 7th for three years now. He would have joined earlier, but twelve was the youngest you could become a Scout.

Geographically part of the Americas, Cuba was economically dependant on Russia and politically allied to communist China. Relations between Cuba and the rest of the Americas had been rapidly declining with the ever-increasing tension between the world's superpowers. Fear of what the future might hold for the small communist island grew stronger for each passing year. Many Cubans tried to flee to Argentina, Mexico, and the USA, hoping to pass themselves off as natives of those countries. Most just waited, though, and prayed that things would get better.

Carlos's parents decided to try and find a boat to take them to Miami. Once there, they would be able to disappear amongst its large Black and Latino population.

At last, their prayers were answered. They had found a fishing boat in a small port on the south coast whose captain was willing to smuggle them out—for a price.

The boat was packed with over seventy men, women, and children. Wrapped in blankets and clutching their few belongings, they huddled together in the hold.

As night fell, *La Paloma* left the harbour. If they survived the sea, if pirates didn't attack them, and if the U.S. Coast Guard didn't turn them around and escort them back to Cuban waters, then maybe there would be a future for them in the USA.

La Paloma was running blind. Captain Fernández navigated by the stars, keeping the North Star ahead of him. His boat was carrying too many passengers. It lay low in the water but not dangerously so. The waves were high but not so high as to make him worry. Spray limited his field of vision—although there wasn't much too see out there, he thought: just the endless black sea and, thankfully, the stars in an even bigger, blacker, night sky. He had ordered all lights on-board to be extinguished. It would be a fateful decision.

Tony Howard, captain of the freight ship, the *Diana Rose*, stood at the helm. The *Diana Rose* was an Ultra Large Container Vessel at over 1200 feet in length.

It had been a long trip from Liverpool to Boston. From there they had sailed to New York and on to Miami where the last of their containers from England had been unloaded. In Miami they'd loaded new containers and were now on their way back to England.

Soon home, Captain Howard thought. Seems like I think about land more than the sea these days.

The sea had been good to him—giving him work, a career and the means to provide for his wife Joan and their four children. The kids were all grown up and married with families of their own now. Still think of them as *the kids* though... Always will, even if they've all moved away from Liverpool. To be honest, we're not much of a family anymore, he thought. The passion and sense of adventure he'd shared with Joan as they struggled to raise children, pay off the mortgage and be a happy family had dulled with the passing years. Both of them were in their mid-fifties now; they were used to each other and would probably stick together for the long haul. More out of habit than any remnants of romantic love, he admitted to himself. The physical attraction had worn off a long time ago, although they still went through the motions now and again. Pretending for each other—and for themselves—he supposed.

Lost in his thoughts, Captain Howard didn't see the dim silhouette of the fishing boat.

"Tony! Watch out!"

His steersman, Jack Burroughs, had just come back from the galley where he'd brewed yet another pot of tea. He resisted the urge to grab the wheel.

"Dead ahead!"

Captain Howard was startled into action.

He wrenched the wheel sharply full to port. It was pointless—and they both knew it—but what else could he do?

Jack Burroughs sounded the klaxon, swearing and praying at the same time. Their only hope was if the fishing boat could turn in time.

Ships in the night... Tony Howard thought. *Christ!* Where did that come from?

But they weren't destined to pass each other. The *Diana Rose* clove *La Paloma* in two. Twenty passengers and crew on board *La*

Paloma died immediately. Thirty-two more, including Captain Fernández and Carlos's parents, drowned before rescue dinghies from the *Diana Rose* could save them. Of the twenty-five survivors, six more would die of their injuries.

Quite how Carlos survived was something of a miracle. An unconscious one-year-old afloat in the cold of the Atlantic Ocean could only stay alive for a few minutes. He was lucky. Very lucky.

A strong hand grabbed him and lifted him out of the water, passing him straight on to the next man. These sailors knew the sea and just how dangerous the cold was. They had to act quickly.

Literally tearing Carlos's clothes from his tiny body, the merchant sailor known to his mates as 'Big Fred', wrapped the child in an aluminium survival blanket.

It wasn't enough. Carlos's body temperature was so low that he couldn't generate enough heat to keep him alive. He was turning blue.

Realizing what was happening, Big Fred quickly unzipped his survival suit, tossed the aluminium blanket aside, and pressed the boy to his chest. Knowing every second counted, he pulled the zip fastener shut, closing his survival suit over the both of them.

Big Fred's body warmth was just enough to keep Carlos alive.

Ten days later, the *Diana Rose* docked in Liverpool. There was no Cuban embassy in England, so the Cubans were taken to a refugee centre where they would stay until it was decided what was to be done with them. The USA put pressure on the British government to return them to Cuba. As they usually did with requests from their mighty ally, the British agreed. Only the orphaned Carlos and a pregnant nineteen-year-old girl were eventually allowed to stay in Britain. The government didn't want to be seen as being too heartless in the eyes of the national newspapers that had picked up on the story. Two weeks later, the remaining seventeen Cubans were bustled into a chartered plane and flown back to Havana.

Cuba was becoming a quasi prisoner-of-war camp, its coastline heavily guarded by the US Navy. No more boats would flee to Florida.

Anne Hadley, the Social worker who had been taking care of Carlos, had become quite attached to the skinny little black child with beautiful, big brown eyes. She didn't want to see him sent off to one of Liverpool's tough orphanages.

Anne was originally from North Wales. As often as she could, she went back to visit her sister who still lived in their childhood home in Fengwidditch. When Anne told her of Carlos's plight, she promised to check with the local orphanage to see if they had room for him.

There had been a certain amount of red tape to cut through, but in the end, no one else really cared what happened to the little boy. Anne drove Carlos down from Liverpool to Fengwidditch and handed him over to the orphanage.

It would become the only home he would ever remember.

The orphanage was run by Mrs. Jennings. She was strict, both with the children and her staff, and stood no nonsense. Deep inside, though, she was a kind, warm-hearted woman who took care of the orphanage with a fierce passion. She was careful not to let anyone know this, though. Especially not the children. Well, that's what she thought. They knew anyway.

Mrs. Jennings decided straight away that 'Carlos' wasn't a good name for the little newcomer to grow up with in Wales, so she promptly rechristened him 'Charlie'.

And now Charlie was near the top of one of the mountain ranges that stretched all the way across the island of Crete. It was a fantastic morning. The sun was shining; the air was crisp but not cold. Charlie felt more alive than he'd ever felt before.

The long hike from base camp had pushed him physically. Being one of the oldest children, his rucksack was packed not only with his own clothes but with a sizeable share of the troop's camping equipment and food as well. The donkey path they'd been following had become steeper and rockier the higher they climbed.

Dave Anderson was the only Scout leader with them on the hike. His wife, Jane, had stayed at base camp with two of the girls who had come down with pretty nasty colds. Luckily, all the other kids seemed to be fine. Dave reckoned he could always phone the local police if anything happened to them up there. They knew the mountains well and could come and help a sick child back down if necessary.

Conditions were perfect. All the kids were used to hiking, having been on the troop's five-day trip along part of the BP-path earlier that summer. What made Dave proudest of all was to see how the older children helped and encouraged the younger ones. The kids from the orphanage seemed especially quick to help if someone was struggling. All of them seemed to rally around Charlie as well. He wasn't the oldest or the strongest, but there was something about his natural enthusiasm and big smile that affected everyone around him.

Ah, to be young again, Dave thought. He was only forty-five, but a long and distinguished rugby career had taken its toll. He wouldn't let on to the kids, but the occasional twinge from his right knee and his general stiffness certainly reminded him which side of his athletic career he was on.

Up front with Charlie was his best mate, Johnny. A strong, squarely built and quiet lad from an old welsh mining family, Johnny was a year older than Charlie. Even so, Johnny would follow Charlie wherever the younger boy led—even if it got them into a tight spot. Truth be told, Charlie's exuberance and quest for adventure had landed them in more than just a couple of those tight spots over the years. A bit like Robin Hood and Little John, Dave chuckled to himself.

From their vantage point, Charlie and Johnny could see all the way across the island to the magical, shimmering Aegean Sea beyond.

More like King Arthur and Lancelot surveying their realm, Dave thought.

The sky in the east was beautiful, but strange. Thick red and grey layers of clouds stretched out across the horizon. Above the clouds, the sky was a perfect blue.

Never seen a sky like that before, Dave thought. It doesn't look natural. Must be something atmospheric.

Two

The massive thermonuclear explosions across the world had triggered intense seismic activity in the Earth's crust.

Earthquakes ripped landscapes apart, and volcanoes became suddenly and violently active, spewing lava and toxic gases into the atmosphere. Tectonic plates shifted under all these forces, sending whole coastlines into the sea. Shock waves of unimaginable power spread across the face of the Earth like ripples on a pond, leaving forests and cities flattened in their wake.

Deep beneath the Mediterranean Sea, the Earth's crust tore apart. The energy that was released created a huge wave that surged outwards at over a thousand kilometres per hour. It was hardly detectable far out to sea, but on reaching shallow coastal waters there was nowhere for it to go, but up.

A wall of water over a hundred metres high hit the shores of the Mediterranean and its islands. The Japanese name for these mega waves is *Tsunami*.

Johnny saw it first. The wave reared up as if out of nowhere. With an incredible roaring sound, it crashed into the island, sweeping onwards and upwards. Everything was flattened. Nothing that stood in the path of the mass of seawater survived the onslaught. Dave Anderson heard someone screaming—then realised it was his own voice.

The wave swept up the island's valleys and gorges, smashing everything and drowning everyone. Most of the island of Crete was gone. Destroyed. Only a few people living high in the mountains survived. As well as seventeen children and one Scout leader from Wales.

After the horrendous sound of the tsunami, there was an eerie silence for a minute or two. Then everything went back to normal. The sea became tranquil and sparkled brilliant blue, birds chirped and sunlight dappled through the leafy trees. Only to the east, where the sky had taken on an even deeper hue of red, did anything seem strange.

The Scouts gathered together. No one wanted to break the silence.

Dave fumbled in his jacket pocket for his cell phone and pressed the speed dial. Nothing. The local network was gone, as were most of the communication satellites that circled the earth. He looked back down the island. My wife is also gone, he realised. No one could have survived the tsunami.

He knew that thinking about his wife was selfish. He had to take charge and do something about the situation they were in. They had food and camping gear. That was good. But we need help… I'll head for the port, he said to himself. If help was going to arrive, it would be from the mainland. I'll go on my own. It'll be quicker. The kids will be safer here, too.

"Troop, listen up. I'm going back down to try and find help. Wait here. Don't go anywhere. I promise I'll be back. You've got food and water, so you'll be fine. You can make camp over there…" He pointed to a sheltered glade just off the path. It was a good spot. The mountain face protected one side, and it was big enough for them to pitch all their tents on.

"I promise I'll be back," he said again.

He quickly sorted through his rucksack, keeping some food and other stuff he'd need for the next few days but leaving behind the rest of his gear as well as the pots, pans and cooking utensils he'd been carrying. There'll be no time to make camp either, he reckoned, so he left his tent as well. A sleeping bag would be enough.

By now the children were all talking amongst themselves. The older ones tried to explain what had happened to the younger ones. Some of them were crying. They wanted to go home.

Dave prayed that he wasn't leaving them to die.

Hoisting his rucksack onto his back, he told them he would

hurry. That he would be back. There was nothing else he could say.

Turning quickly so the children wouldn't see the tears in his eyes, he set off down the track. After a few hundred yards he turned and looked back.

The children had gathered together and were sitting in a circle. Only Charlie and Johnny were still standing up—gazing out across the island. Dave looked up at them. More like Jesus and Peter, he thought as he turned away.

He kept a steady pace for the rest of the day, coming closer and closer to the destruction line: the highest level the tsunami had reached. He'd been stumbling more and more frequently, almost loosing his footing a couple of times on the rocky path.

I must rest a bit, Dave told himself. Just for a few minutes.

Finding a flattish spot, he lay on the ground and rested his head against his rucksack. A minute later he was asleep.

The moon rose deep red in the east. An owl hooted. The earth turned slowly beneath billions of stars in the heavens.

Tremors from the earthquake had loosened a rock higher up the mountain. It started to roll, bouncing and gathering speed on its way down.

It was a fluke accident. A chance in a million.

The rock hit Dave on the head and continued rolling down the hill. He was knocked instantly unconscious. Severe bleeding in his brain sent him into a coma. Twenty minutes later he was dead.

Dave Anderson, leader of the 7th Fengwidditch Scouts, would never keep the promise he had made to return to his troop.

Apart from the few who had survived on islands in the Mediterranean, most of the world's population was now to be found in northern Scandinavia. Early snowfall had stopped the nano-virus from spreading further north than Stockholm.

Other small pockets of humanity across the globe had survived as well, but for most of them, surviving the war was no more than a prolonged death sentence. Famine, drought, infectious diseases and radiation poisoning, as well as the brutal violence that desperate and panicked people inflicted upon their own neighbours, would soon wipe them out.

Scandinavia and the Mediterranean islands would be isolated from each other by the barren wasteland of continental Europe for thousands of years.

Three

The Fengwidditch Scouts watched Dave walk down the trail.

Charlie couldn't help feeling that they would never see him again and that there would be no help coming. Later he would wonder how he could have been so certain. It had just been a feeling: one of those things you can't explain but that are usually right. Something had gone terribly wrong. It wasn't just the tsunami.

"I think it's World War Three," Johnny said. "The world's been blown up. That's why the sky is red."

"But why are we still alive then?" Charlie said.

"I don't know. Guess they missed us. What are we going to do now?"

"Make camp, I guess. Wait for Dave."

"But what if he doesn't come back? What if no one comes to rescue us?"

"I was thinking that too. Feels like we're pretty much on our own."

"So what do we do?" Johnny said. "What the heck do we do?"

Charlie didn't say anything for a few moments as he gazed out over the blue sea.

Then the answer came to him as if from nowhere. A strong feeling seemed to wash over him, almost rocking him off balance as his whole world shifted subtly. Everything changed in that instant.

His eyes never left the horizon, but he was seeing beyond it. Way beyond it.

"Survive," he said softly. "Survive."

Johnny and the twin sisters, Jen and Gwen, were all sixteen years old. Steve, the school's number one bookworm, was just a few days younger than Charlie. Two of the other girls, Helen and Nina, were fifteen as well. The rest of the kids were pretty evenly spread out in age down to the twelve-year-olds: Alison, Angie and Dick. About a third of them lived at the orphanage, but they all went to the same school: the Fengwidditch Middle School. Being such a small town, Fengwidditch had mixed-age classes whose size depended on how many children there were in each age group.

Scouting didn't attract that many of the town's youth, but those it did were a mixed bunch as well. Over half of them were girls, which was unusual for a Scout troop. Jane had thought about starting a Girl Guide group, but she and Dave had agreed that having a mixed troop was much more fun for all of them.

It was mainly due to the influence of Jane and Dave's twin daughters, Jen and Gwen, that there were so many girls in the Scout troop. The two sisters almost forcibly dragged their friends along to the Friday evening Scout meetings.

Jen and Gwen were both true carrot-top redheads, with all the freckles to go with their hair. It would have been almost impossible to tell them apart, but luckily Gwen kept her hair cropped short, whereas Jen wore hers long and most often tied into a huge ponytail.

The term 'tomboy' could have been invented for them. In fact, most of the boys their own age couldn't keep up with those two. Not many of the older ones, either! If there was adventure to be had, mischief to be made or trouble to get into, then you could be sure the Anderson twins would be leading the charge with huge grins on their freckled faces and more often than not with scraped up knees to rival any of the boys'. The younger girls adored them. Worshipped would actually be a more fitting description. They would follow them anywhere, however scared they might be themselves. Thanks to the twin's legendary escapades, the town's boys were mostly in awe of them—even a bit scared. No one could forget what had happened to Jeremy Hill and Ewan Greyham last year.

Jeremy was a bully. He had been ever since he'd realised that because he was a little bit bigger, stronger and meaner than the other kids his age, that he could get whatever he wanted: extra pocket money, sweets, comics… He just took them from the other children. What he loved most was seeing the fear in their eyes as he closed in. What a feeling!

Last summer Jeremy and his friend Ewan had made a big mistake.

It was the last day of term. Summer holidays! That magical time of sun, and play, and freedom.

Dawn Williams was eleven years old. When she'd been five years old, she'd been in a terrible car accident that had crushed her legs and hips. She knew she would never be able to run or play like the other children but had come to terms with it. Her friends took her along with them whenever possible and made sure she didn't feel too left out of their games.

Trevor Walcott, Dawn's part time personal assistant, had wheeled her out to the school's parking lot where she would be picked up and taken home by a wheelchair accessible taxi. It wasn't due to arrive for another ten minutes, so after making sure that she was alright, he popped back to the staffroom to pick some things up.

Dawn sat in the sun with her eyes half closed, enjoying the warmth on her face. Like all the other children, she was looking forward to the summer holidays. In two days time she would be going down to the south of Portugal with her father and brother; her mother had been killed in the car accident that had left her a cripple. She loved Portugal. They had a villa there with a pool where she could swim, and they took trips almost every day to different places along the coast or into the countryside.

Jeremy and Ewan snuck up behind Dawn's wheelchair. They each grabbed hold of one of its wheels and jerked upwards.

Dawn fell hard, hitting her cheek on the asphalt. Tears of pain and fear burst from her eyes.

"Look at little fishy on dry land!" Jeremy taunted. "Whatcha gonna do? Get up little fishy!"

Dawn tried to push herself up. Laughing spitefully, Ewan

rushed in and kicked one of her arms away. She fell flat again.

"Poor little fishy. Can't get up and walk on dry land. Ain't got no legs!"

"Poor little fishy! Poor little fishy!" they both chanted.

Ewan didn't see it coming. Gwen's fist slammed into his jaw, breaking it with a loud snap. He collapsed unconscious to the ground.

Then she turned to face Jeremy. He was taller and stronger than her, but like all bullies, deep inside he was a coward.

The wild look in her eyes made his heart jump. Still, she was only a girl, wasn't she?

He put his fists up. *"Come on then!"*

And she did. Her foot smashed into his groin. A lightning bolt of pain doubled him up. Then she was all over him. A straight punch to his face broke his nose. He went down.

Instinctively, he drew his knees up to his stomach and tried to protect his head with his arms. Punches rained down on him.

Her fists smashed into his head and body, again and again.

And then, just as suddenly, it stopped.

Trevor had come out of the school building just in time to see the whole fight but too late to do anything about it… It had happened so quickly!

He ran over as fast as he could and grabbed Gwen in a bear hug from behind, pinning her arms to her sides. She fought to get free, trying to kick him and get loose.

She bit him hard on his upper arm. That hurt, but Trevor didn't let go.

Finally, the fight went out of her. She went limp in his arms.

By now other people had arrived. Someone picked up Dawn's wheelchair and helped her back into it. A teacher had started giving the two boys first aid. Someone else had rung for an ambulance.

At last, Trevor released his hold on the young girl.

Gwen turned around to face him.

"Is Dawn okay?" was all she said.

Four

"Listen everyone. We'll make camp over there. Come on!" Jen said.

She slung her rucksack onto her back and started walking over to the clearing that Dave had pointed out.

The others gathered their gear together and followed her lead. Charlie and Johnny took the big pots and the other cooking gear that Dave had left behind. They were all fairly quiet. The first shock of seeing the destruction the tsunami had caused had worn off. Everything seemed to have returned to normal.

The glade was about fifty yards across. Long ago, part of the mountainside had sheered off, leaving what was in effect a huge ridge sheltered on one side by the mountain face. A large pine tree stood in the middle, and in a rough circle around the outer edge, smaller trees and bushes had grown where they could catch more sunlight. Covering the whole area were dead branches and pine needles. On the far side, the ground fell away: gently at first, then more and more where there were no roots to support it.

It was a great place for a campsite, Jen thought. Her mind was already racing, working out what they would need. She had also thought about the possibility that Dave might not be able to find help. That they might be on their own.

She called the troop together near the big pine tree.

"We're going to pair up and put our tents up. We'll put them in a big circle with the openings facing towards the middle. Makes sense?"

"Yes," everyone said.

They'd all been carrying either a complete two-man tent or part of one: poles and pegs, the main tent or a flysheet. All in all, they had eight two-man tents plus Dave and Jane's tent, which was a bit bigger. If three of them shared that tent, it would leave one of the small tents over.

"We can put all our food in the extra tent so bugs don't get to it," Jen said.

"I'll mark out where the tents should be," Steve said.

"Great! Make sure you measure accurately."

Steve gave her a withering look. He was best at maths, and everyone knew it.

He found a stick and started to trace lines in the ground, radiating out from the pine tree. Some of the others helped him, calling out whether he should move a bit to the left, or a bit to the right so that the tents would be perfectly positioned. None of them could have said quite why it was so important to put the tents up in such an orderly fashion, but it gave them something to do, and well, it just felt right to do it like that.

"Hang on!" Jen said. "We should clear the ground before we start pitching the tents."

That got all the others into action as well—even those who had just been looking on. Soon, nine patches of ground had been cleared of all the sticks and stones, and the Fengwidditch Scouts were busy putting their tents up.

Some worked in pairs, others found it easier when three of them helped each other: two of them holding the poles while the other one draped the inner tent and flysheet over them. After the guy-lines had been attached and pulled tight, they hammered the rest of the tent pegs into the ground.

Johnny and the two youngest boys, Dick and Harry, finished first. The oldest children had intuitively chosen the youngest ones to help them. The rest mostly stuck with their best friends.

Dick concentrated as hard as he could on following Johnny's instructions. He was an impish boy, dark haired and full of energy. He looked up to Johnny and wanted nothing more than to follow the older boy's lead and prove himself useful. Harry, Dick's best friend, was a year older. The two were inseparable, going everywhere and doing everything together.

Their tent stood straight and stable. And first! It wasn't a race, of course, but Dick and Harry beamed with pride at their achievement. Johnny had already gone off to help a group of girls with their tent.

Finally all the tents were up. Steve was pleased. His measurements had been spot on, and all the tents were perfectly aligned. Well, as perfectly as the ground allowed, he said to himself.

With all their rucksacks piled at the base of the central tree, the camp looked organised and tidy.

"Troop Meeting!" Jen called out.

The kids who weren't already there joined the others by the pine tree and sat down.

"I know we're all hungry," Jen said, "but we've got to get organised before we eat. Has everybody decided who they want to share tents with?"

"We'll take Dave's tent," Johnny said, speaking for Dick and Harry as well.

"Good. Anyone not sure who they're sharing with?"

No one spoke up.

"Right then. We've got to decide on who's to be the leader."

"You're doing a pretty good job," Charlie said.

"Thanks, Charlie, but we must vote on it."

"Shouldn't we have one leader for the boys, and one for the girls?" Gwen said. "Like Dave and Jane, I mean."

"Good point, Gwen. What does everyone else think?"

Steve put his hand up. "I think it's a good idea to have two leaders. There's a lot to be done. Dave should be back in a couple of days… but what if he isn't? What will we do then? We'd be on our own."

Up to then, Charlie had been sitting down with the others. Later he wouldn't remember making the decision to stand up.

Everyone looked up at him.

"We'll do two things," he said. "We'll help each other, and we'll survive."

Five

Growing up in an orphanage could be tough. There were always bullies, like Jeremy Hill, who could make life a misery for other children. Mrs. Jennings knew there were fights from time to time. Treating the children's bumps and bruises was part of her job, but none of the kids would ever tell her if they'd been hurt by someone else. Being a 'rat' was the worst possible label anyone could get. Most of the time, though, just the threat of violence was enough to uphold the bullies' power over the other children.

Charlie had been picked on pretty badly. Being the only black kid in the orphanage made him an obvious target. Physically he never stood a chance against the sturdier built Welsh boys.

Other kids were naturally drawn to him, though. They always went to him when they didn't feel so good, knowing that he would listen to their problems and their longings. Charlie offered advice where he could and helped them join in games if they felt left out. He had lots of friends. This made the bullies hate him even more, of course, but it protected him too. Anytime Charlie was cornered, other kids would gravitate towards him. They wouldn't be openly hostile or anything, but just showing up in number made a difference. It made the bullies nervous. Most times they would end up just walking off—calling Charlie names to save face, of course. In time they came to the realisation that it was better just to leave him alone.

Charlie would always remember what this had taught him though: strength comes through helping each other.

In the end they didn't vote to elect leaders. There was no point. It was obvious: Jen would be the girls' leader, and Charlie the boys'.

"Has anyone got a pen and paper?" Steve asked.

After a bit of rummaging around in rucksacks, he was handed a pad and pencil.

"We've got to make a list of things to be done and split up into groups to do them," he said. He lowered his head and started writing.

Gwen put her hand up.

"First I'd say we ought to make a fireplace and collect wood," she said. "So we can cook some food."

"Yes, any volunteers to make the fireplace?" Charlie asked.

Hands shot up.

"Pete, Kev, find some rocks to make a ring. Make it big enough so that we can have a proper campfire and can all sit round it. Maggy, Sarah, Nina, will you collect firewood? We need small sticks and bigger branches. Don't go too far, and don't be gone too long at a time, okay?"

"I'll go with them too," Gwen said.

"Great!"

The six Scouts jumped up, ready to go about their tasks.

"The rest of us will get everything unpacked and sorted into the tents," Charlie said. "Anything else really important?"

Steve looked up from his notes. "Well, yes, actually. A latrine is a high priority."

"Right. Of course. How many spades do we have?"

"Two. I've been carrying them. They're in my rucksack."

"Good. If we have two teams, we can take turns digging. It'll be hard work. Johnny, can you take three others and find a good spot back down the path a bit? But not too far…"

"Sure. I dug latrine pits at camp last summer, so I know how to do it. Let's see… How about you three dwarves? You look strong," he said to the three youngest boys, Dick, Harry and Tom.

"Oh no!" Gwen doubled up in laughter. "I don't believe it! The Three Dwarves! *Tom, Dick and Harry!"*

Her laughter was infectious. Soon everybody was laughing hysterically—even Tom, Dick and Harry. Some of them had to hold their stomachs, trying hard to stop laughing as tears ran down their cheeks.

The laughter was like medicine. All the fear and worry they'd kept bottled up inside came bubbling up to the surface and exploded into laughter before evaporating into thin air.

From that day forth, Tom, Dick and Harry would be known as *The Three Dwarves*: a name they bore proudly.

All the Scouts went about their tasks: collecting firewood and rocks, digging latrines, sorting out sleeping bags and pads, and putting all their gear into the tents.

Jen had taken command of the food tent. She and two others collected all their rations and water bottles together and lined them up in orderly rows. All the while, she had been mentally calculating how long their food would last. When they'd left base camp, they'd had more than enough for three days. So we should be able to stretch that into an extra day, she reckoned. Maybe even more. I'll talk to Charlie about it when I'm done sorting, she said to herself.

Steve had taken charge of stacking the wood into three piles: small sticks, medium sticks and bigger branches that would have to be chopped down to size.

Lighting the fire was no problem at all. The wood they'd collected was dry and burned easily. Steve was a bit proud that he'd only used a single match to get it going.

"Charlie, come over here, will you?" Johnny said.

"Sure. What is it?" He walked over to the fireplace where Johnny stood admiring the fire Steve and the girls had built.

"I've been thinking. Say Dave doesn't come back and we really are on our own like we talked about?"

Charlie nodded.

"Well, we've got to have a fire to cook food and keep warm, but what do we do when we run out of matches and the lighters are empty? We've only got two lighters and one box of matches. Have you ever made a fire by rubbing sticks together or anything?"

"I tried once, but it was impossible. I tried for hours, then gave up even though I thought I was doing it right. Dave helped me too. We made a bow to turn a stick on top of another piece of wood. It got really hot from the friction, but we couldn't get the tinder to light… and you know what? Dave said he'd never got it to work either."

"Guess we'll have to practice."

Steve had come over as well. "I've made a list," he said. "But it really comes down to three important things."

"Go on," Charlie said.

"Food, fire, and water. There's seventeen of us. We're going to need a lot of food. I think we should start trying to find some straight away tomorrow. Not wait until our rations run out."

"Yes, you're right. We should have a big meeting and get organised. Later though—after we've eaten, okay?"

"Okay. We're going to run out of water even sooner, so we'll have to find a stream, or a well or something. I saw a couple of small brooks on the way up, but they're too far back down for us to carry water all the way up here. I think we should send a team out to search before it gets dark."

"Good thinking, Steve. Why not the three of us? It'll give us a chance to scout the land out a bit as well."

At last, everybody had finished what they were doing, and they were all gathered together by the campfire.

"Quiet everyone!" Jen said. "Listen. We've got two big pots, right? How about we make a big stew out of all our rations. Just throw everything in and mix it with water. What do you think?"

"Sounds horrible!" Dick piped up.

"But a good idea," Steve said.

"Even the Mars bars?" someone asked.

"Yuck!"

Jen laughed. "Yes, everything! And when we find other food, we just chuck it in and keep the stew going. We're going to have to change the way we think about food," she said a bit more seriously. "It doesn't matter what it tastes like as long as it keeps us alive. Everyone must eat as much as they need, of course, but not pig out, so there'll be enough to go round. All agreed?"

Everyone nodded.

"We should call ourselves *The Tribe of the Two Pots!*" Gwen said.

That made everyone laugh.

"Jen's right. Help each other and survive," Charlie said, repeating the words he'd spoken earlier that day.

"*Help each other and survive!*" Dick shouted.

The others joined in. "*Help each other and survive!*"

Jen raised her voice to be heard. "Come on then! A big group hug, then let's get this stew on!"

They all clapped and cheered.

They didn't know it then, but that first stew in the two big pots would become the stuff of legend. A tale told for generations to come.

The name *The Tribe of the Two Pots* would stick as well. It soon became shortened to *The Two-Pot tribe*, and later—much later—they would just call themselves *Tupots*.

It was late in the afternoon by the time they'd finished eating. The sun was sinking in the sky. Too late to start looking for water, Charlie decided.

Steve presented the plan for the next day. "We'll split into teams of three and start scouting the area out," he said. "Water is the number one priority. Hopefully we'll find a stream close by. Otherwise we'll have to keep on searching and then move camp closer to it when we find one."

There were a few groans. It had been a lot of work pitching the tents, building the fire and digging latrines. Everyone was tired.

"Maybe Dave will turn up with help," Jen said.

Charlie put his hand up.

"We shouldn't hope too much. I've been keeping an eye out and haven't seen a single boat on the sea… No aeroplanes either," he added. "Anyone else?"

The question was met with headshakes.

"I know it's scary, but if we *are* on our own, I think we can make it. Anyone got any questions?"

"Have you tried the cell phone?" Maggy asked.

"Yes, still no signal. None at all."

"What do we do if we get attacked?" Dick asked. "You know, by wolves, or vampires or whatever?"

"Good question. Though I don't think there are any vampires up here. What do you think, Johnny?"

Johnny was a bit annoyed. He should have thought of that himself.

"Well, we've all got our Scout knives, haven't we?" he said.

"Yes," everyone replied.

"I'm not sure if I could kill a wolf with my knife," Alison said.

"Don't worry. We'll protect you." Johnny said.

He looked around at all of the boys one at a time.

They all seemed to straighten their backs, returning his look with slight nods. There was something focused and determined in their eyes. A bit like the look you get just before a rugby match, Johnny thought. But more. It was deadly serious now.

"Count on us," he said.

If he could have seen into his own eyes, he would have seen that same determined look. A deep, peaceful feeling came over him… *I would die fighting to protect my people…* The thought just came to him. But it made so much sense. This is who he was. This is what he would do—protect his people.

Charlie spoke up again. "No one should go anywhere alone. Well, not further than the latrines. And not out of sight of the camp. Okay?"

"Okay," everyone said.

"I've got an idea," Jen said. "It's better if we keep the fire alight all night. We've got more than enough wood. Those big logs will burn for ages. It'll keep wild animals away… and vampires!" She laughed, looking at Dick. "We can take turns in pairs to watch over the fire and keep a lookout for anything else that might be dangerous."

"Great idea, Jen. I'll take the first watch," Johnny said.

"With me!" Dick said.

The talking went on until long after the sun had set.

When they finally started to feel drowsy, the Fengwidditch Scouts went to their tents and climbed into their sleeping bags.

"We'll keep watch until we're too tired, then we can wake two of the others," Johnny said.

Dick put his hand on his sheath knife. I'll never get tired, he said to himself.

Two hours later, though, his eyelids became very heavy.

Johnny nudged him gently. "Come on, Dick, let's go and wake

Charlie and Harry up… I'm tired."

"Mmm…" was all Dick managed to say.

Soon he was crawled up deep inside his sleeping bag and sound asleep.

Six

The dawn chorus had woken Charlie up about an hour earlier. He'd slept pretty well and was glad to hear the birds singing. It had been strange the day before when everything had been so quiet after the tsunami.

I guess Dave could have made it down by now, he thought. It was an empty thought, though. Somehow, he just knew that no help was coming. That was scary in many ways. Could they survive? Would they find water? And food?

At the same time, he had a feeling of independence—of freedom, and adventure, and of a purpose—to stay alive. No, it's not just staying alive, he thought, it's *feeling* alive. Anyhow, no point lying here thinking about it, I'd better get up and start *doing* something!

He crawled out of his tent and yawned. A bird chirped high up in the pine tree.

"Good morning, Bird," Charlie said, and smiled up at it.

As he walked down the grassy slope to the latrines, he felt the coolness of the dew beneath his bare feet. He stopped and rubbed his hands in the grass, then wiped the last of the sleep from his eyes. The dew felt so fresh and pure. This really is the start of something new, he thought.

Nina had already put some more wood on the fire and hung the two pots over the flames.

"What's for breakfast?" Charlie called out on his way back.

"Well, you have the choice of freshly baked French croissants and strawberry jam… or Two-Pot stew!"

"Hmm… I'll take the stew!"

He sat down at the fireplace. The morning hadn't warmed up

yet, so it was great to sit by the fire and feel its heat on his face.

"One stew coming up!" Nina said, handing him a bowl.

"Thanks!" Charlie said.

One by one, the others came and sat around the fire. Nina gave each of them a bowl of stew.

Last to get there was Johnny. In the early hours of the morning he'd taken a second guard watch on his own—he hadn't wanted to wake Dick. When he'd finally gone to bed, he'd managed to sleep for another hour until the sounds of the camp had roused him.

"Morning, everyone!" he said.

"Morning, Johnny!" came the chorus of voices.

After everyone had eaten, Charlie stood up.

"We've got two main things to do today," he said. "First we've got to find water. We'll send out a few groups. If we find a stream, we can take all our water bottles in a couple of rucksacks and fill them up. Okay?"

There were nods all round.

"And the other thing is food." He paused. "I think this is going to be our main duty. We're going to have to spend a lot of time looking for food."

Sarah had put her hand up. "Charlie?" she said shyly.

"Yes, Sarah."

"You know my mum's the biology teacher?"

"Yes."

"Well, she's taught me to recognise a lot of plants and herbs. We used to go collecting every summer with my grandmother and then make scrapbooks with the Latin names written under the pressed flowers. And I thought that might be useful…"

Jen jumped up. "Useful? *Useful!*" She wrapped her arms around the small girl in a huge hug, lifting her straight off the ground. "Useful? You silly girl, that's *wonderful!* You might have just saved our lives!"

Seeing the look of surprise on Sarah's face, everybody started laughing. Not used to being the centre of attention, Sarah wasn't sure how to react, but realising they weren't laughing at her—that they were just happy—she started to laugh as well.

"*Useful!*" Dick shouted, making everybody laugh again.

"We've got to kill things too," Johnny said.

Everyone turned to look at him.

"Has anyone ever killed an animal before?"

"I usually ring the neck of a chicken for Sunday dinner," Mark said, "and I've seen my dad butcher a pig, but I've never done it myself, so it's not like hunting or anything. And fishing of course…"

"Anyone else?"

No one said anything.

"We'll have to learn, then… and make weapons."

"What kind of weapons?" Charlie asked.

"Easiest is a spear. You just lash a sheath knife to a long stick. The other thing I came up with is this…" He pulled something out of his pocket.

During the night he'd made a catapult. Using the jagged teeth on the side of his knife, he'd sawn off a branch about six inches from where it forked into two. Then he'd shortened the other two ends to about the same length, leaving a sturdy Y-shaped stick. Two notches near the top held a piece of elastic cord that he'd taken from his rucksack, and he'd even laced a small square of nylon he'd cut from a groundsheet onto the cord.

"Look, I'll show you," Johnny said. He picked up a stone. "See that tree over there?"

Everyone looked at the tree he was pointing at.

Taking careful aim, he pulled back the cord, froze for a second, then let fly. The stone flew straight and hard. It missed the tree by about a foot.

Someone booed. Then everyone joined in.

Johnny looked sheepish. "Well, I need to practice—" he started to say, but the booing had turned into loud cheers and clapping.

There wasn't a boy there who didn't want to start making a catapult of his own right away. And a spear!

It felt as if a heavy weight had lifted from Charlie's shoulders. We can hunt, and we can gather food, he thought.

He caught Jen's eye. The slightest of nods passed between them. We can do this, they both thought. We can survive.

A group of four girls took off to start looking for plants, and two pairs of boys went off in different directions to try and find water. Sarah went with the plant gatherers, of course. They'd all agreed to be back by noon when the sun was directly overhead, so as not to go too far.

It was almost too lucky to be true. Steve and Kev had decided to continue up the donkey path and hadn't been gone for more than ten minutes when they saw water bubbling out of a crack in the rock face by the side of the path. It was like a tiny waterfall.

The water was cold to the touch and looked clean. Kev cupped his hands and tasted it.

"I think it's good," he said.

Steve held his hands together under the spring and gulped some as well.

"Yes. It tastes good. This far up it should be pure. Let's hope so anyway."

The water ran down the hill for a bit before seeping into the ground.

"It probably joins up with other sources underground and turns into one of the streams we saw further down," Steve said.

They both drank some more. It was delicious.

"We'd better get back and find the others," Kev said. "This is perfect. No point looking any further."

The two boys hurried back to camp to tell everyone about their find.

Everybody wanted to go and see the spring, of course. Johnny and Dick said they'd go and look for the other water hunters and bring them back. Steve and Helen volunteered to stay behind and watch over the fire. All the others who'd been at the camp took their water bottles and marched up the hill behind Kev. Charlie and Jen took up the rear.

"We've been lucky," Jen said.

"Really lucky," Charlie agreed. "A good campsite, and now water close by."

"Some of the younger kids are homesick and scared."

"I know. But I don't think there's any *home* left—or any way to get there even if there was. There's been no sign of Dave or anyone else back down the island. No boats or planes. Nothing. I think we're on our own."

"It could have been worse, couldn't it? At least we've got our camping gear with us. But apart from that, it's like we're back in the Stone Age or like a tribe of Red Indians…"

When they reached the spring, everyone was taking turns drinking and washing their faces.

"Perfect!" Jen and Charlie exclaimed in unison.

Johnny and Dick had found the other boys and even bumped into the girls who were foraging in the woods. Gwen jumped for joy when they told them about the freshwater spring.

"That's great!" she said. "But we'll stay out here and keep looking for plants. We can go and see the spring later."

It would be another couple of hours before the foragers returned to camp with everything they'd found.

"Can someone fetch a groundsheet and lay it out?" Gwen said.

Johnny went to get the groundsheet that he'd cut a piece out of for his catapult. They lay all the berries and flowers on it. There were even a couple of roots they'd dug up. Sarah had been able to identify quite a few different plants, but there were many more she didn't recognise.

"Maybe we could make a scrapbook and press the flowers and leaves so we can all learn them?" she said.

"That's a great idea," Jen said. "Gwen, you've got a college block, haven't you?"

"Yes, I'll go and get it," her twin sister replied, and headed off towards her tent.

For the whole of the rest of the afternoon, Sarah talked them through the different plants.

They sat in a half circle near the fire. It was almost like being in school—but with a thirteen-year-old teacher!

She held up one flower at a time and told them what was special about it: its colour or shape, how many petals it had, or something about its stem or leaves. Some of the flowers were edible as they are, she said, but you can only eat the leaves or stems of others. The flowers that grow over edible roots are very important, as roots are very nutritional even if they don't look so tasty. You have to dig them up with a stick. They can be roasted, or put…

"*Into the pots!*" everyone shouted.

After a flower had been passed around, Gwen neatly sellotaped it onto a page in her college block and wrote its name and anything else that Sarah had said was important underneath it.

After the flowers, they went on to the berries. The berries couldn't be pressed—that would have just made a mess of course—but Sarah said that the most important thing was to check that the leaves were right. Some edible berries looked very similar to poisonous ones, but by comparing the leaves you could tell them apart.

"Never, *never,* eat anything you're even the slightest unsure of," she said. "If in doubt, bring it back to camp so we can check it first, okay?"

"Why didn't you pick any mushrooms?" Harry asked.

"We will," Sarah said. She was getting more confident about talking in front of the group and answering their questions now. "But mushrooms are especially dangerous if you eat the wrong ones. My mum said they don't have so much nutrition in them either."

"No bananas?" Tom asked.

"No! No bananas. But we did find these wild apples," she said, picking one of them up and holding it out for him to inspect.

At last they'd gone through all the plants they'd collected and written them up in *The Plant Book*. It was too much for everyone to learn at once, Sarah said, but soon they would all recognise the most common flowers and plants.

"What do we do with them all now?" Jen asked with a grin.

"*Into the pots! Throw 'em into the pots!*"

'Into the pots' had quickly become a catch phrase. Little could they imagine everything that would eventually make it into the pots.

Jen spoke up again. "Are we all agreed then? Never eat anything you're not absolutely sure is safe. It's never stupid to ask one time too many. And *nothing* gets thrown into the pots until Sarah has okayed it. Agreed?"

"Agreed," everyone said.

That evening the stew was delicious—Although it could do with some meat, Johnny thought. We'll do something about that.

Most of the boys spent the evening talking about the weapons they would make the next day. Spears and catapults were at the top of the list. Bows and arrows would be harder, but they could always try, they all agreed. They would have to practice shooting and throwing as well.

The girls were less interested in weapons and hunting. There was even a lively discussion as to whether this was natural—whether it was because of instincts or genes, or if it was just the way they'd been brought up. It was hard to ignore the fact that girls and boys had different interests, Steve had summed up, but hard to know if that was natural or not. We didn't exactly grow up in the jungle, did we? he'd said.

In the end, they agreed that the girls would concentrate on gathering plants and the boys on hunting. Everything ended up in the same pots anyway, they said, so we'll just try to keep them as full as we can.

Night came quickly as they sat around the fire.

It was hard to think that they might not be saved. That Dave might not turn up with rescuers. That they wouldn't soon be on a plane back to Wales…

In time, though, Fengwidditch would become just a memory—like a dream they had woken from—distantly remembered but not thought about so much.

Seven

Just before the sun rose, Charlie was woken by a hand shaking his shoulder.

"What is it, Jen?" he whispered, not wanting to wake Mark and Kev.

"Come outside, Charlie. Quick. I need to talk to you."

He pulled his trousers and shirt on and snuck out of the tent.

"What is it?" he asked.

"We've got a problem. Alison is sick. You know she's got diabetes, don't you?"

"Yes."

"Well, she takes insulin every day. She had more at base camp, but now hers is used up."

"What does that mean? What happens if she doesn't take it?"

"I asked her. She's scared. She said she would die without it."

"Die!" Charlie was wide awake now. "When? How?"

"She said you just get tireder and tireder because your body can't take up any sugar. So eventually you just fall asleep… and die."

"There must be something we can do." He was thinking fast now. "We'll have to go back to where the base camp was and see if we can find her insulin. If we're lucky, the tsunami didn't destroy it… Or in Heraklion. There must be insulin there. In a hospital, or a chemists or something. We can't let her die, Jen. I'll go straight away. I mean, *we'll* go. I'll wake Mark and Kev up."

"We haven't got any rations that you can take. Everything's been put in the pots, but if you eat now, maybe you'll be okay?"

"We'll have to be," Charlie said.

"Do you want me to come with you?"

"No, stay here and look after Alison."

"Shall we tell the others?"

"Yes, I think it's better that everyone knows. Try to keep them occupied with other things if you can, though."

Jen went back to Alison's tent. Charlie hurried to wake Mark and Kev. He told them what they were going to do.

"We'll take as little as possible with us so we can move quickly. It's warm enough at night, so we don't need a tent or sleeping bags. We can sleep in our clothes. Have you both got your knives with you?"

Mark and Kev nodded.

"We'll take a small rucksack so we can collect stuff. Anything else you can think of that we *must* have with us?"

They both shook their heads.

"Right then. Grab a bowl of stew and let's get going."

The sun had just cleared the horizon as they started off down the track. Jen watched them go and said a silent prayer. Please, please let them find some insulin and get back safely.

It was late in the afternoon by the time they got to where the tsunami had reached. It was much higher up than their base camp had been.

The three boys looked out over the destroyed landscape. There wouldn't be anything left of the base camp—that much was obvious. The tsunami had flattened almost all of the small trees and bushes that grew further down the island. Only a few of the tallest trees still stood. The receding seawater had washed everything away, leaving just mud and debris behind.

Mark went off the path to take a leak, so Charlie and Kev sat down to wait for him.

They'd hardly had time to get comfortable before Mark appeared again. He was waving his hands frantically.

"*Quick, guys! Come here!*"

Charlie and Kev rushed to where he was.

"It's Dave!" Mark said.

It was obvious that he was dead. One side of his head was split open, and they could see where blood had run out over his shoulder and arm. Dave's eyes were closed, and his skin was a chalky white colour. There was no doubt. He was dead.

"What shall we do?" Mark asked. "Bury him?"

"No," Charlie said. "We haven't got time. We'll have to do that later. We've got to find insulin for Alison… But we can take his rucksack with us on the way back. We'll take his boots and trousers as well. We might need them."

Getting Dave's clothes off wasn't easy. It felt strange doing it as well—none of them had ever seen a dead body before. It was a bit easier if they didn't look at his face.

"What do you think killed him?" Kev said.

"I don't know," Charlie said. "Looks like someone bashed his head in. But they didn't take his gear or even his knife. I don't know…"

They put everything into Dave's rucksack and hung it from a tree on the other side of the path.

"No point in lugging it with us," Charlie said. "Take his knife, though. A knife is too valuable to leave behind."

The three Scouts explored the area on the other side of the path and found a good place to sleep for the night.

"We'll stay here until morning," Charlie said. "There's no point going further in the dark. We won't find anything until daylight anyway."

It would be a restless night. They were all wide awake hours before sunrise, just as the sky was beginning to get a bit lighter. It had been a bit too chilly to sleep without sleeping bags too, so they all agreed that they should get going. None of them said it out loud, but they all wanted to get away from the place where Dave had been killed, and were glad to set off down towards the ruined city.

Once past the level where the tsunami had struck, the going got tougher as there was no visible path to follow. The only way down was by clambering over fallen trees where they could or skirting around the ones that were too big to climb over. They passed the place where the base camp had been without even noticing it—there was nothing left of it at all.

After a short break in the middle of the day, they carried on.

Normally it would have been lunchtime, but they had nothing to eat.

Closer to the city there were fewer fallen trees to get past but much more debris blocking their way.

Finally they made it to the city itself. Furniture and rubble from crushed buildings filled the streets. Smashed up cars and lorries lay all over the place, and there were dead bodies everywhere. The giant wave had left them lying around like discarded rag dolls: broken, lifeless.

The smell of decaying flesh was almost unbearable, so they tied their Scout scarves over their mouths and noses to keep from retching. It helped a little. Crows and seagulls feasted on the dead bodies. Their croaks and calls were the only sounds that could be heard.

Most of the buildings had been destroyed. Only a few of the biggest and best built ones still stood. Some of Heraklion's roads and streets could even be followed, although they were all covered in slimy mud and seaweed. Constantly watching their footing, so as not to slip and fall, they made their way to what used to be the city centre.

If we're going to find anything, it'll probably be there, they thought. By the look of things, though, the chances of finding any medicine—let alone insulin—were almost next to none. Everything in the shops had been washed away or ruined. Stuff lay everywhere.

Maybe we'll be able to search for useful stuff next time we come, Charlie thought.

As they turned the corner of a tall building, they saw a strange sight: a huge container ship had been dumped across the street, crushing buildings on both sides. It was still more or less the right way up itself, but most of its cargo had been ripped off and swept away.

After the first shock of seeing the ship, Charlie realised it could be the answer to their prayers.

"What do you think? Shall we go in and explore?" he said.

"Ships always have some medical stuff. A clinic or something, don't they?" Mark said.

"Yeah, let's do it," Kev said.

Getting onto the ship wasn't so easy, as they had to clamber up the hull. Luckily there were foot and handholds built into the side, but like everything else, they were covered in slimy, smelly mud. It was a slow climb.

Charlie led the way. "Careful guys, it's a long way down!"

"As if we don't know!" Mark called back.

They finally made it to the container deck. It only sloped a bit, so it was okay to walk on. It was slippery, though, so they still had to be careful.

They made their way as quickly as possible to the superstructure where the bridge and living quarters were, and set about searching the cabins and other rooms. Almost all of crew must have been on land when the tsunami had struck, as most of the cabins were empty. But not all of them. They found a number of dead bodies—men who had been smashed to death or drowned. In the ship's canteen there were more dead crewmembers.

The boys were getting used to seeing dead people, but they still looked away from those that were the worst mangled.

Kev had gone ahead down one of the corridors and had found a room marked with a red cross.

"Over here!" he called out.

Charlie and Mark hurried to where he was.

The door to the ship's infirmary was either locked or jammed. It took them ten minutes to break in. First they battered the hinges with a metal pipe, then took turns ramming the door with their shoulders until the hinges broke off.

"No!" Mark said.

The room was a wreck. Bits of broken furniture lay everywhere. What had once been the medicine cabinet was smashed to pieces.

"We've got to search anyway," Charlie said. "This might be our only chance."

It was hopeless. There was nothing of any use to be found. After just a few minutes of rummaging, they knew they had to give up.

"Let's go search somewhere else," Charlie said.

"Where, Charlie?" Kev said.

"I don't know. We'll search through the city centre. Maybe we'll find a hospital—"

"But everything's ruined!" Kev said. He kicked the broken door. He was close to tears. "Isn't it!"

"We've got to keep searching," Charlie said. "We'll keep on until it gets dark. Then…" He trailed off. Then what? How long should they keep looking? They probably wouldn't find any insulin—and even if they did, how long would it last? Sooner or later Alison was going to die.

They climbed back down the hull with the help of a long mooring rope that they'd flung over the side. Charlie was the last one down; Mark and Kev had already started off along the street.

"Hang on, guys! Come back! I think I've seen something."

The side of one of the buildings that the tsunami had thrown the container ship into had been ripped away. Inside, Charlie had seen a flight of stairs leading down below ground level. What had caught his eye, though, was that the stairs weren't covered in as much mud as everywhere else. The ship must have blocked the seawater from flowing past, he thought.

"Let's go down and look," he said.

There was a huge steel door at the bottom of the stairs.

Mark grabbed its handle and pulled. The door swung open.

Inside, everything was untouched—seawater hadn't even seeped over the floor. The huge room was filled with rows and rows of bookshelves.

A large sign in both Greek and English hung on the wall: 'Heraklion University Library Archive'.

There was a computer on a table in the middle of the room. Kev pushed the '*on*' button, but nothing happened, of course.

Charlie walked up one of aisles. Most of the books were in Greek, but there were lots of English ones too.

"This'll make Steve happy," he said. "He's always got his nose stuck in a book."

"Yeah, but it's not going to help Alison," Kev said. "Let's get out of here."

They went out and closed the door securely. The library had obviously been designed to protect the books in case of fire or flooding.

Books, Charlie thought. What can we do with books?

The seed of an idea had formed in his mind but hadn't surfaced to become a conscious thought yet. It was, however, to be the beginning of the path he would tread for the rest of his life.

The three boys spent the rest of the day, and all of the next, searching the city. They found lots of stuff that could be useful, even some food in the ruins of a supermarket. At the end of the second day, though, they still hadn't found any insulin.

Even if they had, it wouldn't have made any difference. Alison had died the night before.

Eight

Everybody was sitting around the fire when Jen came out of Alison's tent. They'd all been up for hours after nightfall, talking in soft voices or just staring into the fire.

Johnny had been restless the whole time. He'd walked slowly round and round the perimeter of tents with his spear in his hand as if he could single-handedly keep death from invading their camp.

Jen and Gwen had taken turns sitting beside Alison. She slept, but her breathing had become shallower and shallower. At one point Gwen thought she'd even stopped breathing. She'd grabbed the small girl's shoulders and shook her—gently at first, then a bit harder. Alison had opened her eyes and said 'hi' in a tiny voice before falling asleep again. Gwen just held her hand and cried.

It would be another two hours before Alison's young life slipped away.

"She's gone," Jen said.

For a long while, no one said anything; they just cried and hugged each other.

Johnny stopped his prowling. He stood perfectly still and stared out into the dark night.

He remained standing there even after the others had gone to bed. The only other person awake was Gwen. She sat by the fire, gazing into its glowing embers.

At last she went to him. Not wanting to startle him, she gently called his name.

Johnny didn't reply.

Saying his name again, she wrapped her arms around him.

They stood like that, with Gwen resting her head on the back of his neck, for what seemed like forever.

"It's okay," she said softly. "It's not your fault. There was nothing we could do…"

Slowly, very slowly, the tension went out of his muscles. Johnny turned around, tears streaming silently down his face, and put his arms around her. Gwen gently kissed his neck and cheek, tasting the saltiness of his tears.

He turned his face slightly to look into her eyes. Their lips touched.

Softly, as if searching for an answer, they kissed.

The kisses lingered, almost stopped. All they could feel was their breath on each other's lips.

They lay down on the pine needle covered ground and tenderly helped each other off with their clothes.

Gently, they made love.

They slept, arms wrapped around each other, until the cool morning air and the call of wood pigeons woke them.

Gwen put her hands on either side of Johnny's face and softly kissed his cheeks… a memory of last night's tears.

They dressed and went to sit by the fire, then watched the flames and the sunrise, until one by one, the others joined them.

Alison was buried near the top of the mountain.

Jen and Gwen lowered her naked body into the hole they had dug.

Handful by handful, they all threw earth over her until she was completely covered and the grave was filled. No one said anything. Nothing was left to mark the grave. No stone or cross. Those were the old ways, none of that mattered anymore. Now they only had the woods, the earth, the sky… and each other.

Last to leave the grave was Alison's best friend, Angie.

Nine

Johnny had gathered all the boys together. He was showing them a better way to lash their knives onto sticks to make spears. There was an air of determination about them. They were going hunting. If they didn't eat, they would all die.

Johnny had hoped that Charlie, Mark and Kev would have made it back from Heraklion before they set off to hunt. He would have preferred to have Charlie along with them. He would know the best places to look, Johnny thought. Well, who knows, maybe we'll be lucky anyway. The stew in the pots could certainly do with some meat.

Clutching their spears grimly in their hands, the four hunters set off.

The girls had split up into groups as well. Three of them, including Sarah, were going to search for plants. Jen told them to keep to the other side of the path than the hunters, so they wouldn't be mistaken for animals and have spears thrown at them!

"Hang on a minute," Johnny said just before they all set off. "We haven't seen anything dangerous here yet, but we don't know what might be out in the woods. If anyone is in danger, then make a call like this…" He cupped his hands to his mouth and let loose a loud Indian war cry. "Everyone can do that, can't they?" he said. *"Try!"*

The whooping cries that followed made them all laugh. But it was good. They would be able to hear each other from quite a long way away.

"Use it only in an emergency, okay?" Johnny said. "Right then, let's go catch something!"

That was a lot easier said than done though. The boys spent the rest of the day moving as stealthily as possible through the woods and across areas where there were only rocks and bushes. They all carried their spears at the ready. Johnny even had his catapult tucked into the top of his trousers.

A squirrel ran up a tree, but by the time Johnny had pulled a stone from his pocket and loaded his catapult, it had already climbed far too high above them and was well out of range. When they heard birds singing or calling to each other, they moved towards them but couldn't get close enough before they flew off.

The boys' spirits sank as the day went on, and by the time the sun reached the treetops, they all felt disappointed and frustrated. Johnny decided it was time to start heading back, even though none of them wanted to return empty handed—least of all him. They kept their eyes open on the way back anyway… just in case.

"There's a rabbit!" Harry said.

"Where?" Johnny said.

"I thought there was. Can't see it now though…"

They moved on.

Hungry, tired and with heads hanging, Johnny and his fellow hunters walked into camp.

Charlie, Mark and Kev were already there. They'd been told about Alison's death and, in turn, had told the others about finding Dave.

There were more tears. The hunters' failure didn't seem to matter now. The older children comforted the younger ones. You've been so brave, they told them. Now you have to be even braver…

Now they really were on their own. No one was going to rescue them. No one was going to take care of them.

"What killed Dave?" Johnny asked.

"I suppose it could have been a bear," Charlie said. "He hadn't been robbed or anything."

"Wouldn't a bear have eaten him?" Steve said.

"I don't know. Maybe, I guess."

"I didn't think there are bears on Crete. Wouldn't Dave and Jane have told us if there were?"

"I don't know," Charlie said.

We'll have to be on guard all the time, Johnny thought. It might have been a bear… or a human. S*omething* killed him, and it could be a danger to us.

"Wear your knife at all times, Charlie," he said.

"Yes, I will… I think we should even practice how to fight and defend the camp as well."

Johnny nodded in agreement.

Charlie looked over at Gwen. "Not just the boys, either. The girls can fight as well, can't they?" he said.

"Huh! You talking 'bout me?" Gwen said.

He smiled at her. "Just saying you're a good fighter!"

"Just don't make me mad," she said, trying to match his smile but only managing a wry grin. "You remember Jeremy and Ewan?"

"Of course I do!"

"They were lucky I didn't have a knife."

"Seriously, Gwen?" Charlie asked.

She didn't say anything. The look in her eyes was answer enough.

Johnny broke the silence. "We were out trying to hunt today but didn't see anything. Well, apart from one lousy squirrel who got away. What did we do wrong?"

"I don't know," Charlie said. "I'm no hunting expert either. Maybe you scared them off?"

"We tried to be as quiet as possible."

"Animals have incredible hearing and sense of smell," Gwen said. "Maybe tomorrow you could try hiding and lie in wait for them."

"Can't be any worse than we did today," Johnny said.

That evening the stew tasted great thanks to the new plants and herbs Sarah and the other girls had collected. It was still a bit watery, though—more like soup than stew.

"I've got an idea," Dick said.

"Go on," Charlie said.

"Well, look, I've been thinking. When I was little—"

"You *are* little!" Gwen said, and laughed.

"Ha-ha! No, but seriously. When I was little, I used to dig up worms in the orphanage's garden and eat them."

"That's gross!" someone said.

"Yeah, that's what Mrs. Jennings said too. But the thing is, they're not actually that bad. Bit slimy, but we can put them in the pots. They're food, aren't they?"

"Yuck!" someone else said.

"No, Dick's right," Jen said. "If we don't eat, we'll starve to death. We could try it tomorrow in just one of the pots… Dick, can you organize some worm catchers?"

Dick beamed. "Ants aren't so bad either!" he said.

That made everyone laugh.

"Okay then!" Jen said. "Dick has to taste *any* funny insects we find *before* they go into the pots!"

Dick stuck his tongue out at her but followed it up with a big smile.

"I'm off to bed. Lots of worms to catch tomorrow!"

The next day, Johnny, Charlie, Kev and Mark went off to hunt. Tom, Dick and Harry said they would go 'grubbing' as they called it: looking for worms, ants and any other insects that Dick deemed edible. They didn't want to take their spears, as they would have been in the way, so they unbound their knives and wore them on their belts instead. Gwen and Helen said they would fetch water. All the other girls took bags with them to collect plants, leaving Steve and Pete to guard the camp.

The stew was too thin. They had to find more food.

The hunters had been walking for about half an hour and hadn't seen any signs of animals. Charlie was beginning to worry.

"Johnny, if we can't catch anything up here, we're going to have to move down to the coast where we can try fishing. We can't live on flowers and worms forever."

"Don't worry, Charlie. We've just got to learn how to hunt properly. Like you said, we probably scared them off."

"How about finding where they go to drink? A pool or stream or something?" Mark said.

"Good thinking," Johnny said.

"And keep an eye out for droppings," Charlie added.

They explored for another half an hour, still getting to know the woods surrounding the camp, but didn't even find a place that seemed worth waiting at until an animal came along.

The three dwarves were having much better luck. They'd gone up to the spring with Gwen and Helen, then followed the watercourse for about ten minutes down to a place where the ground levelled out.

Dick, the self-proclaimed worm expert, announced that this was prime worm territory. The earth was soft and rich.

They dug with sticks.

He was right. One after the other, they pulled juicy worms from the ground and put them in a sealable pot they'd brought with them. Dick tasted one of the worms, 'just to be sure' he said—but mostly to show off—"Delicious!" he proclaimed.

For a while, the three boys were silently engrossed in their grubbing.

Harry looked up. He thought he'd seen something out of the corner of his eye.

A goat stood not more than thirty feet away. It wasn't doing anything, just standing there looking dolefully at him.

"Guys, be quiet. Look over there…" He tilted his head slightly to show them where he meant.

"What do we do? We mustn't scare it off," Dick whispered.

Harry took the lead. He stood up as quietly as possible. Tom and Dick did the same.

Trying to move as carefully as they could, they walked slowly towards the goat. It was unperturbed. It turned its head to look around a bit, then back at them.

Harry closed his fingers around the handle of his sheath knife and released its catch.

"I'll go for it," he said.

Tom and Dick froze. They held their breath as Harry took another few steps towards the goat… He was getting close now.

He held out his free hand as if offering it something to eat. Seeming to recognise the gesture, the goat took a step forward and stretched its head out.

Its hairy lips grazed his fingers.

In a flash, Harry pulled his knife from its sheath and plunged it into the goat's neck. Bright red blood gushed out.

The goat tried to leap away, but its legs buckled. It fell to the ground.

Harry took a step forward, holding his bloody knife in front of him. His whole arm was covered in blood.

"What do we do now?" Tom called out.

"I don't know!" Harry called back.

The three boys just stood there, watching as the goat's life bled into the ground. It kept trying to stand up, but it was getting weaker and weaker.

At last it lay still. The boys were entranced, not quite believing what had happened.

"It's dead," Harry said.

"You did it! You killed a goat!" Dick shouted.

"Into the pot with it!" Tom joined in.

That broke the spell. They all started laughing and hopping up and down for joy.

"How do we get it back to camp?" Harry said when they'd all finally quietened down a bit.

"We don't have to go back up to the spring and down the other side," Dick said. "I think if we just go round the side of the hill, it'll bring us more or less to camp. It shouldn't be too far."

Tom and Harry each took hold of one of the goat's hind legs and started dragging it behind them. The goat wasn't that heavy, but it was a bit awkward as there was no real path through the trees and bushes. They took turns either clearing the way ahead or dragging the goat. By the time they got to camp, they were all spattered with blood.

Dick got there first. He had a huge grin on his blood-smeared face.

"We found some worms."

Everyone stopped what they were doing and looked at him.

"And…" he said, dramatically flourishing his arms just as Tom and Harry entered the clearing, "Dinner!"

Everyone rushed to look at the goat. There was back clapping and smiles all round.

"Let's call the hunters back," someone said.

"We can't use the danger signal," Jen said, "but if we all shout their names at the same time, they might hear us. On the count of three: *One... Two...*"

Her *'Three'* was drowned out by the shouting.

It worked. In less than ten minutes, the hunters came running into camp. It took them a couple of moments to understand what all the commotion was about, but when they did, they joined in the celebrations.

"We'll have to take it somewhere else to butcher it, then bring the meat back here. Otherwise it'll stink and there'll be flies everywhere." Steve said when everyone had quietened down a bit.

"Who's up for butchering, then?" Charlie asked.

"I know how to do it, sort of," Mark said.

"I'll help," Gwen said.

"Me too," Johnny said.

"Right then. Let's drag it down to the latrines... but not too close either. We can bury the innards and stuff down there."

Butchering the goat was a messy business. By the time they were done, they were all soaked in blood. They separated the goat's legs from its body so they could roast them over the fire. Then they cut as many chunks of meat off as possible to be thrown into the pots. In years to come when they thought back to this first butchering, they would laugh about how much of the goat they'd wasted. They didn't know any better back then. In time they would learn.

That night the Tribe of The Two Pots feasted. The roasted meat was wonderful. When no one could eat any more, the three dwarves had to tell the story of how they'd killed the goat... again and again! Dick even pretended to be the goat. He stood on all fours as Harry showed the others how he had closed in and killed it. Dick's death throes were definitely worth an Oscar, everyone agreed. Their play-acting was rewarded with a standing ovation.

For an encore, Harry and Tom dragged the poor Dick by his legs around the campfire. Everyone howled in laughter. Even Dick.

"Hang on," he said when he'd been let back up again. "Just a second..."

He disappeared into his tent and came out holding a plastic container. With a dramatic flourish, he lifted its lid and grabbed one of the worms, shaking it so everyone could see.

Before anyone could protest, he ceremoniously dumped all the worms into one of the bubbling pots.

Oh well, they all thought, and gave him another round of applause.

It would take several more days before a hunting party brought anything back. They'd begun to realise that hunting was a skill you learnt slowly. Any mistake would scare the animals and birds off, leaving you empty handed.

Ten

Steve and Charlie were sitting together by the fire. It was late, and everyone else had gone to bed. In the east, a blood-red moon was rising. There were just a few thin clouds in the sky.

The moon would be full in a couple of days. It would mark their being alone on the island for three months.

"We're doing pretty well, aren't we, Steve?"

"Yes, three months on our own, and we're still alive. Except for Alison… But there was nothing we could do to help her, was there?"

"No, nothing…"

They sat silently for a while, both of them lost in their own thoughts.

Steve broke the silence. "It's December now, but I think it's warmer than it should be. Even for Crete, I mean. Something in the weather has changed. If we're right, and they blew everything up with atom bombs, it could have caused the climate to change. I suppose we're lucky. I don't think it ever gets really cold here. Not like in Wales, I mean. But we're quite high up, so winter should be colder here than down by the coast, but it doesn't even feel like autumn. More like the end of summer… Do you think we're the last people left on earth?"

"I don't know," Charlie said. "That's hard to believe. We haven't seen any signs of anyone else though. No boats or planes, and Heraklion was empty. The only thing I can think of is that other people might have survived on some of the other Greek islands. Unless the tsunami wiped them all out too."

"Thank goodness we had our camping gear and knives," Steve said.

"Yes, and those hiking rations and the pots… We've been working really well together, too, haven't we?"

Steve laughed. "Sure. Hardly any squabbles. Not bad for a bunch of kids. A lot of it is thanks to you and Jen, though. The kids follow your example. You know, always helping each other."

That surprised Charlie. Being a leader came so naturally to him that he hardly thought about it, or that he was setting an example.

"Huh! Thanks Steve. But everyone's done their part, haven't they? I kind of see Johnny as the leader, not me. He seems to be the most grown up, you know, leading the hunters and guarding the camp. He doesn't say much, but you can tell that's all he thinks about."

"Yes, that's true, but he looks to you to make the big decisions and organise things.

"Yes, I suppose so…"

They both fell silent and stared into the fire, each of them thinking about how much their lives had changed.

The moon rose higher and higher, casting a silvery light over the woods. Somewhere an owl hooted… Far way, another answered.

Steve broke the silence again. "I really want to know what happened," he said.

"What do you mean?" Charlie said. "If it was World War Three?"

"Well, that's part of it, of course. But I mean more about what went wrong with mankind, I guess… I want to understand if this was meant to happen, if it was unavoidable or if we took a wrong path somewhere in our history and it led to this. I don't know quite what I mean, but I want to understand."

Charlie thought about what Steve had said. It was interesting. It sparked something in him.

"It's true," he said at last. "Lots of people said they knew why we're alive. Everyone seemed to have their own theory about what life is about. But what if they were all wrong? What if no one had worked out why we're alive, and that's why it ended up like this? But how are we going to find the answer? If there even is one at all…"

Steve looked at him. "We could study," he said.

"Study? Study what?" Charlie asked.

"Look. What do we do all day? Hunt, gather plants, collect wood and water, sit around the fire… That's about it, isn't it? Well, the main things anyway. We haven't got to go to school or go to work when we get older. This is all there is, Charlie. We live off the land like Red Indians or Cavemen. We've been thrown back hundreds, or even *thousands* of years, to when there were no cars, or electricity, or machines or anything like that. It's not bad at all. Like you said, we're doing well, but we need something to stimulate our minds. To learn, and teach each other, I mean."

"Like having a school?"

"Yes, sort of. But not with all the subjects we used to have. We could study what went wrong as well. Does that make sense?"

"I'm not sure. I think so. With the books from the library?"

"Yes! It's all there. The basic material anyway. About the way people lived, what they believed in, and everything they knew. If we study that, we might find the answer to why it went wrong…"

"So where do we start?"

"I don't know," Steve said. "First off, we can go back to the library and bring back some books. Just start there. Read and talk about it. Maybe that'll lead us in the right direction."

"But why would we be able to find the answer if no one has found it before?"

"I don't know. Maybe they never really believed it would go wrong. I mean, they might have *said* so, but maybe deep down they didn't really believe it. Maybe they hoped they could sort it out. That everything would carry on anyway."

"But we know," Charlie said, picking up on Steve's train of thought. "Right? Not just think, or believe. We *know* it went wrong."

"Exactly!"

"So, we're the ones who can find the answer?"

"Maybe," Steve said. "Maybe. We should at least try…"

The two young men looked into each other's eyes.

There was something they recognised. Something they saw in each other. Something they both knew they were looking for in their own different ways.

The moon shone clearly above them.

Eleven

Days rolled by. The pots were full more often than not.

The boys were getting better at tracking and hunting. They'd caught rabbits, birds and even other goats. They gradually learnt the ways of the different animals: where they might find tracks, what time of day they were on the move, and when they might go to the streams to drink. The more they learnt, the easier it became to think like the animals and find them.

Catapults had become a favourite weapon. Dick was the best shot. Johnny and the other bigger boys were stronger and could shoot further, but Dick had a knack of knowing which way an animal was going to move—or if it would stand still. His shots often hit, rather than just scaring their prey off.

Rabbits were the easiest animals to track. They left droppings that could be followed back to their warrens. Then the hunters had to wait.

They spread out, hiding behind trees and bushes around the rabbit holes. When a rabbit came out of its hole, it would be very nervous at first: sniffing the air and looking around for any signs of danger. Any movement or sound would scare it back into its hole—and the waiting would begin again. The trick was to keep perfectly still and quiet until it ventured further afield. When it did, the hunter who was closest would let fly with a shot. Even if it missed, all was not lost. The surprised rabbit would bolt back towards its hole. Expecting this, the others would jump out from their hiding places, cutting off its escape route. Scared and confused, it would freeze in its tracks—and be hit by a barrage of stones.

It was very rare for a shot to kill a rabbit directly. One or more good hits would stun it or knock it down though, giving them the precious seconds they needed to leap forward and thrust their spears into it. They'd tried throwing spears but missed more often than not. The rabbit was finished off by having its throat cut.

Patience was the key to a successful hunt. Even so, some days the hunters would return empty handed and disappointed.

For their part, the girls were becoming experts at identifying all the plants Sarah had shown them. They always kept one of every kind they had never seen before, so it could be pressed and put in the plant book.

There were still many plants that they didn't recognise: ones that might or might not be edible. Sarah had grown up learning about the wild plants and flowers that grew in Wales. On Crete, there seemed to be a much greater variety—or maybe it just seemed like that because she didn't recognise them. The plants that grew in the more open and rockier places were a lot different than anything that grew in Wales. But which ones were edible, and which ones might be poisonous?

Her grandmother had taught her how to test unknown plants. Sarah had never tried doing it herself, though. First you rubbed the leaf or stem between your fingers, her grandmother had said. If there was no rash after an hour, you wet your lips and held a piece between them for a few minutes. Any horrible taste or tingling on your lips and that was that. If not, you waited another hour. The next step was to take a little piece and put it on your tongue. If after a few minutes it was still okay, you could chew it and then spit it out. If there were *still* no side effects, then after yet another hour, you could eat a small piece, chewing it thoroughly first. Only after a few more steps, eating increasing amounts and waiting to make sure there were no bad effects, could the plant be deemed to be non-poisonous—and hopefully tasty.

Although this was a good way of testing, it could still go wrong. Once, after eating the stalk of a purple flower, Sarah got really sick, vomiting again and again. When she finally recovered, to no one's surprise, she declared the purple flowers to be unfit for the pots!

Mushrooms were the most dangerous, her grandmother had

said. They can pass the test and taste good. Then up to a week later you could fall ill. Often the longer it takes to get ill, the greater the risk that you will die… Sarah showed them the few kinds of mushrooms that she knew were edible and told them to leave any others they found well alone.

Slowly but surely, the plant book filled up, and the stews became tastier and more nourishing. The Tribe of the Two Pots became leaner, losing any fat they might have had, but not unhealthily so. They were eating well, and surviving.

All through the winter it never really got cold, and it never rained. Not until the end of January, that is. Then the skies became covered with thick grey clouds and the rain came bucketing down. It kept on raining almost non-stop—day after day, and week after week, for almost a month.

Keeping the campfire alight wasn't easy. Even deadwood from beneath the trees with the most cover was soaked. It had to be stacked around the outside to dry out before being put on the fire. A lot of work went into splitting logs to get to the dry wood on the inside as well. To keep the rain from putting the fire out, they built a slanting roof high over it by lashing a row of logs together. It was held up by poles on either side and kept most of the rain off.

One night, the fire went out anyway. It took all morning to get a new one started. Luckily their lighters still worked. This worried Steve. What would we have done if we didn't have the lighters? he thought. We're going to have to learn how to make fire…

It was hard to hunt as well. All the animals and birds had taken shelter from the rain, and their tracks were washed away. The Two-Pot tribe's stew became thinner and thinner.

Then one day, the skies cleared and the sun came out again.

Twelve

Charlie woke with a start. It was the middle of the night, and everything was quiet. He'd been sleeping outside by the fire, under a moon that shone brightly in the cloudless sky.

His heart beat fast. Why did I wake up so suddenly? he asked himself. Maybe from a dream?

He lay absolutely still in his sleeping bag, trying to listen for any sounds. A long way away, he heard the baying of a dog—or a wolf. Maybe that was what woke me up? he thought. The first howls were joined by others—and then by barking.

Dogs, he thought—and they sound closer now. Feeling a bit worried, he got dressed, then opened the flap to the nearest tent where Kev and Mark were sleeping.

"Get up, guys. I think we've got trouble."

Charlie went back to the fire and waited for his friends to join him. He could still hear the dogs. They're much closer now, he thought.

"Come on," he said when Kev and Mark came out. "Let's wake the others."

The three of them grabbed their spears and put catapults in their pockets. Then they went from to tent to tent and woke everybody up. The barking was much louder now. It was hard to tell how many dogs there were—but quite a few, Charlie thought.

They all gathered by the fire.

"Jen, keep the girls together. You've got your knives with you, haven't you?" Johnny said.

"Yes," she said. "And sticks." She pointed to the pile of firewood.

"Good. We'll make a ring around the camp and fight the dogs off if they come here. They've probably smelt our food. If they break through our defences, it's up to you, okay?"

"Yes."

Johnny quickly got the boys spread out around the edge of the camp. They all had their spears at the ready. The barks were very close now.

Mark saw the pack leader first. It was a big, black dog with eyes that gleamed in the light of the moon. It glared at him and bared its fangs. Growling from deep in its throat, the dog moved slowly forward.

Behind it, the rest of the pack came into view.

The dogs had once been belonged to people who lived in the mountain villages. Driven desperate by hunger, they had reverted to their wild nature.

The other boys had realised where the danger was coming from and moved closer to Mark.

"Stones!" Johnny commanded.

Most of the boys already had stones in their pockets. Those that didn't, bent down to pick some up. They kept their eyes on the dogs all the time.

"Load … Steady … and … *Fire!*"

A barrage of stones whipped into the pack of dogs.

Those that were hit yelped wildly. They retreated into the woods. One of them limped badly. A stone had hit it hard on the leg.

"Be ready. They'll be back," Johnny called out. A few stones weren't going to keep the dogs from the meat they'd smelt.

The dogs spread out, keeping safely out of catapult range.

Instinctively, Johnny realised what they were doing.

"Spread out! They'll be coming from all directions!"

The black dog had circled around to the opposite side of the camp

Barking wildly, it rushed forward, straight towards Johnny.

This was the signal for the other dogs to attack the ring of boys. About even in numbers, it was going to be a vicious fight.

Johnny lifted his spear and lunged at the dog running towards him. In the last split second, it swerved, narrowly avoiding being stabbed, and ran past him towards the centre of the camp.

Thinking it was going for the girls, Johnny turned and raced after it.

The other boys were doing well—stabbing, slashing and beating the dogs with their spears.

The spears were effective weapons that gave them a big advantage over the dogs' only weapon: their teeth. But the dogs were fast. Both Charlie and Tom were bleeding from bites. Their wounds weren't serious enough to stop them from fighting though.

The dogs were faring worse. Two had retreated with nasty wounds, and one lay dead, speared through the heart.

Snarling and barking, the other dogs held their ground, waiting for a new chance to attack.

The pack leader that had broken through the boy's defences gave them that chance. Running straight past the girls, it took a huge leap and landed right on top of Charlie's back. The weight of the dog knocked him to the ground.

He screamed in pain as the dog sank its teeth deep into his shoulder.

If Johnny had reached him just seconds later, Charlie would have died. The dog was going for the back of his neck. One more bite from its savage teeth would be enough to kill him.

Johnny dropped his spear, not daring to throw it in case he missed and hit Charlie, and hurled himself onto the dog's back. Wrapping his arm around its neck, he tried to pull its head up and away from Charlie's neck.

Mark and Dick were the closest to the fight. They rushed in to help. This left another gap in the boys' defences. Seeing their chance, the other dogs broke through and raced towards the fire.

Screams pierced the night. The young girls were terrified.

Gwen and Jen didn't back down. Instead, they ran at the dogs, beating them wildly with sticks and screaming at the top of their voices.

A dog managed to grab Gwen's stick with its teeth and wrestle it from her grasp. In desperation, she pulled a burning branch from the fire. As the dog lunged at her again, she swung the branch, hitting it hard on the nose. The dog yelped in pain.

Before it could run off, Gwen brought the burning branch crashing down on its back. The dog fell, barking madly in pain and fear as its fur started to burn.

Johnny held on, but the black dog was strong. It thrashed its head from side to side, trying to bite him.

All of a sudden it let out a tremendous howl.

Dick had seen an opening and with all his strength had thrust his spear straight through the dog's eye. A second later it was dead.

Charlie was bleeding badly.

Johnny grabbed the spear that Charlie had dropped when he'd been attacked. He ran towards another one of the dogs.

In one slashing stroke he cut it deep along its belly, killing it.

Battle frenzy shone in his eyes. A blood-curdling snarl came from his throat. He turned and faced another dog.

The pack leader and three other dogs were dead. Two more were badly wounded. The dogs knew they were beaten.

Still barking, they turned tail and ran off into the woods.

Johnny took Dick by the arm. "You could have stabbed me or Charlie when you got that one through the eye," he said, pointing at the dead dog.

"I'm sorry, Johnny…"

"Don't be sorry, you idiot! You saved Charlie's life. Maybe mine as well. I'm *proud* of you!"

Even though he was the shortest of the boys, Dick felt as if he was ten feet tall. He was a warrior. He'd killed a dog. Johnny was proud of him!

They dragged the four dead dogs to the edge of the camp. No one wanted to go any deeper into the woods that night even though they could tell from the sound of occasional yelps that the rest of the pack was already far away.

Charlie's wound was the worst. After it had been cleaned with fresh water and soap, they could see that even though the dog's teeth had gone deep into his shoulder, only skin and muscle had been injured. It hurt like crazy, but no bones had been damaged.

The wound would heal, leaving a ragged scar that Charlie could be both proud of and which would always remind him that they should never let their guard down.

No one slept for the rest of the night.

The rising sun found the Two-Pot tribe sitting around the fire, recounting the battle, praising each other for their courage and talking about how they could have been better prepared. Most of all, though, they were all relieved that no one had been seriously injured or killed.

The next day, they butchered the dead dogs and threw the meat into the pots.

Thirteen

"Charlie?" Jen said. "Can we talk?"

"Sure. Of course. What's the matter?"

"No, I mean, can we talk in private?"

"Okay. I guess we could go to my tent. Is something wrong?"

"Come, I'll tell you there."

They left the fire and went over to his tent.

Jen sat down on Charlie's sleeping bag. Charlie rolled Kev's bag up and sat on it with his legs stretched out. He'd twisted his ankle in the fight with the dogs, and it was still a bit swollen and painful.

He didn't say anything. He could see that Jen was struggling to find a way to start telling him about whatever it was.

"Well…" she said, and trailed off.

"Well, what?" Charlie said.

"Well, I think we have a problem, Charlie. It's Angie and Maggy."

"Huh? They seem fine," Charlie said. "I saw them at dinner. They didn't look sick."

"No, they're not sick. It's not that…"

"What is it then, Jen?"

"Well," she said. "It's like this. This afternoon I went into their tent, and they were, well, you know…"

"Huh?" Charlie said. "What? No, I don't know."

"Charlie! They were getting off. You know…"

"So?"

"*So!*" Jen looked at him with wide eyes. "Is that all you have to say, Charlie?"

"Well, yeah." He was silent for a moment. "*So what,* then?" he said at last.

"*So what!*" Jen exclaimed. "Don't you think we should do something?"

"Do something? What do you mean, 'do something'?" Charlie said, a bit surprised.

"I don't know. Talk to them, or something."

"Or something? Like what something? Put up a sign that says girls can't get off with each other? Or make a law and banish them to the woods? Come on, Jen. Like I said, *so what?*"

"So what? So you think it's okay if girls get off with each other?"

"Yeah. So what?"

"Or boys with boys?"

"So what?" Charlie said again, and shrugged his shoulders.

"Or a big group orgy?" Jen said, getting into it now.

"Yeah, so what?" Charlie laughed.

"Or if the three dwarves have a ménage à trois?" She couldn't help laughing out loud at this thought.

"*So what!*" they both cried out.

Charlie couldn't stop laughing now. "*So! … What!*" he just managed to gasp between heaves of laughter.

"Or if *we* screw each other?" Jen said, sending them both into howls of laughter again.

"*So! What!*" Charlie gasped, trying to catch his breath.

Their laughter was making such a noise that the others at the fireplace couldn't help noticing. They had no idea what was going on, but the laughter was infectious.

"Yeah! So What!" Jen said, pulling her shirt off.

She snapped her bra buckle open, then went for Charlie's belt.

Minutes later when she came with Charlie deep inside her, she let out a huge cry of … "*So what!*"

Having heard exactly what was happening in the tent, this sent the others into more fits of laughter.

Afterwards, Jen and Charlie lay with their arms wrapped around each other, holding and touching each other, and occasionally murmuring a soft 'so what'.

"We can do anything we want, can't we, Charlie?" Jen said at last. "No parents. No teachers. No rules… We're free, aren't we?"

"Yes, well no, I'm not sure," Charlie said. "We're free to do whatever we want. But it feels like we still have to learn how to allow ourselves to *be* free as well. To be really free. Truly free."

"Maybe," Jen said. "It'll take some practice." She laughed, stroking him hard again.

"Come here, Charlie."

"Ouch! Mind my shoulder, Jen!"

Fourteen

They'd had to put off the expedition to the library in Heraklion until it stopped raining. Steve was raring to go, now that the days were sunny again.

"I'll go with Mark," he said to Charlie. "He knows the way."

They were eating stew and watching a pale crescent moon rising slowly in the clear blue afternoon sky.

"Three of you should go together," Charlie said. "If one of you gets hurt or something, then it's better to be three."

"Why should we get hurt?"

"You never know. You could fall and break a leg, or get attacked by the dogs or by whatever killed Dave. It's better to be three."

"But that leaves fewer of you guys to protect the camp. It's more likely that the dogs will come back here. We'll be careful."

"What do you think, Johnny?" Charlie said.

Johnny looked up from his bowl of stew. As he usually did, he took a few seconds to gather his thoughts before speaking. Steve and Charlie waited patiently. There was never any point in rushing him.

"Most important is to protect the camp," he said at last.

"So you mean Steve and Mark should go on their own?"

"Well, yeah. It's a bit more dangerous for them, I agree," he said after another short pause. "But we've got more to lose if we don't guard the camp."

This was always Johnny's first priority. Sometimes it seemed as if protecting the others was all he thought about.

Even though they'd kept guard at night before the dog attack, it hadn't seemed so important. Now they knew better. One of them always stayed up after the others had gone to bed. Then they would take turns until the sun rose and the camp came to life. They'd become good at telling the time by where the stars were in the night sky.

Quite often whoever was on guard would be joined by Johnny, who 'just happened to be up', as he put it.

Johnny loved the sounds of the night: the crackling of the fire, the wind in the trees and the occasional hooting of an owl. He could sit for hours just staring into the darkness.

Even the deepest and darkest nights would be lit up by tiny flashes of light: a ray of moonlight, a reflection in the eyes of a night predator, fireflies blinking in the bushes or a shooting star burning across the sky. Johnny watched and listened.

Every now and again, he would get up to stretch his legs and walk around the camp's perimeter, listening to the sounds of his tribe: the gentle snores, someone turning in their sleep, hushed whispers, and the soft rustle of love-making.

"Okay. If you're sure then, Steve?" Charlie said. "But don't be gone too long. Just get some books and head back. If you see anything strange, or whatever, then come back to camp so we can work out what to do. Agreed?"

"Agreed," Steve said.

It was the books he wanted to get his hands on, so he could start studying. Johnny's thoughts were taken up with the safety of the tribe, Steve's just as much with the question he and Charlie had talked about: Why had it gone wrong?

There were some obvious answers, of course: politics and economics, religious fanaticism and irrational nationalism. Those had been the cause of war and conflicts throughout history, but Steve had a feeling that there was something else—something deeper—the root of the problem. To find it, he would start by studying history and politics in the light of what they now knew, he thought. Then see where that led. But where to start? he asked himself… I'll sort that out when I get to the library, he decided.

At daybreak, Steve and Mark set off. They took two bottles of water and two roasted squirrels with them in case they didn't find any food in the city. The sky was clear. It was going to be a great day.

Steve had a big grin on his face as they waved goodbye. He'd been looking forward to going to the library for what felt like ages. Both of them had unbound their knives from their spears and now wore them on their belts. The spear shafts made good walking staffs and could still be used in a fight if need be. Not as deadly as a spear, of course, but nonetheless.

Mark set the pace. Steve was right behind him. They'd agreed to camp above the tsunami line. Mark had said that the city was creepy, so they didn't want to spend the night there. Better to sleep in the open.

"I have an announcement to make," Jen said when Steve and Mark had left. "Listen up, Tribe! Today is a day off!"

"A what?" someone asked.

"A day off, silly! No gathering and no hunting. The pots are full. So we get a day off!"

"What do we *do*, then?" someone else asked.

"Anything! You can do whatever you want. Or don't do anything at all if you don't want to. I've got an idea, though, if anyone is interested?"

"What? Tell!"

"We can have a *Making Day*."

"A what day?"

"A Making Day. We can *make* things."

"What things?"

"That's up to you, Jen said. "Think of something you want, or something that could be useful. Then work out how to make it. We can all help each other with ideas or work in groups. How does that sound?"

"Can it be something to play with?" Maggy asked. "Like a doll?"

"Yes! That's perfect, Maggy. Anyone else got an idea?"

Everybody started talking at once. Ideas were discussed. Some were discarded as being too hard or because they didn't have the right materials. After a while, they broke off into groups of twos and threes and started *making*.

"What are you going to make, Johnny?" Jen asked.

"A bow and arrow. I've been thinking about it for a while. I think it can be done. I just need a bit of help—"

"Not from us!" Tom, Dick and Harry said in chorus. "We've got something else we're going to make!"

Johnny laughed. "Well, I'll make it on my own then! But don't come asking to borrow it later!" he said with a grin.

"What about you, Jen?"

"Oh, I've got lots of stuff to make," she said somewhat mysteriously.

"And you three?"

"Not telling! You'll see!" the three dwarves called back as they rushed into the woods.

"Huh! Oh well, if no one's going to tell me anything, I might as well get to work," Johnny said.

Fifteen

Steve walked slowly up and down the library aisles. Where to start? he asked himself. Where on earth do I start?

"Got to start somewhere," he said out loud, looking at the row of shelves in front of him.

He was in the section for international politics. Many of the books seemed to be far too specialised, covering only very narrow subjects. Others seemed more prophetic: about how the future of nations or economic systems might develop. The ones that predicted a catastrophic end to humanity were the most interesting.

At last, he decided to take one of those books *The Death of Civilisation*. He put it in his rucksack along with what looked to be more like a university coursebook *A History of Political Systems*.

In the meantime, Mark had been wandering aimlessly through the library, occasionally looking at books that caught his eye.

When Steve called out that he had found a couple of interesting books, Mark was in the biology section looking at the pictures in a book about great apes: gorillas, orangutans, chimpanzees and bonobos. He put the book back on its shelf and was about to go over to where Steve was, when a book on the bottom shelf caught his eye. It was a slim book, squeezed in between two thicker ones. It had a bright green sleeve. Maybe that was why it had stood out. Thinking about it later, he couldn't really explain it, though.

"Hang on, Steve. Just a second," Mark called out as he bent to pull the green book off the shelf.

Its title leapt out at him, instantly making his heart jump. He couldn't believe it. In bold letters it simply said: *Edible Plants of Greece*.

"Steve! Steve! Come here! Quickly!"

Steve hurried over to the aisle where Mark was.

Mark held the book up so he could see its cover.

One look at it told him all he needed to know. He grabbed the book, opened it in the middle and quickly flicked through the pages.

"*Yes!*" Steve said, and gave Mark a mighty slap on the shoulder.

The two lads grinned at each other.

"You think Sarah will like this?" Mark asked.

"You've got to be kidding! She'll go crazy! This is *gold!* I think our stews just got a heck of a lot tastier!"

"We should get back to camp with it as soon as possible. Shall we head back straight away?"

Steve would have loved to stay for hours, or even days, exploring the library, but he realised that Mark was right. This book was too important. They had to leave.

They wrapped the precious book in a plastic bag they'd found in the library's reception area. Steve put it in his rucksack along with his other books. They didn't have any food to carry, as they'd eaten the roasted squirrels the night before, but even though they were hungry, they were far too excited to worry about looking for food in the city.

Closing the library door carefully behind them, they set off for home.

Sixteen

The Two-Pot tribe was hard at work, *making*.

Angie and Maggy huddled together in the shade of the tree in the middle of camp. They had both found forked branches which, when cut and carved, had the rough shape of a doll—if you had the imagination of a thirteen-year-old girl that is! Gwen had helped them cut through the thickest parts of the branches. Now they were carefully whittling them, trying to give the wood a face, fingers and toes. Hair was going to be a problem, but they had decided to sort that out later.

Gwen was glad that the two young girls seemed to be adapting to their new life. Angie and Maggy had been the most homesick at first even though the older children had been really good at looking after them. After Alison had died, Angie hadn't said another word about home or her parents. It was as if she had decided that this was her home now, and that everything else was gone forever—to be forgotten about.

Maybe that's what got us through, Gwen thought. When you have to take care of other people, you stop thinking about yourself so much. We've really changed in such a short time. Not just the caring for each other, but having to manage on our own without any grown-ups to come and help us if we get into trouble. It had been easier for Tom, Dick and Harry. They'd latched onto the older boys, and having each other seemed to make everything seem like a big adventure. Where are they anyway?

She wandered into the woods, vaguely in the direction that the three dwarves had gone off in. She didn't have to go far before she found them in a rocky clearing.

They had laid out about twenty branches of different lengths on the ground. Now they were busy stripping them of leaves and twigs. Tom had even started scraping bark off with his knife.

"Hi, guys! What are you making?" Gwen called out as she got closer. She had no idea what it could be.

"Promise you won't tell Johnny?" Tom said.

"Sure, of course not."

"We're making him a chair," Harry said. "You know how he's up almost every night guarding the camp? Well, we thought he might like a comfy chair to sit in and watch the sun go up in the morning."

"He is getting old, you know," Dick butted in. "He's almost seventeen!"

That made them all laugh.

"How are you going to tie the branches together?" Gwen asked.

"That's really easy," Tom said. "We found a glade over there…" He pointed into the woods away from the camp. "There's loads of creepers hanging from the trees. They're all sorts of thicknesses. Some of them are thick enough to climb up."

Gwen laughed. "I bet they are. For monkeys anyway!"

"Yeah, yeah…" Tom said, "When you're at the top, you just cut the thin creepers off."

"You are careful, aren't you?" Gwen said. "So you don't fall down, I mean…"

This just got her three withering looks.

"Anyway," Harry said, "the only thing we haven't worked out yet is what to use as a seat. The branches won't be that comfortable to sit on without something soft."

"Maybe I could help you with that," Gwen said. "We've got a goatskin that's been scraped clean. If we made holes round the edges, you could tie it to the chair. I think it's big enough to cover the back as well."

"That would be great!" Dick said. "Can you get it now?"

"Sure," Gwen said, smiling at them. "I think Johnny will love the chair."

"Great! Thanks!" the boys said in unison.

"Hiho, hiho, it's back to work you go!" she sang as she turned around and headed off towards camp.

Charlie had also gone off, but he was already back and was now sitting at the fire with Angie and Maggy. He had his head bent over and was obviously concentrating hard on whatever it was he was making. He had two pieces of wood: a thick flat one which he'd made by splitting a bigger log, and a thinner stick which he was in the process of scraping smooth.

"Hi, Gwen!" Charlie said, looking up as she came into camp.

"Hi!" she said, and gave all three of them a hug. "What are you making, Charlie?"

"Fire."

"Wow! Really? How?"

He held up the stick he'd been working on. "By friction… Look, this is a hard wood, and the flat piece is a soft wood. What happens, hopefully, is that by rubbing the hardwood stick in a groove in the soft wood it'll get hot enough to light some tinder. That's the theory anyway," he added a bit sheepishly.

"That's great, Charlie."

"Thanks. We'll see if it works when I'm done. What about you? Are you making something?"

"Yes, I've started making a wooden flute. I think it'll end up being more like a recorder."

"Can you play?" he asked

"No, but I'm going to teach myself. I can't do that without making one, though, can I?"

"No!" Charlie laughed. "I guess not!"

The day seemed to have gone so quickly.

When the evening light finally got too weak to see by, the tribe tucked into bowls of stew. Time had flown by so fast that they'd all forgotten to eat. It had been a great day. None of the projects were finished, so they unanimously decided that the next day would be a making day too.

"But then it's back to hunting and gathering," Johnny said. Hopefully, I'll soon be hunting with my bow and arrow, he thought to himself, although he had to admit that it was turning out to be much harder than he'd imagined. He'd already tried, and discarded, three types of wood for the bow. They would either snap if he bent them too much or not bend enough.

Helen and Sarah had spent the day scraping rabbit skins clean. They were going to make collecting bags out of them. They had whittled sharp sewing needles from small sticks, but their first attempts at sewing hadn't been a great success. They'd tried using the stalks from different plants to make thread, but nothing was strong enough to work with. Dick had told them about the vines they'd been using for their secret project, but he thought they'd be too thick for sewing.

"We'll have to experiment some more tomorrow," Sarah said.

"Yes, something that can be used as thread and string would be useful for a lot of things, wouldn't it," Helen said.

"What have you been making, Pete?" Gwen asked.

He'd been gone all day and hadn't brought anything back to show for it. He seemed to be thinking hard about something as he ate his stew.

"Me? Oh, me and Nina have been making a clock."

"You've what!" someone said.

"We're making a clock," Pete said. "And a calendar. We thought they'd be useful, or interesting, at least."

"But how?"

"We're still working on the theory, but basically it's a sundial. You tell the time by the shadows caste by the sun. That's the clock bit, anyway. But then we thought that because the sun moves slowly north in summer and south in winter—"

"The equinoxes!" Jen said

"Right… Well, by marking those positions as well, it would make a calendar. It'll take us a year or so to get it finished, though," he said with a laugh, and looked over at Nina.

"We're making it in the clearing by the spring, where the sun shines all day," she said.

"The moon changes every month too, doesn't it?" Maggy asked.

Nina smiled. "That's right, Maggy. It's more or less twenty-eight days from new moon to new moon, so it takes two weeks from new moon to full moon, then two weeks back again. We should track that as well…"

As if on cue, the first rays of a new moon shone over the horizon.

Seventeen

"Sarah, close your eyes and hold out your hands," Steve said.

"Huh! Why? It's not my birthday or anything…"

"Just do it, silly!"

"Okay," she said. She closed her eyes tight and held out her hands.

"Not so wide," Steve said. "Good! Here… You can look now."

Sarah opened her eyes and saw the book's cover.

Her eyes widened even further.

"No!" she said, quickly opening the book he had given her. "*Yes!* I mean. It's wonderful! Look! That one I didn't know… and *those* I've seen… Here, look!"

There was no stopping her babbling now. She was so excited that she could hardly stand still. So she sat down instead—and started reading.

By the light of the fire, she read the book from cover to cover, flipping back and forth to compare flowers and plants.

Much later that evening, she gently closed the book and let out a sigh. It really was too good to be true, she thought. Gathering will be so much fun now. So many different things to find!

"Oh!" she said. "I forgot!"

She ran over to Mark's tent

"Hi, are you still awake? Can I come in?"

"Of course. Come on in," Mark said. "Steve's here. We're just talking."

Sarah went into the tent and gave them both the hardest hugs she'd ever given anyone in her whole life.

"Thank you, thank you," she said. "This is so great…" Tears rolled down her face.

Mark held her in his arms. "Hey, it's okay, Sarah. Shush. We know. It's great for all of us."

"Yes, I know," she said. "It's just, it's just… I've been so worried that we wouldn't find enough plants. But now there's so much more. It's great!" She sniffed and wiped her eyes. "Sorry, I've cried all over your sleeping bag!"

As it turned out, the book was also a Rosetta stone: a key to translating between Greek and English, as every page was written in both languages. Steve quickly worked out the Greek alphabet; most of the letters were fairly similar to the English ones.

As was his way, he buried his nose in the book whenever he could and steadily gained a grasp of the new language. He'd realised that knowing Greek would let him read all the books in the library. Having no idea how to pronounce the Greek words properly, he pronounced them as he would in English or however seemed to fit the closest when he was unsure.

While Steve was studying Greek, Charlie set about ploughing through the other books Mark and Steve had brought back. His quick mind raced with new ideas which he took every opportunity he could to discuss with whoever was up to it.

Often his thoughts bubbled out faster than the others could keep up with. At times, even Steve had to tell him to slow down.

Although naturally highly intelligent, Steve used his intellect more like a battering ram: breaking down problems bit by bit, then putting his thoughts together in a logical step-by-step order.

Charlie's brain worked differently. He made intuitive leaps of reasoning, jumping over logical steps and reaching conclusions without the plodding footwork Steve needed to catch up with him. Once Charlie had seen where a train of thought was leading, he could almost instantly see its furthest consequences. Only then did he backtrack to fill in the missing logic and reasoning. At this point, though, Steve gave him no rein. Any illogical thought or ungrounded assumption—however minor—would immediately be seized upon and shot down without mercy. This unavoidably led to hours and hours of sometimes quite heated discussions. Neither of them would give an inch. A minor point could lead to a discussion that went round and round, sometimes for days on end. The slightest nuance of the meaning of a word, or concept, would be debated, argued and relentlessly picked to pieces. At times it seemed as if they were getting nowhere. Then one or the other of them would bring up another point, and off they would go again, deep into another battle.

To those who listened to them, it seemed as if they could never agree on anything. This wasn't so. They were simply whittling away everything that wasn't perfectly logical or that seemed to lead to a dead end. What was left might be true—or at least it might lead them in the right direction to something else that might be.

Eighteen

"Johnny! Come over here, Johnny!" Tom, Dick and Harry all shouted at once. They were standing shoulder to shoulder at the edge of the camp.

"Nah! You come over *here!*" Johnny called back from where he sat by the fire. He had a mug of Sarah's chamomile tea in his hand. It was mid-morning. He'd been up half the night, and when he'd finally gone to bed, he'd slept deeply.

All morning, Tom, Dick and Harry had been putting the finishing touches to the chair they'd made. It stood behind them now, hidden from view.

"No! *You* get over *here*, old man! We've got something to show you!"

"Old man, huh!" Johnny said. "I'll show you what an old man can do, you mischievous imps!"

He put his mug of tea down and walked purposefully towards the three boys. "Well then, little people. What is it?"

He couldn't help laughing, even though he was trying as hard as he could to look ferocious.

"It's like this," Tom said. "You spend a lot of time at night staring at the horizon when you're not patrolling the perimeter, right?"

"Yeah, so?"

"You see, we thought we could make life a bit more comfortable for you."

With a dramatic swooshing noise—as if pulling theatre curtains open—the three dwarves stepped aside.

"*Ta-da!*"

The chair was truly magnificent. The vines they'd lashed it together with had made it strong. They'd woven thinner sticks together to make the seat and back, then stretched the goatskin over it and tied it down with thin vines to keep it taught.

"Go on! Try it!" Harry said.

Johnny sat down in the chair.

It didn't wobble at all. They'd spent a long time making sure the legs were all exactly the same length.

"Not bad," he said.

"*Not bad!*" Dick cried out.

"Nah, not *bad*. More like... *Fantastic!*" Johnny admitted with a grin.

Tom, Dick and Harry beamed.

Praise from Johnny was rare. It had to be well-earned but that made it all the more valuable.

"Thank you, guys," Johnny said. "Now, will one of you run to the fire and get me my tea? I think I'll just sit here for a while."

They all laughed as Dick ran off to get Johnny's tea.

Nineteen

It was a beautiful morning.

The sun had just risen over the horizon. Its first rays turned the dewdrops on the grass into thousands of tiny rainbows.

Jen was the only one awake. She sat with her back to the fire, watching the sunrise and the dewdrops. Every time even the slightest of breezes blew through the trees, the leaves of grass would sway, making the dewdrops shimmer ruby red, orange and yellow, emerald green, sapphire blue, indigo and violet.

"So beautiful. So fragile," she said softly.

The sun would soon warm the earth, and the tiny beads of water would evaporate.

Their lives are so short, then they are gone. So short a time, but so beautiful… The wonder and the sadness of this thought caused a single tear to form in the corner of her eye.

She didn't see it herself, but just for a moment the sun reflected in the teardrop, and it sparkled with all the colours of the rainbow.

Our lives are fragile too. We are born. We live and grow old. Then we die… Life goes on, day by day. For millions of years, people have lived and died on the earth. Struggling to survive like we do. Giving birth to children in an endless chain that links us to the very first humans. Then further back to the animals, and plants and everything else. So many lives. So many deaths.

Why? she wondered. Are we meant to find something? Or do something? Become something, or feel something? Or is this it? We live because we do. Is life its own reason?

Her thoughts wandered back through the ages. Such a long time. So many lives all joined together… and we are part of it. Just a small part, but we are alive now, being part of it… like the dewdrops.

She hadn't really noticed the others who had come to sit by the fire. They hadn't wanted to disturb her. It was obvious that she was deep in thought, so they quietly put more wood on the fire and stirred the pots.

It was the smell of the stew that finally roused her from her reverie. It smelt tangy from all the new herbs they'd learnt from the plant book. It smelt delicious.

"Oh, hi! Sorry everyone, I was daydreaming. I should have stoked the fire."

Charlie smiled at her. "No problem, Jen. Here, have some stew."

"Thanks." She took the bowl and smiled back at him. "Is everyone here?" she asked, looking around the fireplace.

"Except Dick. Why?" Charlie asked.

"Tom, go wake Dick will you?"

"Easier said than done!" Harry said.

But they had their ways to wake him up. From the sound of shouting and laughter that emerged from their tent, it entailed a certain amount of tickling!

"I've got something to say," Jen said when the now not-so-sleepy Dick had been dragged to the fire and given a bowl of stew.

They all turned to look at her.

"I'm pregnant," she said.

"What!" Gwen cried out. "Why didn't you tell me?"

"I'm telling you now. I wanted everyone to know. In about six months I'll be having a baby."

"That's good, isn't it?" Steve asked.

"I'm scared stupid," Jen said, "but yes, it's good."

"I hope it's a girl," Angie said.

"No! We need more boys!" Dick said. "Guess we'll find out when it's born," he added.

"Who's the father?" Gwen asked.

Jen looked at her twin sister. She didn't say anything. Instead, she looked at the boys, one at a time.

"You all are," she said.

"Huh?" Tom said.

"No, she's right," Johnny said. He'd got it first. "We're all going to protect the new one, aren't we? So we're all fathers. Right, Jen?"

"Yes, Johnny. That's exactly what I mean."

"And we're all going to be mothers," Angie said. "I mean, we're all going to take care of the baby."

"Yes, Angie," Jen said, smiling warmly at her. "We're all going to be mothers."

Just under six months later, Jen gave birth. Not to one baby, but twins: a girl and a boy. They were both healthy, greeting the world with loud screams. Both of the babies had freckles. Not just a few freckles on their noses, either, but all over their bodies—from top to toe.

After much discussion, they decided on names for the new twins. Gwen had suggested that they shouldn't be given regular names, but Two-Pot tribe names taken from nature.

In the end, they agreed that the boy would be called Sunray, and the girl, Dewdrop. Jen said that the names would always remind her of the morning she'd told the tribe she was pregnant—and of the tiny rainbows in the dew.

Twenty

"Jen, are you happy?" Charlie asked.

She looked up from the bag she was sewing. "Of course I am… Oh hang on. You want to talk about something else, don't you?" she said, and grinned.

Charlie grinned back.

"Okay then. What do you mean 'happy'?" she asked, taking the bait.

"Well, that's just it," he said. "I've been thinking a lot about happiness. What it means to be happy. What happiness *is*."

"Go on," Jen said.

"Okay. Well, it means that you feel good, right? But that depends on lots of different things, doesn't it?"

"I suppose so," she said, not quite able to see what he was getting at.

"I mean, there are a few basic things we need to feel happy, aren't there? Food, water, warmth… Like now. We're sitting by the fire, it's nice and warm, there's enough stew in the pots for everybody and we've got water to drink. That feels good doesn't it?"

"Of course." Jen said. She still wasn't sure where he was going with this.

"Those are the basic things, but it wouldn't feel so good if you were sitting at the fire all alone, would it? If you were the only person in the world, I mean."

"No, of course not. You would feel horribly lonely. It's nice being on your own sometimes, when you're thinking, or when you're making something, but it would be horrible if you were the only person left in the world. No one to talk to, or be able to do things together with… or make love with!"

"That's what I mean. We can add that to the list: Food, Water, Warmth, Other people."

"Shelter. Don't forget that. Like our tents… Shelter from when it's cold at night or during the rainy months. That's almost the same as 'warmth' though, I suppose."

"Yes, good thinking, Jen. I hadn't thought of it like that before."

"But why do we need each other. It can't just be so we won't feel lonely, can it?"

"No. I think it's a lot more than that. Take Sunray and Dewdrop, for instance. They need you to survive, don't they? Without your milk, they would die within days."

"That's obvious. But that's food and drink, and warmth from my body. That's all on the *happiness list* already."

"There's more," Charlie said. "You'd protect them from danger, wouldn't you?"

"Of course!" Jen's eyes widened. "I'd kill anything that tried to harm them or take them way."

"Why?"

"*Why!* Because they're my babies, stupid!"

"That's not an answer," Charlie said. "Well, it is, but not a very good one."

"Oh, okay, I see what you mean. I'd give up my own life to protect them. They are more important than me, because…" She paused for a moment to gather her thoughts. "Because they're the future, Charlie. They'll go on after us. Without babies, the tribe would die out. And babies can't protect themselves. So *we* have to protect them… That's the way nature works. So that life can go on."

"So we survive. Or our genes do, even when we're dead. Our children need us to survive, and we need them to survive—as a species, at least."

Then it came to him. It was obvious once the thought was clear.

"Everything we do is about survival, Jen! Everything! That's why we help each other… That's why we boys protect you girls. So there can be more babies. Even if some of us died protecting you, our genes would carry on anyway. But that's not all. Everything we do—living together, studying, exploring, playing, making—in the end, it's all helping us survive… The better we do all these things, the happier we are. When we have all we need, *then* we're happy. That's it. That's all! Think about it. That's what animals do, isn't it? They just do whatever they have to—to survive. That's what instincts are for."

"So you mean they're happy?"

"Yes! They must be. They're all happy! Following their instincts. Following their nature."

"But what about people, Charlie? We've grown out of our instincts, haven't we? Think about what people do—or did—I mean. There were as many different ways of living as there were different people. You can't say they were all following their instincts, can you? We all did different things. Just compare city people to farmers, or people in Britain to those in, I don't know, Africa or India. Or just how different people are from each other. What they wanted, and liked, and everything…"

"Yes, but that's just it, Jen. They *weren't* following their instincts. Which means they weren't happy… Which means they were *un*happy. And instead of doing everything they had to, to survive, the things they did led to the opposite. They destroyed the world and killed themselves in the end."

"Yes," Jen said. "But *why* didn't they follow their instincts, or nature or whatever you want to call it?"

"I don't know," Charlie said. "But I'm going to work it out. I think we're on the right track, though."

Jen looked at him. It seemed like he was glowing with excitement… and something else, she thought. Yes, 'discovery'.

"Yes, you are, Charlie," she said, brushing her lips gently against his cheek. "I've got to check up on the freckle twins. They're probably hungry again," she said, and then laughed. "Gotta survive, eh!"

Twenty-one

"Hi, Johnny," Harry said.

Johnny was sitting in his chair, peering out across the island.

"Hi, Harry."

"How's your bow and arrow coming along? That's why we made the chair, you know? So you could sit in it and shoot the dogs if they come back in the middle of the night… Not just sit here and be lazy!"

Johnny laughed. "Lazy! I'll give you lazy!"

Harry laughed too. He knew that no one worked harder than Johnny.

"How's it coming along? The bow, I mean."

"It's coming along," Johnny said. "It's just been really hard finding the right kind of wood. You can't tell if it's going to bend enough, or snap, until you've carved it. If it's no good, then all that time was wasted, and you have to start all over again. I think I've found a good piece now. It's from an olive tree. It feels right. I think the most common wood for bows was from yew trees. Sarah knows most of the trees that grow here, but I'd like to learn more about them too. Maybe we could get a book from the library about trees as well?"

"Good idea," Harry said.

"Hey, Steve!" Johnny called out to the group at the fire.

"What?" Steve called back.

"Pick up a book about trees?"

"Sure. We'll check the library when we're there. I was thinking about going down tomorrow. Harry, you want to come with me?"

"Do I ever!"

Being picked to go to the city with Steve was a great honour.

Steve always went himself, as he had a knack of finding just the right books, but he was always fair when it came to picking who was to go with him, so no one felt left out.

Steve and Charlie had worked their way through a number of subjects already: from contemporary politics and modern political history to doomsday books and ecology. One time Steve had brought back books on world religions. Another time he had found a fascinating book *The Wonder of Reality*. It explained science in a very clear and easy-to-understand way with really great pictures.

Not everyone was interested in reading the books he brought back—or discussing politics, science or philosophy either—so Steve brought back storybooks as well. It was a university library, so there weren't any children's books or that many works of fiction either. He did find some, though, like *The Iliad* and *The Odyssey*: mythical tales from classical Greece that had been written over three thousand years ago.

Although they'd heard some of the stories at school, no one had read the originals—not even Steve. The story of Jason and the Argonauts' search for the Golden Fleece became a favourite. The stories made them feel as if they, too, were part of an ancient Greek adventure on the island of Crete.

The next day, Steve and Harry set off for the city. Steve knew the way really well now, having made the trip at least ten times before. He'd even found the perfect spot to camp overnight—not far from where Dave's body had been found and where they'd buried him.

It was in a small clearing just off the path. On a previous trip they'd made a fireplace with a ring of stones there.

Steve had one of the lighters with him. They always used them very sparingly, even starting fires with just the sparks so as not to waste the lighters' gas. Charlie's efforts to make fire with a rubbing board and stick had *almost* been successful. He'd managed to get small piles of tinder to smoke, and even catch fire a few times, but it was hard, and he was never sure if it was going to work. He was still trying though: experimenting with different woods and different ways of rubbing them together.

Steve and Harry sat by their small fire, chewing on strips of roasted rabbit meat.

It was a beautiful evening. There was just a hint of a warm breeze. The moon had already set, and the sky was slowly filling up with stars. The only sound they could hear was the soft purring of crickets.

"Steve, do you believe in God?" Harry asked.

"Big question, Harry. I guess I don't believe in the god we learnt about at Sunday school—the one who sits in the sky and watches everything we do and listens to our prayers," Steve replied. "And I'm not sure about Jesus either—walking on water and turning water into wine and all that. Seems pretty far-fetched. Weird that so many people really believed it just because it was written in a book a couple of thousand years ago… What about you?"

"It's all *rubbish!* Harry said. "My parents tried to stuff it into my head all the time, telling me how much Jesus loved me, or that God was angry with me if I'd done something wrong. It's all just meant to make you feel guilty and do what they want you to do—"

"Hey, take it easy, Harry. No need to get worked up. We can talk about it, if you want. Just slow down, okay?"

"Yeah, sorry. I didn't mean to sound so angry. It's just my family was really religious. My sister was the worst. She carried a bible around with her and believed all that stuff they told us in church. That's why my parents loved her more than me."

"Don't say that, Harry. You don't know…"

"Yes, I do. She was always a goody-goody. You know, always did her homework and got top marks in school. She talked about Jesus and the bible all the time. I think that's what makes me so *anti* all of it. Worst was when I got into trouble and my dad had *serious* discussions with me. He tried to make me feel bad. He said that Jesus was disappointed in me, or that I had to be afraid of going to hell. When that didn't work, he'd get really mad and punish me. I'm so glad I'm free of them."

"You don't miss them at all?" Steve asked. "I miss my family at times."

"No," Harry said. "I love the tribe and the way we live now. It's much better."

"Yes, I love the tribe too," Steve said. "I worry sometimes that we won't find enough food when it rains for weeks on end. But we're doing well, and I feel like I belong. I never really did before. Not at school, or anywhere really. I was just the bookworm that no one really wanted to be friends with. I didn't belong. Now I do."

"Me too. It's great to belong… and to care about each other," Harry said softly.

They munched on their rabbit meat for a while, each of them thinking their own thoughts.

"It's strange with the scientists, though," Steve said after a while. "They don't believe God created the universe. There's the Big-Bang theory that everything just started from nothing with a huge explosion. But no one's ever explained *why* it started like that. They just say it did… But that's just like the religious people who believe God made the universe. Just two explanations for something that no one has the answer to. Know what I mean?"

"Yes, I think so. But if there isn't a god who started it, and it didn't just start on its own, then maybe it never started at all… I mean, it may have always been there, or it doesn't exist."

"What do you mean, 'it doesn't exist'?"

"I don't really know. It's just a feeling. That maybe it's all an illusion, or a dream or something. We're part of it, so we believe it's real. But it isn't. It just seems to be."

"Hmm, maybe," Steve said. "That's interesting. I've never thought of it like that before. I'll have to give that a good thinking through. But not tonight. I'm beat! We should sleep. We've got a long day ahead of us tomorrow and a lot of walking to do."

"Yeah, I'm tired too," Harry said.

Steve couldn't sleep. He lay in his sleeping bag staring at the stars. Do they go on forever? he wondered. What's out there? More planets with life on them? Plants and animals and beings that think like us?

A shooting star shot across the sky, leaving a trail of light behind it.

"Wow!" he said. "See that, Harry?"

But the younger boy was already sound asleep.

There's so much to understand, Steve thought. Not just what's in the books—the science and everything—but even like Harry had said: that it might be an illusion, because it *feels* that way. Where do those feelings come from? Even this, just lying under the stars thinking about it is important.

With all these deep thoughts late at night, he finally fell asleep.

The two boys got up at sunrise. They packed their gear together, made sure the fire was out and headed for the city.

They went straight to the library, not stopping to explore anything else on the way. Harry was just about to open the library door when Steve grabbed his arm.

"Did you turn the handle, Harry?"

"No, I haven't touched it."

"Are you sure?"

"Of course I'm sure. Why?"

Steve gently pulled the handle. The door swung open.

"It shouldn't be like that," he said. "You have to pull the handle *down* to unlatch it, and *then* open it… Someone else has been here! I know I closed it properly last time I was here. I always do. I know I did."

"But nobody's been here without you."

"No one from the tribe. Someone else."

"Someone else is alive on the island?"

"They must be. There's no other explanation."

"Maybe they're still inside then?"

"Yeah, maybe… We'll go in, but stick together. I'll go first."

Holding their staffs at the ready, the two boys walked as silently as they could into the library.

Months of hunting had sharpened their senses. Turning their heads slowly from side to side, they listened for the slightest of sounds, even making sure to look upwards as they did when hunting for birds and squirrels.

"Nothing," Steve whispered.

"Nothing," Harry whispered back.

They reached the middle of the library and crouched down—utterly still. Any sound or smell, or even the slightest movement of air, would alert them if someone else was there.

After a few minutes, which felt like an eternity, Steve said, "Still nothing…"

"Nope," Harry agreed.

"Let's grab a few books and get back to camp. Keep together, and stay alert, okay?"

Harry nodded.

Steve led the way towards the philosophy section. They both kept their eyes peeled. Harry glanced backwards now and again. You never know, he thought. Whoever it is might be good at hunting too.

The discussion they'd had the night before had left Steve curious. He scanned the titles on the shelves. He always searched this way—just going to the section of the library he was interested in and looking until a book's title caught his attention. It wasn't an infallible system; he often replaced books after reading their back cover or inner sleeve. Nonetheless, he trusted his instincts. This time a book with stars on its cover caught his eye *The Genesis of the Cosmos*. He read its back cover. Exactly what we were talking about, he thought. He chose two more books *A History of Modern Philosophy* and *Philosophers of Ancient Greece* and put them all in his rucksack.

"Steve, don't forget the tree book for Johnny."

"Ah, right! I'd almost forgotten. Thanks. We should find one over there," he said, and headed over to the biology section. With each visit, he found it easier and easier to find his way around the library.

The best book about trees was too big and heavy, so they settled on a smaller one.

"It'll do," Steve said. "Johnny can check out the big book next time he's here himself. Or we can lug it back to camp if Sarah says she really wants to have it."

They left the library, double checked that they had closed the handle properly and walked swiftly out of the city, only stopping to cut open a bicycle tyre they'd seen on the way there. The rubber inner-tube would be perfect for catapults.

What they didn't know, though, was that when they'd left the library, they'd been seen—and were being followed.

Twenty-two

Georgios and Antonio Papadopoulos had grown up in the hills of Crete. Although now in their forties, the two brothers still lived with their mother in the stone hut where they'd been born. Their father had left them when they were babies. Now they had to look after their old mother. The hills were the only home they knew, and they knew them well, having herded goats there for as long as they could remember.

Their mother made goat butter and cheese to sell at the weekend market in Heraklion. She came back with fruit and vegetables, and sometimes even clothes and other things they needed. When the boys were old enough, they made the trips to the market themselves. Georgios and Antonio had never gone to school and had hardly ever met other people before that. They had each other, their mother and the goats. That was all they knew, and all they wanted. They sold their produce from an old rickety table, exchanging as few words as possible with their customers and the other sellers. Their butter and cheese was of the highest quality, though, so it always sold well.

The destruction of most of the island hadn't affected the brothers' lives so much. They still had their goats.

At an early age, Georgios and Antonio had discovered the pleasure of the strong Greek spirit, ouzo. They always brought a few bottles of the cheapest brand back with them from the city.

It was their need for ouzo that had brought them down to the ruins of the city. They'd found a case of it in the basement of a ruined supermarket and quenched their thirst before wandering aimlessly around. They'd even found the university library and gone inside, but it was a disappointment. Georgios and Antonio could neither read nor write, so books were totally useless to them.

They were also on the lookout for painkillers for their mother. She was old and sick. Her back hurt constantly, and she got terrible headaches. In the throes of her headaches, she would rant and rage at her sons. She kept a stiff stick in the kitchen to beat them with. She always had.

Once, when he was eleven years old, Antonio had grabbed hold of the stick to stop a beating. His mother had wrested it back from him, and the beating that followed had made Georgios fear for his younger brother's life. It had left him coughing blood and with four cracked ribs. For days, Georgios had taken care of Antonio's wounds. It took weeks for the worst bruises to heal. Never again did they dare to stand up to their mother's anger, the stick, or her madness.

In secret, Antonio fantasized about slitting her throat like a goat's. Then he would throw her body off the cliff behind their hut, and he and his brother could live in peace…

Georgios and Antonio saw Steve and Harry come out of the library. Without a word they hid from view.

"We'll follow them," Georgios said.

He was the oldest. Antonio always obeyed him. Georgios's fists had taught him early on in life that this was the way it was to be.

The brothers followed the unsuspecting boys as they headed out of the city. They stayed far enough behind, and well out of sight, so they wouldn't be discovered.

Steve and Harry reached the glade where they would spend the night. They didn't have any food left, so they decided to go to sleep straight away.

"We'll get up really early and get back to camp," Steve said.

"Yeah, no point sitting up and just being hungry," Harry agreed.

The Papadopoulos brothers watched the two boys get into their sleeping bags, then moved a fair bit further away from the path to find a place to sleep for themselves—they didn't want their snoring to give them away. First they needed some refreshment, though. Greedily, they shared a bottle of ouzo before falling into a drunken stupor.

Steve and Harry woke with the very first bird calls of the morning chorus. It was still dark as they rubbed the sleep from their eyes and rolled their sleeping bags up. Just a few minutes later, they were ready and set off up the donkey path.

It would be another hour before Georgios and Antonio woke up. Ignoring their hangovers, they backtracked to the glade, only to find it empty.

"*Malakas!*" Georgios spat the swear word out through clenched teeth and cuffed his brother as if it was *his* fault that they had overslept.

Glaring with bloodshot eyes at the flattened grass where Steve and Harry had slept, he realised there was nothing they could do, so he trudged off up the path with Antonio following behind him. Luckily for them, that was the only way the boys could have gone. They hoped they weren't too far behind.

As it turned out, they needn't have worried. The donkey path that led to the tribe's camp was easy to follow. There were no major branchings or alternative paths, so even if they didn't see any actual signs of Steve and Harry all day, they knew they must be going the right way.

Alerted by the sound of the Two-Pot tribe's camp up ahead, Georgios and Antonio moved off into the woods by the side of the path—still following it but using the trees and bushes to keep out of sight.

Sarah and Helen had gone off in search of the thin, flexible branches that were perfect for making twine. It took a lot of work to make it, though. First the branches had to be stripped of bark, then carefully split into very thin strips. After that, long, thin fibres were pulled off and braided together. When it was finished, the twine was surprisingly strong and much suppler and easier to work with than the vines that the three dwarves had used to make Johnny's chair.

Unknowingly, the two girls were heading straight towards the Papadopoulos brothers.

Georgios and Antonio glanced at each other. They didn't have to say a word. Georgios pointed first at himself, then at the blonde girl, Helen. Antonio nodded. As always, he would follow his brother's lead.

Sarah and Helen walked straight past the men's hiding place.

Georgios moved first. He was surprisingly quick for a man of his size. Coming up from behind, he wrapped his huge hand around Helen's face. Antonio did the same with Sarah but missed her mouth, managing only to grab her around the chin.

Instinctively, she bit him—then screamed.

With a yelp of pain, Antonio released his grip, then smashed the back of his hand into her head. Sarah crashed hard to the ground, knocked out by the blow.

Georgios forced Helen to the ground.

She couldn't fight back. He was too strong. The big man's weight pressed down on her back, crushing her so hard that she could hardly breathe.

With one hand pressing on the back of her neck, Georgios found her belt with his free hand and unbuckled it. Brutally, he pulled her trousers down. She was trapped. She couldn't move. He fumbled with his own trousers then grabbed her between her legs, forcing them apart. With a loud grunt he pushed into her.

Helen felt as if she was being ripped apart. The pain, the smell of sweat and the stench of alcohol on his breath made her throw up. She was choking—drowning on her own vomit as he raped her.

Charlie had heard Sarah's scream. Grabbing his spear, he ran towards where he thought it came from. Dick was right behind him.

When he saw them, he didn't stop running. Holding his spear in front of him with both hands, Charlie charged at the man on top of Helen.

Georgios never heard him coming.

Charlie rammed the spear into the back of Georgios's neck. The force of the attack pushed the blade high up into his brain, killing him instantly, before lodging in his skull. Charlie tried to pull his spear out, but it was stuck. It wouldn't budge. Unarmed, he turned to face the other man.

Antonio stood astride Sarah. She was still unconscious. He'd been watching his brother. It would be his turn next. Not so much fun with the one just lying there. Maybe they could tie her up and use her later… He knew how to do that. At thirteen he'd fucked his first goat. He'd quickly learnt the best way to tie their legs so that they couldn't kick him. He'd taught his older brother how to do it too. One time, their mother had caught them in the stone shed with a goat. She'd just turned and walked away without saying a word. Best of all was a goat that was to be slaughtered. They would slit its throat and fuck it as it thrashed about, dying.

The swiftness of Charlie's attack on his brother had left Antonio standing with his mouth open and his trousers halfway down. Quickly regaining his wits, he pulled his trousers up.

Seeing that Charlie didn't have a weapon, he bent down and pulled his knife out from the inside of his boot.

This would be easy, he thought.

For a moment they just faced each other. Charlie stood still, not wanting to rush into the knife.

Antonio took a step forward—and was knocked off his feet.

Dick had barrelled into the back off his legs, buckling the big man at the knees. Seeing his chance, Charlie leapt forward. He landed on the back of the man's head, hitting it hard with his chest.

He managed to grab the man's wrist so he couldn't use his knife, and wrapped his other arm around his neck, pressing down with all his weight: choking him.

Antonio was the stronger of the two. Normally, he would have wrestled the younger man off his back, but he couldn't get any leverage thanks to Dick who was holding his legs in a bear hug for all he was worth.

Still, the tough mountain man fought. He had to let go of his knife so he could twist his hand free from Charlie's grasp. He clawed at the arm around his neck. For an instant the pressure lessened, and he gasped for air. But it wasn't enough.

Now that Antonio had dropped the knife, Charlie's other hand was free, and he could use both of his arms to exert even more pressure on the man's throat and the back of his neck. The more Antonio weakened, the more Charlie could shift his weight and strengthen the stranglehold.

Dick hung on as well—for ages it seemed.

At last, the man lay still. He didn't seem to be breathing.

Charlie slowly released his hold, ready to tighten it again if he moved. He didn't. He was dead.

Helen sat on the ground crying. She stared at Charlie with wide, scared eyes.

"Dick, go help Sarah," Charlie said. He went over to Helen and knelt down in front of her, opening his arms, offering to hug her but waiting for her to come to him.

"It's over," he said.

She flung herself into his arms. Tears gushed from her eyes.

She hung onto him. Not saying a word. Just crying.

Others had come to help, but there wasn't much they could do. Sarah had regained consciousness and seemed to be okay.

They dragged the two dead men a bit further off into the woods and dumped them. Let the dogs have them, someone said.

When Helen's sobs finally became a bit softer, Gwen went over to where Charlie still held her. Kneeling behind the young girl, she wrapped her arms around her as well.

Encompassed and protected, warm and safe, Helen slowly drifted into a deep sleep. Later, Gwen carried her to her tent and lay beside her—holding her close all the time. They slept that way all night: Gwen's arms wrapped around the young girl, keeping her safe… never letting go.

They kept the men's boots and knives, but the ouzo was deemed too horrible to drink on its own. It did give the stew a lovely tangy taste of aniseed though.

Georgios and Antonio Papadopoulos's mother died of thirst two weeks later. She had been too sick and weak to fetch water herself. Her last days were spent cursing her worthless sons.

Twenty-three

"You okay, Charlie?" Johnny said.

"Sure. Why?"

"I mean, you killed two men today."

Charlie looked at his friend. "Yeah, had to."

Johnny returned his look. "Wish I'd been there to help you."

"Didn't need you. Had Dick, didn't I?"

Johnny reached out and gripped his arm.

"You did well," he said.

"So did Dick."

"Hah! I think he knows. He's been telling the story of the fight over and over. I thought *I* was his hero, but I've got some serious competition now! Let's go find him—and get you some stew. You've earned it!"

After they'd eaten, Johnny and Charlie sat together talking quietly.

"There's a difference, isn't there?" Charlie said.

"Umm, difference between what?"

"Between killing in self-defence and murdering someone."

"Of course there is," Johnny said. "One's natural, the other isn't."

Charlie turned his head to look at him. "What?"

"I said, one's natural, the other isn't. I mean, it's like animals. If you corner or attack them, they'll always fight back."

"But they fight about other things as well, don't they?"

"Depends what animal it is, I suppose. But they all fight to defend themselves if something's trying to catch them and eat them… Apart from that, you mean?"

"Yes."

"Well, a mother will fight to the death to defend her young. And a pack of animals defends its territory—same as we do. We protect the camp and the girls, and the freckle twins, of course."

"Anything else?" Charlie said.

Johnny gathered his thoughts for a few seconds. "Puppies and cubs fight all the time. But that's only practicing—learning how to fight. Like we do, wrestling with each other or practicing shooting with catapults... Animals fight all the time over food, but it's not really fighting, just the hierarchy of who gets to eat first. They share as well, within the pack at least, so in the end they all get enough to eat. You know, like a pack of lions."

"Pride."

Johnny laughed. "Right, sorry. Pride."

"Is that it?"

"I guess so. No, hang on, we've forgotten one."

"What? Go on."

"Males are fighting over females all the time, aren't they? To see which one gets to mate."

"Right. Of course. It's so the best genes carry on," Charlie said. "What about us? Humans, I mean. We fight over lots of things. Countries attack each other for territory, or oil, or because they have a different religion..."

"Yes. And people would hurt and kill each other over just about anything, wouldn't they. Because they were jealous or felt insulted, or because they were drunk or just because they enjoyed it..."

Charlie looked off into the distance. "They must have been sick," he said. "It wasn't just the psychopaths either, was it? It was all of them. You'd *have* to be sick to do things like that, wouldn't you?"

"Well, not all of them."

"No, maybe not, but everybody justified war and violence, didn't they. Even if they didn't do it themselves, they still let it happen."

"What about us then, Charlie? Are we sick too?"

"I suppose we must be. Why should we be any different? It's just we're so busy trying to survive that we *have* to help each other. Otherwise we'd be just like them."

"So you mean at the moment we're like animals defending our territory?" Johnny said. "You think that will change? That we'll start fighting over stupid things, like who owns what, or whatever?"

"Maybe."

"What can we do about it then?"

"I'm not sure. Maybe we're doing it right now... talking about it, trying to understand. If it's sick to be violent, then we're going to have to heal ourselves."

"How do we do that, Charlie?"

"I think trying to understand what's wrong with us is the first step. When we know that, I guess it's easier to control it, and maybe heal. Animals all follow their instincts and their nature. It's all they do—all they *can* do—because they're *healthy*. They fulfil all their needs." Charlie stopped and thought for a moment... "And that means they're *happy!* That's it! That's it, Johnny! It must be!"

Charlie was excited now. It made sense. More sense than anything he'd ever thought of before. He stood up and started pacing round the fire. So many things fell into place.

"I was talking to Jen about happiness the other day," he said. "But now we have a link between happiness and healthiness. That's the difference between violence and fighting to survive— or natural violence I suppose you could call it. If you're mentally sick, then the reasons you're violent are totally different from the natural healthy reasons for..." He trailed off. "Violence isn't a good word for it. Can you think of a better one?"

Johnny thought for a moment. "I don't know... When you defend yourself, like we did against the dogs or those men, then you're full of adrenaline, aren't you? You know, really aggressive—"

Charlie butted in, "That's a good word 'aggressive'. In a way you're being aggressive when you do anything you have to do to survive, like hunting and defending the tribe, aren't you."

"And fighting over women?" Johnny said, half jokingly.

"Yes, *exactly!*" Charlie said, not picking up on the joking part. "That's natural aggression as well. Like moose bashing their heads together, or dogs fighting over a bitch in heat."

"So why don't we fight over the girls then?"

"I don't know. I mean, that's how evolution works, isn't it? By selecting the best genes. We'll have to think some more about it... I like the term 'natural aggression' though," he concluded.

Twenty-four

"Jen?"

"Yes?"

"Will I ever feel good again?" Helen asked.

"Of course you will," Jen replied softly.

The two girls had just woken up and were lying together under their sleeping bags.

A week had gone by since Helen had been raped. Jen and Gwen had taken turns staying by her side. They spent the days together, gathering or making. At night they slept in the same tent. Helen often fell asleep in their arms.

"It doesn't feel like it," Helen said. "I feel like crying all the time. You've been great. Looking after me. Gwen too… I just keep thinking about it."

"Of course you do. It's going to take time. You'll get better slowly, then one day you'll look back on it, and it'll just be like a bad dream that you vaguely remember, but one that you've woken up from."

"You think so?"

"I know so."

"I'd like that," Helen said. "It doesn't hurt anymore. That helps."

"That's good. How about we talk about good things? Try thinking about things you like the best."

"Like what?"

"You tell me," Jen said. "What things do you like best of all?"

"That's easy. The freckle twins! They're so beautiful. I love holding them and helping to take care of them."

"What else?"

"Well, I like you, of course, and the other girls… The boys, too!" She smiled. "I like little things. I love the flowers and those small lizards in the rocks. Even insects, because they're small, I guess, and fragile... like me, maybe."

"We're all fragile," Jen said. "That's a nice thought, though—loving little things. I'd never thought of it like that before. It's like you want to take care of them, don't you?"

"Yes," Helen said. "Could we go out into the woods and look at little things, Jen? Not gather stuff for the pots or for making things, I mean. Just go out and look at them? I'd like to be one of the little things among all the other little things in the woods. Does that make sense?"

"Yes, it does. That's a great idea."

They got dressed and went out. The tribe was stirring. Charlie and a few of the others were sitting by the fire.

"Morning, girls!" he called out.

"Hi, Charlie!"

"What are you up to?"

"Oh, just little things," Jen replied. "We're going for a walk. Be back in a while."

"Okay. Be careful then," Charlie said. He put the palm of his hand in front of his mouth, imitating the Indian war cry.

Jen mirrored the gesture. "Gotcha," she said.

"Not going to have some stew first?"

"No," both of the girls said, and shook their heads. "We're off then."

"Okay, bye."

"Bye. See you."

Sunlight dappled through the trees, turning the woods into brilliant shades of green.

"It's beautiful, isn't it," Helen said, looking around her. "We've got a beautiful home."

Jen smiled at her friend. "Yes, we do," she said. "Where do you want to go then?"

"I don't know. Just wander... Maybe over there?" She pointed across the woods to where the sun broke through the trees. There was a track of sorts—probably made by goats.

They followed the narrow path, stopping every now and then to look at little things: a flower or a leaf, a brightly coloured insect or a spotty mushroom. In the distance two wood pigeons called to each other.

"I think I'd like to make drawings of little things," Helen said, "or maybe even paintings if we can find some colours in the city."

"Stone Age people used to make paint. You know, to paint on cave walls. Maybe we could work out how to make paint like that. It was a ruddy brown colour, I think."

"Yes, I've seen pictures of those paintings. They painted the animals that lived around them. And people too. I can't remember if there were any flowers. I'd like to start with flowers."

They came to a little brook and crossed it.

Both girls washed their faces and drank some of the crystal clear water.

"I've got to go to the loo," Helen said.

"Okay, I'll wait here," Jen said. She sat down on a rock and listened to the bubbling sound of the water flowing in the brook. Somewhere a blackbird sang. Sunlight warmed her face.

"Jen! Come here!" Helen called out.

"What! You okay?"

"I'm fine. Just come here, will you!"

"Coming!" Jen called back.

She found her way in behind the bush that Helen had gone behind, then stopped and gaped at what she'd found. The bush had hidden the entrance to a cave. It was too dark to see inside, but it looked big.

"Wow!" she said, trying to peer in.

"What shall we do? Shall we go in?"

"No, we haven't got torches, and it could be dangerous. There might be a wild animal in there, or a hole we'd fall into. We must be careful." She thought for a moment. "We'll go back and tell the others, then we can come back with a torch and explore it, okay?"

"Okay," Helen said.

They hurried back the way they'd come. It took longer than they'd thought... On the way there, they'd been so caught up talking and in finding *little things* that they'd wandered much further from camp than they usually did when gathering.

They got back at last.

Charlie turned to greet them. He had a huge smile on his face.

"What's up with you?" Jen said.

"Look! I did it! I've found a better way to make fire!" he blurted out. He pointed to the small fire he'd made in the shelter of one of the campfire stones.

"That's *great!*" Jen and Helen said at the same time. "Have you shown the others yet?"

"No, I just got this one going a minute ago—but it works every time!"

"You'll have to teach the rest of us how you did it," Jen said.

"Of course!" Charlie laughed. "It'll be this afternoon's first lesson."

"We've got something to show you first, though."

"What?" Charlie said, looking at their empty hands.

"No, not here," she said. "Over there…" She pointed into the woods. "Helen found a cave."

"A cave! How big?"

"We don't know. We didn't want to go in… in case there was a wild animal or something."

"But it looked big," Helen said. "From the outside, I mean."

"Wow!" Charlie said. "Hey! Come here everybody."

A few minutes later, all of the Two-Pot tribe who were in camp were gathered around the fireplace.

"Right, listen up everybody," Charlie said. "I wanted to show you the fire I made." He pointed proudly at his little fire.

Everybody started clapping, so Charlie gave them a theatrical bow.

"Yeah, yeah, thank you, thank you," he said. "But that's not the big news."

"What then?" someone said.

"Helen and Jen have found a cave. Maybe a big one."

"Where?"

Jen pointed into the woods again. "Over that way… About an hour and a half's walk, I'd guess. But we need torches to explore it. Have we got any that still work?"

"I've got one," Johnny said. "I think the batteries will hold up for a few more hours."

"Anyone else?"

No one answered.

"Mine will have to do then," Johnny said. "Who wants to go cave exploring?"

Everyone's hand shot up in the air.

Johnny laughed. "That doesn't surprise me! What about if we go in two groups? Half of us first, then the other half when we get back?"

"I can take the first group," Jen said. "Then Helen can lead the second one. Okay, Hel?"

"Of course," Helen said.

"If we hurry, we should all be able to get there and back by nightfall. Right! Split up troop!" Jen ordered.

A few minutes later, the first group set off towards the cave.

Johnny turned to the second group. "You know those old-fashioned torches they had in medieval castles? The ones you burned? We should try making some."

"Great idea!" Gwen said. "We haven't got any oil, but we could use goat fat and rub it into strips of cloth. We can rip Maggy's old Scout trousers up; she's grown out of them, and they don't fit anybody else."

"Sounds good! Let's get to it then!"

"I'll get my old trousers," Maggy said, hurrying to her tent.

"I'll get the fat," Gwen said.

"We'll go find some good sticks," Harry said, looking at Tom.

"Beat you to it!" Tom shouted, and ran off with Harry close on his heels.

Twenty-five

They didn't have to go far into the cave before it became pitch black. Jen shone the torch around. It was maybe twelve feet across.

She led the way further in. They had to be careful. Even with the torch, it was hard to see clearly ahead. They all had spears or knives in case there were animals hidden in the cave. There probably weren't any bears on Crete, but they knew there were wild dogs. Dick reckoned there might even be an ancient coffin with Dracula sleeping inside it.

The first part of the cave was empty. At first, they could walk upright, but the roof got lower and lower further on. The cave seemed to be getting narrower as well.

Stooping more and more, they went in as far as they could.

"That's it," Jen said. She'd come up against a wall of solid rock. It was a bit disappointing. The cave wasn't as big as she'd hoped. Not big enough for the whole tribe to live in, anyway.

"No, wait!" Mark said. He was in the shadow to the left of Jen. "There's an opening here."

Jen shone the torch across the rock wall.

"See. I think it's just wide enough to squeeze through," Mark said. "You go, Jen. You're skinnier than me."

"Okay…"

She turned sideways and felt her way through the opening. She edged her way forward until the gap became wider, then stopped and shone the torch straight ahead of her. There was nothing. Just darkness. At first she didn't understand why the light didn't reflect off the cave walls. Then it came to her.

"Oh! It's huge! Come through all of you! Careful where you tread."

It was hard to judge the size of the cave by the light of a single torch.

"Jen, turn the torch off a second," Steve said.

"Okay, why?" She thumbed the button, and they were all enveloped in blackness.

"Wait..." Steve said, "I thought I'd seen something."

It took a few moments for their eyes to adapt to the darkness.

"Look," he said. "There's a dim light over there."

"What is it?"

"I don't know, but it must be daylight coming in from somewhere. Let's go and see."

Not really being able to see where you were treading was a bit scary, so they walked in single file. Jen led the way, shining the torch on the ground in front of them. When they got closer, they could see that the light came from around another bend. Jen ducked her head and went through the narrow passageway.

When she got round the bend, she stopped, her mouth wide open in total amazement.

She was standing on a ledge about three feet above a perfectly crescent-shaped lake. On the other side of the lake was a sandy beach, and behind the beach were a few small trees and some bushes. Looking up, she saw a circle of blue sky a hundred feet above her... It was a perfect sinkhole.

For thousands of years, water had slowly eroded the soft limestone rock of the hill above the cave, carving out a hole in the ground. It was beautiful.

The water in the lake was a brilliant turquoise blue.

The others had come through the gap now. The ledge was just big enough for them all to stand on.

"Look!" Jen said. She pointed at two yellow butterflies she'd seen. They flew across the lake, weaving around each other before spiralling high up into the air.

"It's magical," Maggy said.

"I wonder how deep the lake is?" Steve said, thinking out loud.

Dick had already started to take his clothes off. "I'll find out!" he said. He grabbed the edge of the ledge with both hands, then lowered himself until his legs dangled in the water—and let go.

With a jolt, his feet hit the sandy bottom. The water came up to his waist.

"Not so deep here," he said, and waded off towards the beach. "Bit cold, though!"

It wasn't far to the other side of the lake: just twenty feet or so.

"Come on!" he called once he'd reached it.

"This is amazing," Charlie said. "I've never seen anything like it."

"You know, if it rains again, we'd be better off living in the cave," Steve said. "We can make a fire inside, near the passageway. I don't think the smoke would be too bad. It would be much nicer being warm and dry, wouldn't it?"

"Oh, yes!" Jen said. They all remembered how miserable it had been at times when it had rained all day every day.

They all took their clothes off and held them above their heads as they waded across the lake. The cold made them shiver, but the sun quickly warmed them when they reached the beach. None of them bothered to put their clothes back on—they'd be going back soon anyway. They were used to seeing each other naked when washing themselves at the spring or scantily dressed around camp when it was hot. It was no big deal.

I doubt if anyone would look twice if one of us went around naked in camp, Charlie thought. In our old life that would have been unthinkable. At summer camp we all had shorts and T-shirts, or at least swimming gear. Now it just didn't seem to matter.

They were all suntanned, even the redheads, Jen and Gwen, who had the fairest skin of them all. I've even got a bit darker myself, Charlie thought. Doubt anyone has noticed, though!

"Come on!" he said. "We ought to be getting back so the others can see the cave."

Later that evening, after Helen's group had come back as well, they sat around the campfire talking.

"There weren't any bats," Dick said, trying not to sound too disappointed.

"Thank goodness!" Gwen said. She slapped him playfully on

the back of his head. "I bet you wished it really was Dracula's cave! Or that there was a monster living there, didn't you?"

"No!" he said, but didn't sound too convincing.

"Thought so!"

After more discussion, they all agreed that they would move to the cave for the next rainy season. Otherwise, they were better off where they were. Living in the cave all the time would be too dark and dingy.

"Our tents aren't going to last forever, though," Johnny said.

"No, I've thought of that," Jen said. "We should start building shelters—huts or something."

Johnny thought for a moment. "You know, there must be a small village, or at least some houses on the island somewhere—"

"But this is our home!" Jen burst out, looking around at the others.

"Yes, you're right, Jen. This is our home." Johnny said.

There were smiles all round. That was how they all felt. The mountains and woods were home.

The next rainy season didn't come for another three months. By then they'd made a few excursions to the cave to clean it out. They'd also built a fireplace and stocked a pile of firewood in the big cavern near the passageway to the magical lake, as it was now called. Steve and Gwen had made a test fire to be sure that it didn't get too smoky.

Torches were made from old pieces of cloth that had been brought back from the city. They were held upright by piles of stones placed around the walls of the cave and burnt really well, lighting up most of the cave. For the most part, though, the light from the fire was bright enough to see by, so they agreed not to use the torches unless they really had to.

The magical lake would become a very special place for Charlie. It was where he went to write.

He had a favourite spot on the beach. When words didn't come quickly, he would raise his eyes from his work and just look at the beautiful colours of the lake.

Most of the time, it was turquoise, but when the sun was directly overhead and shone straight down the sinkhole, it turned a clear emerald green. When clouds passed overhead, it turned deeper shades of blue.

Charlie had a small fireplace on the beach where he boiled water to make herb tea. 'Going to drink tea with Charlie' was all that had to be said to let everyone know you were off to the cave.

When he saw someone wading across the lake, he would put his pen and paper to one side and put the kettle on. There was always something to talk about, and Charlie always had time to talk… and listen.

If it wasn't too late to be back before dark, he would return to camp to be with his tribe. Many evenings, though, he wouldn't notice how late it was getting and would stay all night at the magical lake.

He loved to lie on the beach before falling asleep and gaze up through the sinkhole at the sky, the clouds, the stars and the moon—and let his thoughts wander wherever they may.

Nina and Pete had finished the sundial and the sun calendar. Now they could keep an accurate log of the days and the seasons.

There were only two seasons: sunny and rainy. The Earth's climate had changed so much. At first, the changes in the weather seemed to be fairly random, but as the years went by, they became more consistent and they were able to predict the coming of a rainy season more and more accurately. During the sunny season it would sometimes rain as well, but these would only be short showers, not like the onset of the rainy season.

A few hours before the rains came, thick grey clouds would blow in from the west. Then it got darker and darker, as they rolled over each other. Seeing this, the tribe knew it was time to pack everything they needed and leave for the cave.

Moving to the cave for the rainy season always felt like an adventure—especially for the kids. They loved playing in the magical lake and on the beach.

Anything they didn't need to take with them was stored in the huts.

The first basic stone huts they'd built had been gradually improved upon. New huts were built too. Eventually no one slept in the tents anymore. They'd talked about what to do with them; the nylon fabric would be good to make other things with, but in the end, they decided to just store them in the library where they wouldn't rot.

Twenty-six

Nina waded across the magical lake to the beach, where Charlie lay with his eyes half closed. She was carrying her baby girl in a shawl that she'd tied so that it left her hands free.

"Hi Charlie… Sorry. Were you sleeping?"

Charlie laughed. "No, just resting, umm, philosophising…"

Nina was twenty-four years old now and had given birth to two children. Her first child, Red, was three years old. He'd been given his name on the day he was born. As soon as he'd come into the world, the other women had cleaned him with fresh water. The baby had howled and howled, bunching up all the muscles in his tiny body, so he could make as much noise as possible in protest of this treatment. So much so, that his face had turned as bright red as a tomato. Nina's first sight of her baby made her exclaim: *"He's red!"*

Red was back at the camp with the other children. The women took care of all of the kids as if they were their own—which in many ways they were—and most importantly of all, was how they all felt about them. It was much easier that way too. They all took turns looking after them, which left the others free to do whatever else needed to be done—or to just rest—kids were a lot of work!

The freckle twins, Sunray, who everybody called Ray, and Dewdrop, were the eldest and thus the natural leaders of the children's group. They were adored and looked up to by the younger ones.

The whole group of children was inseparable—playing in the woods together or making up games in camp. At night they all slept together in the *Big Hut*, as it was called. It had recently been made even bigger by tearing down one of its short sides and extending the roof.

There were ten children in all now, counting Nina's newborn baby girl, Buttercup. She'd been given her name thanks to the pure yellow curls she'd been born with.

Nina sat down on the sand next to Charlie and gave him a hug.

"Would you like some tea?" Charlie said. "I made some an hour or so ago, but we can warm it up. The fire's still hot."

"Yes, thanks, Charlie. Tea would be great. How's your work going?"

"Fine," he replied, smiling at her.

"I brought you a new book to write in. That's why I came here. Well, to talk to you as well, of course," she added with a laugh.

She handed him the book she had made. Most of the library books had several blank pages in the beginning or at the end, which could be cut out and made into new books. The knowledge in the books was too valuable to be destroyed, of course, so they never damage any of them—apart from cutting out blank pages. Duplicate books were an exception to this rule.

Angie had experimented with different ways to bleach the pages of duplicate books so that they could use the paper to write or draw on again. She'd had various degrees of success, depending on which plant extracts she'd used to dissolve the ink. Her best efforts had left the pages greyish and a bit crumpled. It wasn't totally unusable, and slowly her bleaching technique was getting better.

The book Nina had given Charlie had been made by gluing blank pages together, then rebinding them with a spare cover. It had about three hundred pages: enough to keep him going for another year or so.

He wrote with a thin, scratchy handstyle that was almost indecipherable if you weren't used to it. Always careful to use as little paper as possible, his handwriting became more and more condensed for every passing year.

Charlie spent a lot of time reading as well. References from books that were brought back from the library often led him on searches for new books. Sometimes he found them, but if not, the search always seemed to lead to the discovery of other interesting books. After a book had been read and discussed by anyone interested in it, they returned it to its shelf in the library. Books would have been quickly ruined if they had kept them in the cave or in camp. Charlie's writings were taken to the library for safekeeping too.

He didn't exactly write books with a beginning and an end, rather, he wrote discourses on many subjects: comparing and contrasting his own theories with those of others. Charlie's theory of the evolution of mankind's nature and subsequent estrangement from nature—the cause of mankind's downfall—grew to embrace many fields of science and other disciplines: biology and evolutionary theory, archaeology and anthropology, psychology, sociology and philosophy.

His theory was continually being updated, altered and improved upon the more he delved into the mystery of human nature. Charlie kept searching and learning. Discussions led to new questions and new insights. Moments of intuitive inspiration led to new tracks of thought, which in turn had to be studied, discussed and analysed. New knowledge—whether refuted or confirmed—enhanced his theory. Thus it grew. Page by page, and year by year…

"Oh! Thank you, Nina!" He laid the empty book carefully on the sand and gave her a hug. "This means so much…"

"We know, Charlie. We know."

"So, what's new?" Charlie asked as he poured tea into two mugs.

"Oh, nothing new, really. We've predicted a new rain period in a couple of weeks—but you know Pete and his sun calendar! He's worse than me! She laughed. "Wouldn't surprise me if he checks the sundial to see if it's time for breakfast!"

That made Charlie laugh too.

Nina and Pete were even tracking the planets—the ones that could be seen with the naked eye that is: Mercury, Venus, Mars, Jupiter and Saturn. Nina did most of the actual stargazing, then by using her observations, she and Pete were able to plot the planets' positions on maps of the night sky.

Nina and Johnny spent many nights together under the stars: Johnny sitting in his chair—Nina lying on the ground next to him. Now and again, she would sit up and make a note or check a measurement in an astronomy book. Now and again, he would take a walk around the camp.

Every time someone was in the city, Nina hoped they would find a telescope or a pair of binoculars, but none had been found… yet! she always said. *Keep your eyes open!*

She loved the night sky: the stillness of the universe, the slow turning of the stars and the passage of old satellites that looked like stars travelling in a straight line across the sky.

"I've been keeping track of some other things too," Nina said.

"With the sun calendar?"

"Yes." She paused for a moment. "Charlie, you know we girls get our period every month… well, every four weeks actually, following the moon month?"

"Yes." He was intrigued by what Nina was going to tell him. "Go on…"

"I've been keeping track of when the girls get their periods—except when they're pregnant or nursing and don't get them. I've got a theory, but I'm not sure if it's correct, and I wanted to talk to you about it and see what you think. Is that okay?"

"Of course it is." He smiled gently. "You know it is."

"Well, a few days before our period—I guess when we're ovulating—we start flirting with all the guys. Not blatantly. Not even something we're conscious of, I think. But even so…" She paused to get her thoughts in order before continuing. "It's not as if we want to get off with you. Maybe just wind you up a bit. Have you noticed that?"

"Not really… Maybe. I hadn't thought about it, but you're right. I know the sort of flirting you mean. It's different from just showing someone you want to get off, isn't it?"

"Yes, that's going on all the time, anyway!" Nina said, and laughed. "The kids are much more physical than us too—as we were as kids, I mean. I think it's because they're so close to each other the whole time."

"Yes," Charlie said, "day and night."

"I don't think they're going to grow up and be jealous and stuff like we were either. I know we got over it, but it took some doing, didn't it?"

"Yes, I think it might have split us apart if we hadn't been so totally dependant on each other."

"Anyway, Charlie, this flirting I was talking about is something different. More sexual, I mean, more *rawly sexual*. For a couple of days each month I just want a guy—or maybe all of them! Not like getting off with someone… know what I mean, Charlie?"

"I think so. Have you talked to the other girls about it?"

"Yes, they know what I'm talking about, but they haven't really thought about it so much."

Charlie didn't say anything for a short while.

"It makes sense," he said at last. "What you're doing by flirting with us is natural. You're turning all the guys on, and maybe we ought to be competing with each other to mate with you—to get you pregnant, I mean—like male animals who show off or fight over a female in heat. That's how the dominant male's genes get passed on. It's good for evolution and strengthens the gene bank… Maybe people were like that before we got civilised and everyone got married and had children in families. I think they used to live in small groups and would have had a different kind of mating behaviour—so that evolution worked. I think our tribe is a bit more like a natural group, and we've developed differently than if we'd lived in families. That's what I'm writing about, I guess—but I wasn't sure about this mating thing, or if it was just physical attraction that led to it."

"But you guys don't feel like fighting over us, do you?"

"No, that's true. Maybe there's another explanation? Like you said, the other girls don't feel it that strongly, so they wouldn't behave so obviously, would they? That would mean that the guys wouldn't react as you would expect, either… or something else is blocking it." Charlie's mind leapt ahead. "Maybe mating behaviour *is* blocked. You know, inhibited in all of us—both girls and boys. First the girls aren't showing the guys that it's mating time clearly enough—and the guys aren't competing over you even if they did get the message."

"Yes, maybe. Or maybe it would be different if it was another bunch of guys who came along? You'd fight over us then, wouldn't you?"

"Of course! I mean, not because we *own* you or anything, but we're the same tribe…"

"Maybe that's it, then? Maybe the fighting would be between different *groups* of men? The losing group would have to leave, wouldn't they?"

"Yes, I suppose so."

"Then the girl would pick a guy from the winning group?"

"Yes! That would work," Charlie exclaimed. "That would keep evolution going. Sorting out which genes would get carried on in the next generation… and so on."

"Makes us sound like a bunch of animals, doesn't it?"

"Well, we *are*. Instincts, survival, evolution… Why should we be any different than other animals? This is great, Nina! I think it's an important bit of the puzzle that I was missing. I'd kind of seen it, but not as clearly as now. Thanks to you!"

Nina opened her shirt and moved Buttercup to her breast. The baby started sucking straight away. "There's instinct for you!" she said, looking fondly at her baby.

Charlie laughed. "It's getting late," he said. "We should be heading back soon."

Another thought crossed his mind, causing his brow to furrow for an instant. Then it was gone. It didn't worry him. He knew it would surface again, sooner or later.

"How does it feel?" he said.

"What?" Nina said, and looked back up at him.

"Nursing. Having a baby suck on your breast."

"It's nice. Turns me on a bit as well. Makes me randy! But in a regular way, you know? Not the way we were talking about. Both are sexual, I guess, but in different ways. There ought to be two different words for them."

A bit later when Buttercup had fallen asleep, Nina and Charlie picked their stuff up and waded across the magical lake.

The sun was low in the sky as they set off home, so it was already dark by the time they got there.

Everyone was by the fire except for a small group of grown-ups who were sitting under the pine tree.

"We've been waiting for you," Jen said when she saw Nina and Charlie.

"Yeah," Johnny said. "I don't like it when someone's out there when it's dark… or even two of you."

"Anyway," Jen said, getting back to what she was going to say. "It's time for the show!"

"The show?" Charlie said. "What show?"

"You'll see. Sit down, the both of you. Quiet everybody! *Let The Show begin!*"

For the next hour they were treated to a pantomime put on by Tom, Dick, Harry, Angie and Maggy.

It was enthralling. The five actors were naked except for loincloths. They had painted different patterns with mud all over their bodies. It changed them—made them not quite as recognisable as they usually were. They didn't utter a sound throughout the whole performance. By just moving and using body language, they told the story of the Two-Pot tribe.

Their audience was captivated, even though they knew the story so well.

In the light of the fire, the actors' body paint made them look eerie and otherworldly. The children let out gasps of fear and excitement—especially when it came to the famous battle with the dogs. Dick, Harry and Angie played the dogs, pretending to attack on all fours, only to be beaten off and eventually to lie dead at Tom and Maggy's feet. The audience cheered loudly.

Even the story of the killing of the two men who had attacked them was re-enacted. Helen watched with tears running down her cheeks, and with something else—something much fiercer—in her eyes.

The day-to-day life of the tribe was mimed as well: hunting and gathering, cooking and making, gathering water and washing clothes.

At the end of the pantomime all the actors curled up together as if asleep.

The cheering and clapping went on for ages. It had been

wonderful. They had captured the spirit of the tribe and brought alive all the feelings and emotions which united them. There was something else as well: something they all felt… something special, something to be proud of.

The children were bewitched. Led by Dewdrop and Ray, they started playing scenes from the play themselves. They imitated members of the tribe: Charlie reading and writing, Johnny guarding the camp, Sarah collecting plants and putting them in the plant book, a girl helping another give birth, boys wrestling… It was fascinating to see just how accurately the children could portray the grown-ups.

"Go wash the mud off, all of you," Gwen said. "We'll heat some stew."

"I'll help you," Pete said. "I could do with some too. You know what? It's been ten years since the tsunami according to the sun calendar."

"Ten years since Alison died," Angie said in a small voice. She had never stopped missing her childhood friend.

"Yes," Pete said. "But we've only had one death… The pantomime was a great way to mark the tenth anniversary of our new life, wasn't it?"

"Yes, it was," Angie said. "It took me back through the years. I felt so close to Alison… and all of you." Her voice broke up as she started to cry.

"Hey, come here, soppy," Maggy said, and hugged her.

The children from Fengwidditch were grown-ups now. They'd all changed in many ways—some that they didn't even fully realise themselves. The show had made them all think about their life on the island. After they'd eaten, they sat around the fire, talking about it.

"We've not become the people we would have," Charlie said to Jen.

"No," she replied. "You're right. But I think I like the people we've become better."

"How so?"

"I really deeply love everyone in the tribe, Charlie. It wouldn't have been like that back in our old life, would it? We would've had a few friends and fallen in love with a couple of boyfriends or girlfriends before settling down and marrying one of them. We'd still have had friends, of course, but it wouldn't be like this—living together, helping each other all the time." She paused. "Really needing each other… That's why it feels so good, because we truly *need* each other. We didn't before. We were taken care of by our parents or at the orphanage, like you, but there was always someone else to take care of us." She stopped for a moment to gather her thoughts. "Do you remember what you said right at the beginning—'We'll help each other and survive'?"

Charlie nodded.

"I don't think you knew then just how right you were. If we hadn't had each other, we would have all died."

She touched his arm gently.

"Yes, I know," Charlie said. "You're right, Jen. Back then I *felt* that it was right. I guess I'd learnt that at the orphanage. But not that it would be *so* important to have to trust and depend on each other like we do. I think that's what love really is—what we feel for each other in the tribe."

"Yes. It means so much. In the old days everyone 'fell in love'. It was a huge rush with all the excitement of sex and thinking about the other person all the time. But even that wore off after a while and you'd break up and start looking for the next one…" She laughed. "Or even that mystical *The Right One* that everyone dreamed of!"

"Yeah, and when you found him or her, you got married and that was that."

"But that was awful too. Like everyone's parents. I don't think they were in love anymore, were they? It was more like they'd given up and decided they might as well stick together because they wouldn't be able to find someone else, or 'for their children's sake'. They knew it wouldn't get any better, but sometimes it got so bad that they got divorced anyway. I think they were all pretty lonely and unhappy in their marriages."

"Yes, I think so too. That's the difference between how they lived, how we live now, and the way it's meant to be."

"The way it's meant to be?"

"Yes, I think we're a bit closer to our nature and our instincts than people in the old world were. But we've still got a lot of 'baggage' from growing up in the old world. It still affects us and the way we feel and everything…"

"Yes, I suppose so. But what about the children? Won't they be different? You know, not having grown up like we did?"

"Yes. As long as we don't mess them up, I think they'll be able to follow their instincts more naturally then we do—and be happy…"

"That sounds good. I hope so."

Steve had come over to where they were sitting.

"Mind if I join you?" he asked.

"No, not at all," Jen said. "Sit down. I'll make some tea."

"Thanks. That would be great. What an evening! The play was fantastic, wasn't it!"

"Ten years!" Charlie laughed. "Can you believe it? We're getting old!"

"You speak for yourself!" Jen called over her shoulder, and swung her red ponytail contritely.

"What were you talking about?" Steve asked.

"Love, I guess," Charlie said.

"Hmm, big topic. What kind of love?"

"All sorts, but mostly the difference between the way people fell in love in the old world and the kind of love we feel for each other in the tribe."

"Right. Everyone used to be desperately searching for someone to love them, didn't they," Steve said, taking the mug of tea Jen offered him. "Thanks Jen… But now it's just being a tribe. Belonging. That's how I feel anyhow."

"Me too," Jen said. She gave Charlie his tea and sat down. "I don't think about it most of the time. We just take it for granted that we belong together. It's not as if we run around saying 'I love you' all the time, is it?"

"No," Charlie said. But we all feel that way, don't we. It doesn't matter who you think about, there's a special feeling—that you'd give your life for them."

"Yes," Steve said. "That's the only way to protect each other. Without each other, none of us would be able to survive, so by protecting each other we're actually keeping ourselves alive as well as continuing the species when we're all dead and gone."

Charlie took a sip of his tea. "Yes, that's love, isn't it," he said. "Belonging and protecting."

Jen laughed. "Not getting married and giving each other rings and roses?"

"No, that seems kind of silly now, doesn't it?" Charlie said, laughing as well.

"Yes, and being 'true', like in 'faithful to each other', Jen said. We're not good at that are we?" she said, laughing even more.

"It just got like that," Steve said. "You remember when you two got into the *'So What'* thing?"

"How could we ever forget!" Jen and Charlie said at the same time, making them all laugh.

"Well," Steve said, "that sort of changed everything. Everyone just sort of thought: 'What the hell. If they can do it, so can we!' And then it wasn't such a big deal anymore."

"There *were* some problems, though," Charlie said.

"Yes, but everyone got over them, didn't they," Jen said. "It's nice not being jealous or scared that you're going to be dumped, or anything. Have you noticed that the kids are much more intimate than we were?"

"Yes," Charlie said. "I was talking about that with Nina today—"

Steve laughed. "Can you imagine the trouble we'd have gotten into if we'd been like that in the old world?"

"They're never jealous either," Charlie said. "It's not as if they control it like we do, but they don't seem to have feelings like that at all."

"It's because they're together all the time," Jen said. "Playing, eating, sleeping, having lessons… everything."

"Yeah, I love the way they all sleep curled up around each other like a bunch of snakes," Charlie said.

"You dare call our kids *snakes!*" Jen said, whacking him playfully on the arm.

"Oops! Sorry, Jen!"

"What are you two fighting about?" Johnny called out as he came over to the small group. "Will you never grow up!"

"Dunno," Charlie said. "I'm not sure I know what that means anymore. Guess that's what we were talking about. How we've changed in the last ten years—and the way our children are growing up."

"That's what we do," Johnny said. "Eat and grow, then make more kids who'll eat and grow. That's what we do."

"Seems like a pretty worthwhile thing to do," Jen said.

"It is," Johnny said.

"We're doing our best," Charlie said. He looked over towards the Big Hut where the kids were still playing pantomime. "I think we're doing pretty well, actually."

Twenty-seven

Dewdrop and Ray were hard at work. It was the rainy season, and the Two-Pot tribe had moved to the cave.

With each passing year, the big cavern had become more and more comfortable to live in. Reed mats covered large portions of the cavern floor, and Tom, Dick and Harry had made low tables from tree trunks. The three dwarves had become really good at working with wood and had developed lots of new carpentry techniques. Like log splitting.

First, a log was cut with an axe to make a shallow crack, then a wedge of sharp stone was hammered deeper and deeper into it, until it split. It hadn't been so easy at first, but like everything else, experimenting and practice resulted in better ways of doing things.

There were lots of things they'd worked out how to do, more or less without any forehand knowledge, but sometimes a technique they'd taught themselves would be useful for making many different things.

Splitting stones to make useful tools wasn't easy either. First you had to find the right kind of stone, and then practice until you broke off a piece that could be sharpened. When a piece of stone was the right size, had a good edge and was comfortable to hold, it would make a tool almost as good as their old Scout knives—and for some jobs even better. Stone tools were definitely better for scraping hides and for butchering. Their extra weight made splitting bone joints and cutting through tendons much easier.

Going hunting in the rainy season was almost pointless. Animals and birds were hard to find, as most of them had found shelter from the rain too. Being outside in the wet all the time wasn't much fun either. The tribe lived on the food they'd stored in the cave—mostly dried berries and roots, salted fish and smoked meat. They'd learnt the hard way that food had to be stored in strong baskets placed high on ledges in the cavern's walls, where rodents couldn't reach them.

Torches made from bundles of reeds and strips of cloth stood along the cave walls. They were much better than their first efforts at torch making. The latest models burned much longer and brighter, and made much less smoke. Step by step, techniques were developed, and skills were learnt and refined. Occasionally, someone would come up with an idea that would make life a lot easier or more comfortable. These great ideas were pronounced to be 'Nobels', after the famous Nobel Prizes!

By the light of the torches, Dewdrop and Ray were painting a section of the cave wall. They used different coloured paint made from ground minerals mixed with plant extracts, or anything else they could think of, to get the right consistency and different colours—even blood and brain matter from dead animals.

Dewdrop, especially, had great artistic talent. Her paintings were neither realistic nor abstract. Their shapes were easily recognisable as the people, birds and animals that she usually painted, but something about their forms, or the way they seemed to move in the flickering torchlight, said something more about that individual or creature. It was if she could capture their essence—their inner spirit—something others could recognise but hadn't seen so clearly before: something deeper that she brought to life.

Ray's pictures were simpler. He liked to paint people in the same way he'd seen in books about the Stone Age. They looked more like stick people. He usually painted the stories that he'd heard around the campfire or just pictures portraying the tribe's day-to-day life. He was a great storyteller too. Everybody loved to listen to him telling stories. He would hold a burning torch to illuminate different parts of his pictures as he went along. From telling to telling, the stories tended to get more embellished and exaggerated. His favourite story was about the dog attack, but if

Ray's latest picture of this heroic tale was to be believed, the tribe had fought off at least twenty or even *thirty* dogs! He explained to the kids that he hadn't finished painting all the dogs that had really been there either!

The children loved to paint too—although usually got quite messy, resulting in many a dip in the magical lake to get clean afterwards. Luckily they didn't have any clothes to wash, as they ran around naked most of the time. Even in the rainy season it never got cold enough to have to wear clothes. The nights were a bit cooler, but they snuggled up to each other under fur blankets to keep warm.

In the sunny season, the youngest children often wore the Fengwidditch Scouts' old mauve and green scarves on their heads to protect them from the sun. The scarves made them look like a mini Scout troop! Like the grown-ups, they always went barefoot. The soles of their feet were hard as leather.

Shoes were only needed on trips to the city, where pieces of glass and shards of metal sticking up from the ground could inflict nasty cuts. Their old Scout boots were saved for these trips and had kept surprisingly well. Anytime the leather looked like it was drying out, they would be rubbed with animal fat to keep them supple.

Dewdrop had finished her picture: a landscape of the camp. In the middle was the campfire, which cast long shadows of the people sitting around it. It was these shadows that were so captivating. The elongated forms somehow exaggerated the personalities and characteristics of the figures sitting around the fire, making them not only easily recognisable, but also revealing what it was that made each and every one of them special. Even the shadows of the trees surrounding the camp that she had painted seemed to capture a special feeling about their home.

Everyone agreed that it was a wonderful painting: one which gave them an even deeper insight into the beauty of the land they lived in and the love they felt for the tribe.

Twenty-eight

"Almost looks like a school class, doesn't it, Johnny," Harry said.

The tribe's children were sitting in a half circle. Angie stood in front them, drawing pictures on the cave wall with a piece of charcoal. She was teaching them about dinosaurs and evolution.

"Why did the dinosaurs die out?" Robin, a five-year-old with a mop of black hair asked.

"No one knows for sure," Angie said. "There are a few different theories. The most likely one is that the earth got hit by a huge meteorite. Does anyone know what a meteorite is?"

Hands shot up.

"Daisy…"

"I know. It's a big stone that comes from space… Nina told me about them. If they burn up they become shooting stars."

"That's exactly right! This huge meteorite hit the earth and there was such a huge explosion that it changed the weather for years and years. The dinosaurs couldn't adapt to the new conditions, so they all died… But I have my own theory as well."

"What is it? What is it?"

"Well," Angie said, raising her voice a bit. "It's like those guys over there…" She pointed to where Harry and Johnny were standing.

"Huh! Us?" Harry said.

"Yes!" Angie said, turning to the kids again. "The dinosaurs died out because…" She paused dramatically. "They had too many muscles, and too little brains!"

The kids all cracked up laughing.

"*Harumph!*" Harry said, glancing at Johnny.

The two men bared their teeth and made claws of their hands. Growling ferociously, they lumbered towards the children.

This made some of the younger ones scream. The others just laughed even louder!

The kids called it *Learning*. It wasn't organised, though. If there was something they wondered about, they just asked one of the older children or one of the grown-ups. Sometimes that would turn into an impromptu class, like the one about dinosaurs. They learnt to read and write both English and Greek so that they would be able to read all the books from the library and learn about anything else they were interested in. The tribe's day-to-day language was still English, but a fair number of Greek words had become mixed in with it.

They also learnt about the old world. To the children it would always seem to be far away in a distant time and place. The original Scouts' memories of the old world and Fengwidditch faded more and more as the years passed by too.

The children were never forced to learn. They had so much natural curiosity about anything and everything that they were learning all the time anyway.

At times their incessant questions would lead Steve to make additional trips to the library to find the answers. He always went gladly, as his own appetite for learning and teaching knew no bounds. In his free time, Steve could invariably be found reading a book, discussing something he'd read or teaching the children.

He'd talked to Charlie about this. The more we know about our world—about everything—Steve had said, the better chance we have of surviving. It will help us adapt to anything that changes. That's what makes us so different from animals. We're able to change both the way we behave as well as make changes to our environment. We can rebuild our world so it suits our needs and purposes. That's why mankind was able to spread out all over the globe: to any part where there was even the slightest chance of survival. Even to the moon!

That's true, Charlie had said, but there's more to learn about than the world outside. We have to learn about what's inside us as well: our feelings, how we develop, who we are… Then there are the big questions: Why are we alive? Where did the universe come from? And *why* is there a universe? Knowing about ourselves—on the inside—will help us find the answers.

Steve had to agree with this. The two men loved to have different opinions though. They would often take an opposing view just to see where a discussion might lead. Either that, or they would reignite one of their old, never-ending ones. It was sometimes hard to admit that the other was right about something, or sometimes to even concede the slightest of points, but after reflecting on their talks later on, they would both redefine their own positions, accept the other's arguments if they fit in with everything else, and move forward. There seemed to be no end to it. Any insight they gained from their studies and discussions opened up even wider horizons full of new questions to be tackled and debated.

Sometimes I think I don't know anything, Charlie had once said. But then I think about how far we've come. I guess if anyone can make any sense of life and the universe, it's us. We're right in the middle of it, aren't we!

Steve was also the hardest critic of Charlie's work. Any new paper Charlie wrote would be scrutinized, questioned and discussed. After that, he always had to go back and rewrite some parts of it, or even the whole thing, taking in mind Steve's suggestions and comments—the ones they'd come to agreement on, at least.

Charlie had once asked Steve why he didn't write himself. The answer he got was a bit surprising: Steve had said that all the stuff he was interested in had already been written. It was all in the library books. Except the stuff Charlie was writing. That was new. It was putting it all together—making sense of it—but he didn't have the insights Charlie did to add anything himself. He could help keep him on track, though, he'd said. That's more than he could ever wish for.

'Wow!' was all Charlie could say to that.

Twenty-nine

The rainy season was coming to an end. Sunlight had broken through the grey clouds. At times it felt like the rain would never stop—but it always did, leaving their world green and fresh.

Everything is so beautiful, Charlie thought to himself. I'm glad I can feel like that. Maybe that's what it's all about… Beauty.

As they always did after the rains, the Two-Pot tribe had hiked to the other side of the island where there was a beautiful sandy beach they'd discovered years before. They usually stayed there for a few days, or even a week, fishing and collecting mussels. These were lazy days, spent basking in the sun and swimming in the clear blue sea. Gwen was the strongest of the swimmers. She'd been the captain of the Fengwidditch Middle School swimming team once upon a time. In a race from one side of the bay to the other, she'd beaten everybody—even the men—much to Johnny's surprise. He'd taken the defeat gracefully, though, congratulating her on having been born with too many fish genes!

The sea teemed with fish that were easy to catch, either from the shore or from a simple raft that they'd made by lashing split logs together. By rowing out past the reef to the deep lagoon, they could catch even bigger fish. It was fun too. The kids loved going out on the raft. They were careful to only go out when the tide was coming in, though, so it would help them get back to shore. Paddling against the tide was hard—even dangerous. Dick and Harry had once got stuck out at sea and had to wait for hours before they were able to paddle back to shore. At full moon the tides were especially strong. Swimming could be dangerous then, as well, due to the strong rip tides: underwater currents which could easily pull someone far out to sea.

When the tide went out, rock pools full of crabs and mussels were left behind. The pickings were good, and delicious. Every evening they made a fire on the beach and roasted the seafood they'd collected. Roasted crab meat was everyone's favourite. Plucked straight from the embers, the crabs' legs and claws were cracked open to get to the juicy white meat inside.

That evening, they even grilled six big fish. The smaller fish they'd caught would be taken back to camp to be dried and salted before being stored in wicker baskets in the cave. It didn't taste as good as fresh fish, of course, but any food that kept them from going hungry was good. Nothing was wasted, nothing thrown away.

After sunset, the fire seemed to burn brighter as the sky and sea grew darker. A couple of children still played on the beach, but most of them had curled up near the warmth of the fire. The long hike, as well as all the swimming and fishing, had finally tired them out.

Gwen played softly on her flute. Somehow she managed to capture the beauty of the evening on her simple instrument: weaving whispering melodies accompanied by the sound of the waves breaking on the shore and the occasional call of a seagull.

The talk around the fire slowly died down and then stopped altogether. The sound of Gwen's flute, the drifting melodies she played and the soft breathing of the sleeping children carried them all off to a dreamy place where memories and feelings blended together. One by one, they let the music lull them to sleep.

Gwen put her flute back into her bag. She smiled at the sight of the Two-Pot tribe sleeping by the fire. The heat of the embers would keep them warm through the night.

Charlie woke up in the middle of the night, needing to pee. He walked down towards the sea, then stopped to gaze in awe at the magnificent night sky. The Milky Way stretched out clear and bright from horizon to horizon. The planets were easily recognisable, as they shone with different colours than the silvery stars.

When he'd first spent nights gazing at the night sky, a few of the brighter stars had fooled him into thinking they were planets. In time, though, he'd learnt to recognise the patterns the stars made. This made it much easier to find the planets as they wandered across the sky from night to night.

His favourite constellation was still below the horizon. Just quite *why* it was his favourite, he couldn't really explain. It was the constellation he sought out when he looked up at the night sky.

It was mostly because of a memory he had of gazing at the stars one night when he was much younger. Those five stars had been right above him, and as he looked beyond them into the depths of space, the sheer beauty of the universe had taken his breath away.

The five stars would always remind him of that feeling.

They were easy to find if they were above the horizon. One side of the Big Dipper pointed to the North Star around which the whole night sky revolved. On the other side, directly across and about as far again, was the five-star constellation. He'd never told anyone about his favourite stars. He wasn't sure why… Maybe they only have a special meaning for me, he thought—because of that night so long ago.

Steve had found a pair of binoculars on one of his trips to the city, so now Nina could study the night sky in even greater depth and make even more detailed charts. She was much more scientifically interested in the night sky than Charlie and called the stars and the constellations by their old Greek and Latin names that she had learnt from the library's astronomy books. In their own ways, though, both she and Charlie were equally fascinated by the vastness and beauty of the cosmos.

A few thin clouds drifted across the sky, making the stars look even further away. The clouds seemed so close.

Still gazing up at the night sky, Charlie walked towards the sea.

"Ouch!" he cried out… He'd stubbed his toe on a rock!

He let the pain wash over him until it receded. Must remember to stand still and look at the stars, he told himself… Said that before, he thought. Some things you just can't learn!

Charlie peed in the sea, then sat down and let the salty water clean the bloody flap of skin on his big toe. That'll be sore for a few days, he thought—but no worse than that.

His cry had woken Jen. She knew exactly what had happened.

As he walked back to the fire, she grinned at him. He stuck his tongue out at her, and was rewarded with an even bigger grin.

Thirty

Charlie woke up on the beach just before sunrise.

"Good morning, World," he murmured.

He sat up under his blanket and watched the orange and red sky become lighter and lighter. Clouds turned gold, then the first chink of the sun rose above the horizon. That first flash of light always took his breath away.

It was a hard feeling to describe: of sitting on a planet spinning at a thousand miles per hour in a huge universe. He was hurtling towards the sun! At sunset, the feeling was similar: of falling backwards, away from the sun until the last ray of light disappeared.

These moments at the edge of day and night were magical.

He walked down to the sea. There were no waves, just ripples on its surface made by the morning breeze.

When he took his first step into the sea, the saltwater stung his toe.

With a last look at the rising sun, he whispered *"Splash!"* and dove into its golden reflection.

He kept his eyes open. Shimmering rays of light shone through the clear blue water. He took three slow breaststrokes underwater, then surfaced and took a deep breath of the crisp morning air. The sun beamed down on his smiling face.

Turning around to look at the beach, he saw that the tribe was starting to stir.

Two of the kids saw him and waved.

Charlie waved back. It's good to be alive, he thought to himself, and dove into the water again, swimming under the surface towards the beach. Coming to his feet, he splashed water onto his face a few times. What a great way to wake up!

"What's for breakfast?" he called out to the boy and the girl at the fireplace.

"*Fish! stupid!*" they called back, giggling.

After breakfast, the Two-Pot tribe packed everything together and headed back up the island. They walked slowly, as some of them were carrying heavy bags of the fish they'd caught the day before. Others carried bags of seaweed that would be boiled and made into carrageen: a sticky but nutritious jelly. The dried fish and carrageen would be stored in the cave, ready for the next rainy season.

Charlie carried one of the big bags of fish over his shoulder. It was quite heavy, but he could swap with someone else later if he got tired. The sun warmed his back as they climbed the hill.

"You want me to take that bag for a while, Charlie?" Tom said, coming up alongside him.

Charlie turned his head, taking his eye off the path ahead of him just for an instant. His foot slipped on the side of a small rock and he lost his balance. He automatically shifted his weight to his other foot to regain it.

The earth beneath his foot was too soft, and the extra weight of the bag made his body twist. With a cry, Charlie felt his leg buckle. Something snapped in his knee. A searing pain shot up his leg.

He hit the ground in agony.

"*Charlie!*" Tom cried out. He bent down to help him up, but by the look on Charlie's face, he could see that it was worse than that.

"Bad?" he asked, and crouched down to look at Charlie's leg.

"Yes, I think so… Not good."

The initial pain had passed, but it still hurt like mad. He tried to bend his knee, but it hurt too much. Tom took hold of both of Charlie's arms and carefully helped him up. He put some weight on his foot, but yelped as another bolt of pain shot up his leg.

"Nope, not good," he finally managed to say. "Something's torn in my knee. I don't think I can walk…"

"Well, we'll just have to leave you here for the wolves then!" Gwen said, making Charlie laugh and grunt in pain at the same time.

"Ouch! Don't do that! Don't make me laugh. That hurt!"

"We'll have to carry him," Johnny said, taking command. "We'll make a stretcher… We'll need two thick branches about eight feet long for the poles."

The three dwarves rushed off to look for good branches.

"We'll have to make a needle," Gwen said, catching on to how Johnny was thinking. "I think we've got enough twine with us to sew a blanket around the poles."

"Good!" Johnny said.

Helen hurried off to find something to fashion a needle out of. She found a suitable twig and whittled it into shape, then threaded it with a long length of twine.

They folded the blanket around the long sticks so that she could sew them together. She even sewed large stitches tightly along the length of the branches so they wouldn't slip out.

"It'll hold," Johnny said when it was done.

They lifted him very gently onto the stretcher.

"Ray, grab the other end," Johnny said. "We'll take turns carrying. It'll get heavy, so we'll swap often. Don't want to drop you, do we, Charlie?"

"I'm sorry," Charlie said.

"You shut up, Charlie!" Gwen said. "Isn't it you who always says we should help each other? … Well, now you're the one who needs help. So…"

"So shut up!" Angie finished for her.

"Exactly!" Gwen said. She bent down and kissed him firmly on the lips.

"On the count of three!" Johnny said. "One, Two, and *Three*."

"This'll work," Ray said.

"Only way to travel!" Charlie said, and laughed. "Ouch!"

All the grown-ups took turns carrying him—even Angie and Maggy who could only manage one end of a pole each.

"How's it feel, Charlie?" Helen asked.

"I'm not sure. It doesn't hurt so much, unless I move. Feels like my knee is really swollen up."

"That's nature's way of protecting it," she said. "I remember once when I'd sprained my ankle. It swelled up too, and that's what Mrs. Jennings told me."

At last they made it to the cave. They decided that Johnny and Mark would stay there with Charlie, and the others would go back to camp.

There wasn't much else they had to take from the cave, and they were all pretty loaded up with fish and seaweed anyway, so they just took the baby quilts they'd made from old sleeping bags with them.

Johnny, Mark and Charlie stayed at the cave for three days until most of the swelling around his knee had gone down. That was a good sign. He could even hobble about a bit by using a stick to take the weight off his leg. He had to take it very carefully, though. It still hurt.

"I'll be okay," Charlie said, but he wondered if his knee would ever really get better. Something was badly torn. One of the ligaments, he guessed. With the help of a medical book—and some prodding and poking—they worked out that it was probably the outer ligament that had been torn off from just under his knee. It might refasten itself in time, the book said. The meniscus on the inside of his knee had been torn as well, and would never properly heal. For the rest of his life, Charlie would walk with a limp. He made himself a walking stick to help him get around. His leg hurt on and off—more than he let on to the others—but in time he got used to it. Just part of living, I guess, he'd say to himself.

A few months later, he tried to run but had to give up after just a few strides; his knee felt like it was going to buckle again. He sat down and stared into the woods.

"Hey Charlie! What's up?" Johnny said. He'd seen what had happened and had come over to sit next to him.

"Just sitting here feeling sorry for myself."

"Your leg?"

"Yeah, my leg. Don't think I'm going to be able to run again… Makes me pretty useless as a hunter, doesn't it?"

"Guess so. Just the way it is…"

"Yeah, just the way it is," Charlie agreed. "Gives me more time to write, I suppose. I'm going to miss running and hunting, though."

Johnny turned to look at his friend. "Going to happen to us all, in time," he said. "We're all going to get old and not be able to run. You're just the first, Charlie. Leading the way as usual!"

"Thanks, Johnny. Just happened to me a bit sooner than I'd reckoned on." There was a note of sadness in his voice.

"Way it goes," Johnny said.

"Way it goes. No point getting too down about it. I'll do my best, anyway."

"Wouldn't have thought anything else," Johnny said, getting to his feet. He offered Charlie his hand.

"Nah, thanks… I can get up on my own," Charlie said, and gritted his teeth together.

Thirty-one

Years went by.

Johnny was almost forty years old. He was still the strongest man in the tribe but had to concede defeat when it came to running against the younger lads, like Ray, and especially Red who was seventeen years old now.

The island was the only home Red had ever known. He was a great hunter, able to blend into any kind of foliage to become almost invisible. He could move so stealthily out in the open that animals never noticed him—until it was too late. Red could track an animal for miles before killing it with his spear, bow and arrow, catapult or knife.

The men hunted in groups. Rabbits, squirrels, birds and goats were their main prey. On moonlit nights, a hunting party could even come across badgers. Tame goats had bred with kri-kris, the larger wild goats of Crete, and their offspring had spread all across the island. They'd learnt to run away from humans too.

On finding an animal's tracks, the hunters would follow them until they sighted their prey. Then they would fan out, careful to keep downwind and as hidden as possible. One or two hunters would then circle behind the animal, which would often prick up its ears and sniff the air, getting their scent. Seeing that it was about to bolt, they jumped forward, scaring it into fleeing away from them—straight towards the main group of hunters. Panicking, it would either try to find a gap between the two groups or freeze. The hunters were ready to spear it if it ran—or close in for the kill.

Johnny had always led the hunt, although recently Red had begun to question his decisions. Johnny had to admit that however good a hunter he had become himself, that Red was better.

Not surprising, Johnny thought. Red had grown up in the mountains and woods, learning to think like the animals. The realisation that his position as hunt leader was being taken over by the younger man made him feel a bit down. At the same time, he was glad that they had taught their children so well. What use is a teacher if their pupils don't get better than them? he thought, shrugging off his mood.

One evening, Johnny sat by the campfire, just watching the glowing embers. He was lost in thought.

Stars stretched across the sky above him. It had been good day. They'd caught a fat goat which would feed the ever growing tribe for a week or even longer. The goat's hide would be made into warm blankets, and its bones and horns into tools. The goat had been fast. Too fast to outrun they'd found out in their first attempt to catch it. Instead, they'd had to track it down.

When they'd finally caught up with it, Johnny had wanted to spread the hunters out in a large circle—the way they usually did—but Red had suggested that they should stick together and approach it from one side. He had pointed to where he meant. That would mean the goat would run in the opposite direction, where he knew there was a steep cliff. By not spreading out, there was less chance that the goat would get past them again. Johnny had agreed that it was worth a try.

Red had been right. The goat ran away from them until it reached the edge of the cliff. Then it had to turn around. The only way the scared animal could go was straight back towards them…

It ran at full gait—straight into their sharp spears.

It collapsed, blood pouring down its chest and neck. Red leaped forward and slashed its neck with his stone knife. Bright red blood covered his arms and grinning face.

It was a good kill—and a great hunting strategy, Johnny admitted, wishing at the same time that he'd thought of it himself.

"Hi Johnny," Red said. "Okay if I sit here?"

"Of course! Good hunt today. Great tactic you came up with…"

Red seemed to understand how Johnny was feeling.

"Hey, don't let it get to you, old man," he said with a smile. "Everything I know, I've learnt from you—*That* I'll never forget."

"Yeah, thanks Red. I guess I know. It's just…" He trailed off, leaving his thought unspoken.

"It's just natural," Red said. "That's how the tribe will survive. New leaders take over from the old ones…" He inclined his head towards the Big Hut. "One day, one of those brats will be better than me. It's just the way it's meant to be."

"You're right. Of course you are, Red. I know… I'm proud of you, don't get me wrong. It's just it isn't so easy when that day comes."

"I'll remember that," Red said with a laugh that sounded more like a grunt.

"Oh, and by the way," Johnny said. "How did you get to be so wise, so young?"

"I dunno!" Red laughed. "Like I said, good teachers, old man."

At this they both laughed and gave each other a hug.

"You stay on your toes," Johnny said. "I'm not done for yet."

"No," Red said. "Never thought you were."

They sat silently, listening to the singing of crickets and the crackling of the fire. Johnny let the peace of the night sink into his bones. The tribe will go on, he thought to himself.

"Shall we take a walk around the perimeter?" he said at last.

"Sure. Good idea, Johnny."

"Got to keep on your toes," the older man said softly.

So softly, that it was more like he was talking to himself.

Thirty-two

"Hi, Charlie, want to go for a walk?"

"Sure, Jen. Where do you want to go?"

"Nowhere particular. Just walk—and talk for a bit. We could head for the cave. There's lots of berries and even some fruit in the woods now, so we can eat along the way."

"Great. Hang on, I'll just get my stick."

They walked along the narrow path, stopping now and again to pick blackberries.

"What's on your mind?" Charlie said after a while.

"The tribe's getting too big, Charlie. Have you noticed how there are almost two separate groups of us girls? Even you guys don't go off hunting all together like you used to."

"Yes, I know what you mean."

"At the moment there's enough food, but we have to split into two gathering groups to cover more ground. It takes us further and further from home as well."

"What do you think we should do then?"

"We've been talking about splitting up."

"You girls, you mean?"

"Yes, Angie and some of the others think they could stay at the beach instead. I think they're right. There would be more food for everybody that way."

"I guess us guys would split up as well then. It would be good to be a smaller group again. We were closer in a way before… What would we do in the rainy season?"

"There's still room in the cave for all of us. If we all stored food there, I think we'd be fine. It's not as if we're never going to see each other again, is it?"

"No, we would still be the same tribe," Charlie said. "We'd just be two different groups." He laughed. "Like two different Scout troops!"

"I'll call a meeting this evening. Find out what everyone thinks, and what they want to do."

"What about you? You want to stay up here, don't you?"

"Yes. And you?"

"Me too."

Later that evening, and long into the night, the Two-Pot tribe talked about splitting up. Many of them said they'd either had the same thought or just a feeling of restlessness—especially the girls, it seemed.

They decided that it would be up to each and every one of them to choose if they wanted to stay or move to the beach. As it turned out, though, it was really simple. As Jen and Charlie had already realised, there was already a natural split in both of the groups.

"At least we won't be fighting over the position as hunt leader now," Johnny said to Red, half jokingly.

"That's true!" Red laughed.

The two men gave each other a hard hug.

"You take care of your people," Johnny said.

"And you take care of yours," Red said with a nod.

They looked deep into each other's eyes—both of them recognising themselves in the other man.

"Be seeing ya, kid!" Johnny said with a smile.

"And you, old man!" Red said, smiling back at him.

Of the original Fengwidditch Scouts, Jen, Gwen, Sarah and Helen said they would stay in the woods. Charlie, Johnny, Steve, Mark and Kev would stay with them.

Angie, Maggy and Nina would go to the beach along with Tom, Dick, Harry and Pete. That the three dwarves would be inseparable surprised no one.

All in all, there would be twenty-four in the *Mountain troop* and twenty-two in the *Beach troop* as they had started calling themselves.

Three generations of us, Charlie thought. Incredible! And now we're spreading out and populating the island! It feels right, he thought. We were too many people in one place. At least we didn't have to fight over our territory.

At the same time he wondered what would have happened if they'd *had* to. Would he have fought if there was nowhere left to go? I guess we'll cross that bridge if and when we get to it… For now, the island is big enough for a lot more of us.

That evening, Charlie couldn't get to sleep. He was still thinking about whether they would have fought over their territory if there was no other way it could support all of them. I suppose we would, he concluded—although we'd do everything to avoid it first. In the end we have to survive and grow. Without food and babies, the tribe can't survive, he thought. We've learnt to do lots of things we'd never have dreamt of doing before, and if the tribe doesn't survive, well, then there's no point in anything at all. Part of him found it strange to think about fighting his lifelong friends. Another part found it perfectly natural.

He slowly drifted off into sleep.

The splitting of the tribe into two troops and all the emotions that went with it gave Charlie lots to think and write about. It was an important turning point: one that clarified some of his theories and raised many new questions to research and contemplate.

In the end, it would be through this experience that he would gain his most important insight into human nature: the natural size and structure of tribes.

Thirty-three

A wood pigeon woke Charlie up.

He'd slept outside by the fire, where he'd fallen asleep watching the stars and the moon. As he usually did, he'd woken up in the middle of the night and gazed into the night sky for an hour or so before falling back to sleep.

There had been a gentle breeze all night, just enough to discourage mosquitoes. On warm nights when there was no wind at all, there was the eternal problem of either being too warm under a blanket, where the mosquitoes couldn't get to you, or lying on top of the blanket—which was cooler—but left you open to attack from the blood-thirsty vampires!

Sarah kept experimenting with different ointments to keep the mosquitoes away. Her most successful repellent was a mixture of hibiscus juice and stinging nettles, although it only seemed to work for half of the night until it wore off. Luckily for the tribe's stargazers, the mosquitoes were very sensitive to even the mildest of breezes.

The wood pigeon was in a tree nearby. It called out again.

"Yeah, yeah," Charlie muttered. "I'm getting up… Good morning, Wood pigeon! Good morning, World!"

He turned onto his stomach and pushed himself up. This was the only way he could get up in the morning, as his leg was always stiffest then. It would loosen up once he got moving about. Not too much trouble, for the most part, he thought.

"Old and worn out," he mumbled to himself.

Everybody else was beginning to wake up too. A baby cried. Moments later it found its mother's breast and was quiet again.

Ah, there's one who's awake! Charlie said to himself, seeing a young girl perched high up in the old pine tree. She peered studiously down at him. It was Amber. She was eleven years old but was small for her age, so she looked younger. Her golden-red hair was braided into two pigtails, which hung over her shoulders and almost down to her waist.

"Hi there!" she called out.

"Hi, Amber!" Charlie called back. "What are you doing up there?"

"Oh, just sitting," she said, and then laughed. "It's nice being taller than everybody else!"

Nimbly, she started to climb down from branch to branch.

"Want me to catch you?" Charlie said.

"No, I'm okay," Amber said, then launched herself the last six feet to land on the pine needle covered ground.

Humph! Wish I could still do that, Charlie thought.

"What are you up to today?" he asked as they walked over to the campfire.

"I want to go to Emerald Cove!" Her face lit up with excitement.

Emerald Cove was a little bay about a mile from where the Beach troop lived. It was the children's favourite place. The sea dropped off just a few feet from the beach and was so deep that they could jump and dive into it from a ledge that stuck out from the cliff on the far side of the bay.

Why not? Charlie thought. They had enough food, so they could take a couple of days off from hunting and gathering. A day at the beach would be great. Do some fishing too...

"Go see what the other kids say," he said.

The grin on her face told him that she already knew the answer to that! She ran off to find the other children.

"Charlie says we're going to Emerald Cove!"

Charlie smiled. Close enough to the truth, I suppose, he thought.

Everyone agreed that it was a great idea.

Be good to sleep by the sea again, Charlie thought to himself.

On the trips to Emerald Cove they sometimes visited the Beach troop. But not always.

There was no stopping the children as they scrambled up the

cliff path and hurled themselves into the sea.

They plummeted through the air and into the clear blue water, whooping, yelling and screaming, then surfaced with huge grins on their faces before striking out for shore. The youngest children were too small to dive or jump from the cliff, so they sat on the beach, half in and half out of the water, enthralled by the diving performance. Their faces were just as tense and excited by the thrill of it all, as if they too were part of the action.

It was a hot day, so everyone was in and out of the water to cool off.

After he'd come back from a swim, Johnny had said that there was a pretty strong current further out beyond the cove's entrance. Better to stay close to shore.

What a lazy day! Swimming, fishing and lapping up the sun…

The children built sandcastles and drew pictures in the sand. When the tide came in, they tried to rescue their works of architecture and art by digging trenches. Unsuccessfully, of course.

The night sky was perfectly clear. A billion stars shone brightly.

Charlie lay awake for a long time, just looking up at them and letting his thoughts wander. We have such a beautiful life, he thought… A tear formed in the corner of his eye.

"Goodnight, Charlie," Jen said.

"Goodnight, Jen," Charlie said softly.

There was something in his voice that made her catch onto the way he was feeling.

She leant over and kissed him tenderly; first on his cheek, then, maybe having seen the glint of his tears, she kissed him even more softly on his eyelids.

Thirty-four

Charlie woke a few moments before the sun crested the horizon.

A seagull landed on the beach just in front of him.

"Good morning, Seagull," he said.

Golden sunlight sparkled on the calm sea and caught the seagull's pure white feathers.

After his habitual morning 'splash', Charlie sat on the beach, watching the sea. Far off, close to the horizon, two dolphins surfaced for a moment, then dove again. They were joined by two more—then even more.

A tribe of dolphins out hunting, he laughed to himself. The feeling of wonder he'd had the evening before still hadn't left him. So much beauty…

"Come on, Charlie! Stop dreaming!" Steve called out.

Charlie waved back. "Coming!"

He turned his gaze once more to the sea.

Beauty is all around, he thought. But it's a feeling—a human feeling—so it's all inside us, too… Even the things that make life hard at times are part of nature. Without the struggle to survive we would never have developed. Without sickness and death there would be no evolution. It's all good. It's all beautiful.

"Hurry up, Charlie!"

"Yeah, yeah! Coming!" Charlie pushed himself to his feet and took a last look at the sea.

An ancient donkey trail led away from the beach and past some old rock formations before winding up the hill. The sun warmed their backs as they walked in single file. Charlie brought up the rear, using his stick to help, but having no problem keeping up with the others. No one was in a hurry that morning.

"Flo, where's Amber?" Gwen said to the girl in front of her.

Flo, whose real name was Sunflower, turned her head to look back over her shoulder. "I don't know," she said.

Helen looked around but couldn't see her anywhere. "Did she run ahead? Johnny, is Amber up there with you?"

"No!" Johnny called back. "No one's ahead of me." He'd taken the lead, of course.

Helen was a bit worried now. "Is Amber back there? Charlie! Did you see her?"

"No! There was no one on the beach when I left."

"Where is she then! Anyone seen Amber?"

Charlie turned around to look back the way they had come. "No one's on the beach," he called out.

All he could see was a solitary dolphin way out to sea.

No! Wait! That's not a dolphin!

In that same moment, he dropped his stick and started running. He hadn't run for years, but his legs hadn't forgotten how.

Pumping his arms, Charlie ran as fast as he ever had. The sea air swept his hair back. There was no pain in his knee, no burning in his lungs.

When he reached the sea, he didn't hesitate. Lifting his knees even higher to clear the low waves, he pounded into the water. He lost his balance and dove forward, trying to keep as much momentum as possible.

Charlie was a strong swimmer. Maybe not as fast as Gwen or Johnny, but his long arms and legs propelled him forward in a graceful front crawl.

On every third stroke, he lifted his head to breathe and check that he was heading towards Amber. He could see her head bobbing up and down in the water. Trying not to think, just concentrating on swimming as fast as possible, he got closer and closer.

She had run off for a last dip in the sea. The tide had caught her, but it wasn't before she was past the Cove's entrance that she'd realised that she couldn't swim back against the current. By then, she was too far away for the others to hear her cries.

She saw Charlie. "Help!" she called out to him.

Yes! Charlie thought. She's alive. I can get to her! This seemed to give him even more strength. He quickly covered the remaining distance and grabbed hold of the young girl. He held her with one arm wrapped around her waist.

Right, take it easy now, Charlie, he said to himself. Keep both our heads above water, paddle backwards—no rush, don't get exhausted…

Luckily, Amber wasn't panicking. Charlie's hold on her seemed to comfort her.

"It's okay Amb, I'll get you to shore," Charlie said. "You okay?"

"I'm okay," she said. "I just wanted a last swim."

"It's okay. Don't worry. Let's just get back, okay?"

"Yes, Charlie."

The badly damaged meniscus in his knee had been stressed to breaking point by the sudden running and swimming. Suddenly, it snapped in half, one jagged edge jamming into his knee joint.

The pain was even worse than when he'd injured his knee the first time. Charlie cried out in agony as his knee locked up and his whole leg cramped and went into spasms. I can't swim, he thought—or even tread water. His head went under.

Not far away, Johnny was swimming towards them as fast as he could… He heard Charlie's cry.

Charlie kicked out with his other leg, breaking the surface.

Amber sputtered and spat out a mouthful of seawater.

He was tiring now. Still holding Amber, he was trying to stay afloat and swim with just one leg and one arm. Charlie sank again.

Fight! he told himself. *Fight!*

He kicked to the surface again.

Amber was being pulled away from him. He tried to hold onto her, but then realising that Johnny had her, he let her go.

His other leg had begun to cramp as well now.

Can't stay afloat, he thought, gritting his teeth against the pain. It didn't help. His head sank beneath the water.

Johnny had a good hold on Amber. He could see that Charlie was in trouble. With his free hand, he grabbed his wrist.

Kicking with his feet, Johnny lay on his back, holding Amber on top of him and pulling Charlie upwards at the same time. He managed to turn her over so that she was facing him, and pressed her close to him with his arm around her back. She locked her arms around his neck. It made it easier to swim backwards.

Charlie surfaced, gasping for air. Realising what Johnny was doing, he tried to help by paddling with his free hand, but it didn't help much. He was in pain, and exhausted. They weren't making any headway against the current.

However strong Johnny was, he couldn't rescue both of them. His grip on Charlie's wrist slipped.

With a last burst of strength, Charlie grabbed Johnny's arm and propelled himself towards him so as not to drag them all beneath the water.

Charlie and Johnny's eyes met.

They both knew there was no choice.

In Johnny's eyes, Charlie saw burning determination—and frustration. They gripped each other's wrists as tightly as they could, desperately trying to stay afloat.

A wave washed over Charlie's head. He coughed and spluttered as the salty water filled his mouth.

He kicked both his legs at the same time—like a dolphin—to rise above the surface. Pain streaked through his body, but he barely noticed it as he spat the seawater out of his mouth and took a deep breath of pure fresh air.

He felt the warmth of the sun on his neck and looked at his friend holding the young girl just in front of him. Johnny's eyes were locked on his.

Worth dying for, Charlie thought. Or did he say it out loud? A big grin lit up his face.

Johnny got it. He grinned back.

Just like two young boys on the adventure of their lives.

Still smiling, Charlie looked deeply into his friend's eyes before slipping beneath the water.

The last thing he saw were rays of silver sunlight streaming through the blue sea—and the sky above him.

When she'd seen that Johnny and Charlie were in trouble, Gwen had thrown her bag down and dived into the sea. She struck out, swimming faster then ever before in her life.

She reached Johnny and Amber.

"Where's Charlie!" she screamed. But she already knew the answer.

Taking a deep breath of air, she dived below the surface.

She couldn't see him.

She came up for air. And dived again—searching desperately.

Another breath of air, and down again.

Again and again... Until she knew it was too late. Charlie had been underwater too long.

Taking a last breath of air, Gwen dived once more. She swam deeper and deeper—down to where the water was a deep dark blue.

Turning slowly, she looked all around, then raised her hand to wave farewell.

'Goodbye, Charlie', she thought silently—words she could never say to him now.

When she had no more air in her lungs, she kicked her feet and swam towards the surface.

Johnny reached the beach with Amber. The little girl was taken from him by helping hands. He sat down on the beach with his arms wrapped around his knees. Salt water and tears stung his eyes.

Gwen came out of the sea and stood in front of him with clenched fists.

"I should have swum out straight away!" she said, tears streaming down her face.

"No, Gwen! Me and Charlie should have saved her easily... But his leg—"

"I should have swum out *straight away!* It's *my* fault!"

Johnny stood up quickly and grabbed her by the shoulders. He held her at arm's length.

"Never, *never* say that again! Gwen It's not your fault! You couldn't have known!"

She collapsed into his arms, shaking and crying.

They sat on the beach for the rest of the day, watching the tide come in.

As the sun set, the sea turned darker and darker blue. Tiny sparkles of light danced on the waves until they, too, disappeared.

When the moon rose, the sea sparkled again.

Gwen curled up and slept—her head resting in Johnny's lap.

Johnny didn't sleep. He kept watch over his old friend.

At sunrise they walked up the beach and set off home.

Johnny picked up Charlie's walking stick from where he'd dropped it when he'd realised Amber was in trouble. Make a good spear for one of the young boys, he thought. Charlie would like that.

Turning one last time to look at the sea, he spoke softly, "Bye, Charlie."

A single tear rolled down his cheek to the corner of his mouth.

The salty taste lingered on his lips as they walked up the hill hand in hand.

Thirty-five

A week had gone by since Charlie had died. It was the night of a full moon. That evening the children were going to perform 'The Play', as it was called.

The Play told different stories of the tribe: from the early days after the tsunami—stories that the children been told about and knew well through having watched earlier Plays—all the way up to things that may have happened just that same day.

The Play changed, depending on who was performing it and which characters they portrayed. It was much more an expression of feelings than a true-to-life representation of events. The children's roles changed too, depending on which stories they played or for whatever best fitted their improvisations. One thing was constant, though: the play was always silent. No words, sounds or songs were used. The stories were told with just body language and miming. Sometimes they dressed up or painted their bodies. That evening most of the children had daubed blue paint in wavy patterns on their skins.

This time, the play started with the actors rushing wildly at the audience, their arms held high above their heads—like a tsunami—before drawing back again.

Some of the children mimed searching for water and the joy of finding the spring. Others weaved and danced around them like small waterfalls. Two children made rain with their fingers waving over the heads of the others—the rainy season. When they mimed fishing, paddling on a boat and diving into the sea, everyone could see that they were at Emerald Cove.

A circle of children sat down and joined hands to make the magical lake where others pretended to bathe. One boy sat on the beach just outside the ring. He mimed writing in a book. Everyone could tell it was Charlie.

All the other children stood up and formed two circles: one inside the other. They waved their arms slowly up and down in undulating waves, bending their knees and stretching towards the sky. The effect was captivating. The children's eyes glistened in the moonlight, full of concentration.

The boy stopped writing and stood up. He started to swim around the two circles of children.

At last he was let into the outside ring. Then into the middle.

As he got to the very centre, he turned to look at the audience.

Smiling all the time, he lowered himself slowly to his knees. The waves drew in around him.

Covering him gently, the children's arms waved slower and slower. The boy disappeared from view. They all became perfectly still.

How did they know? Johnny thought. How did they know Charlie was smiling? He hadn't told anyone about those last moments. Not even Gwen. Tears ran down his cheeks. They just know… They just know he was happy.

For long moments no one moved—neither the actors nor their spellbound audience. Then one by one, the grown-ups got to their feet. They went over to the pile of children and joined hands, making another ring around them. Gently, and in silence, they embraced them.

The Play was over. Something very special had been captured that evening.

Johnny caught the eye of the boy who had played Charlie and nodded. The boy nodded solemnly back… imitating him.

"What a bunch," he said softly to himself.

"Yes, aren't they," Jen said.

He hadn't noticed her standing right behind him.

"They're different than we were," she said.

"They would be, growing up like this," Johnny said. "But it's more than that, isn't it?"

"Yes, Charlie was right. Children need a group of other children to belong to. That's how they develop and mature, learning from each other. Not by being told what to do—or *not* to do—by grown-ups."

"Yes, you can see how the older ones take the youngsters under their wing and how much the young ones look up to them, can't you."

"That's how they learn though, isn't it. By wanting to become like the ones who take care of them. In turn they'll take care of others and teach them."

"And so it goes on," Johnny said.

"Yes, we teach them all the practical stuff they need to know. The rest—the important stuff—they get from each other. They haven't just copied us; they've developed their own ways of doing things. They learn how to love and take care of each other. We don't make rules or punish them. That's what Charlie said messed everybody up in the old world. We were all made to feel guilty about so many things, and then spent our entire lives trying to prove that we were worth loving… Sorry, I'm lecturing, aren't I?"

"No, it's cool, Jen. We need to remind ourselves all the time. They've grown up following their instincts—and that's how they'll survive. Our children, and their children. They're beautiful people, aren't they?"

"Say that again, Johnny."

He smiled at her. "They're beautiful people. Don't you ever regret not growing up like them, Jen?"

"Of course I do! It makes me wonder how far they can go. Sometimes I feel we old ones are still trying to get to the point where they started from… I mean, we're still trying to get over our hang-ups and break free. They're starting off free, without even realising it, and can go so much further."

"Yes. But this is the next best thing, isn't it. Knowing that we're giving them a chance to be the people they're meant to be. It makes our lives worthwhile, even if we'll never be totally free ourselves."

"Yes. That's the most meaningful thing we can do with our lives. Charlie knew that. He saw it first.

"I miss him," Johnny said.

"I miss him too," Jen said. "We all do…"

Epilogue

There was another story as well: one which Mark and Steve had written in the years following Charlie's death.

They had started off by sorting through the thousands of pages Charlie had written, all of which had been safely stored in the university library in Heraklion.

Charlie's theory had developed through the years. Things he'd written early on were amended in later papers when he'd gained new knowledge and new insights. Year after year, his reasoning became clearer—the logic more watertight. Vague suppositions were replaced with sound scientific theories; tentative conclusions were further investigated, analysed and questioned, then either discarded or incorporated into other fields of study.

Still, there was a core that was central to his theory. It ran through all of Charlie's work, becoming clearer and more defined as time went by. In essence, though, it was based on his earliest insights into human nature and how mankind had become estranged from it—as well as the way ahead he had seen for the children of the tribe to live according to their inner nature: to grow and mature, and be happy.

Mark and Steve were so familiar with everything Charlie had written, and the way he thought, that they could work as one to condense this vast body of writing into a more concise summary.

Mark did the actual writing. He copied some parts word for word from Charlie's papers, summarised others, and wrote other parts himself. Steve proofread Mark's work. His analytical, almost pedantic, mind missed nothing.

Then Mark rewrote everything. Neither of them would be happy with anything other than perfection—or at least the very best they could do—even if Steve's corrections did make Mark grumble good-heartedly at times.

The two men were constantly amazed at the depth of knowledge Charlie had fathomed. With honesty and love for the truth, he had pieced together a myriad of facts with his own intuition and experiences.

Charlie had never written a summary himself. Maybe he never would have. There always seemed to be something new that caught his interest and had to be investigated, or a question someone had asked that needed to be answered. He was forever checking and questioning his own theory, discovering new perspectives and finding new topics to write about. He would have kept on all his life. Even if he had lived forever.

It took them three years to finish the book.

Mark had written the final version on spare pages from library books, which Steve was now binding together in a hardback cover.

When he was done he held the book up.

"Now it just needs a title and a cover picture," Mark said. "What shall we call it?"

Steve laughed, "Hadn't thought of that!"

They were both quiet for a short while.

"How about just calling it *Charlie's Book*?" Mark said at last.

"Yes, that's what it is, isn't it," Steve said. He paused for a moment. "You know, Mark, I remember something Charlie said a long time ago: he was sitting by himself, watching the sunset. I'd gone over and asked him what he was thinking about. 'Oh! Just searching for truth.' he'd said." Steve smiled at the memory. "But it was true, wasn't it. Charlie spent his whole life looking for truth…" He was quiet for another moment, recapturing that evening in his mind. "Could we call it that, Mark? *Charlie's Book - In Search of Truth.*"

"Couldn't be better. That's what we'll call it."

The two friends shook hands. They had big smiles on their faces.

The next day, Dewdrop wrote the title on the front cover and sketched a picture of Charlie writing at the magical lake.

"A real book!" Mark had said proudly when he saw it.

"I think you should make a copy," Steve said. "Everybody wants to read it, and it would be good to have a spare copy in the library, wouldn't it?"

"Yes, you're right," Mark said. Then he laughed. "I thought we were finished!"

"Finished? No, we'll never be finished…"

"Huh! What do you mean?"

"Well, we've finished Charlie's Book," Steve said. "The first copy anyway—but we're not finished with searching, are we?"

"Well no, I guess not. We probably never will be."

"Certainly hope not!"

"Stew?"

"Stew!"

Years went by. Babies were born, and children grew into adults. Some lived to be old. Others died in younger years.

The last of the Fengwidditch Scouts to die was Sarah.

She had lived to be almost ninety. Her back was bent with old age after all the years of bending down to gather the flowers and plants she loved so much. In her last years, she no longer gathered food… There were enough youngsters to do that, she would say with a laugh.

Everyone had loved to sit and drink herb tea with her and listen to her stories—especially the story of how the Two-Pot tribe came to be: of all the struggles and the adventures of the first years. Sarah even told them about the old world and of her childhood in Wales.

She also told the story of the flowers.

Every flower had its own story, she would say. How it came to look the way it did, why it grew where it did and what it could be used for: as food, or tea, or as medicine.

The children loved it when they came across a rare flower. Then they would bring it to her and hear her tell its story. Very, very occasionally, one of them would bring one that Sarah had never seen before.

Oh! she would exclaim, her wrinkled face breaking into a big smile and her eyes glittering with joy. Look! she would say, holding the flower in the sunlight to see it clearly from all sides. The joy of discovery was as great now as it had been when she was a young girl picking wild flowers with her mother and grandmother.

Then the questions would begin: Where did you find it? How many flowers grew together? In the sunlight or in the shade of a tree? And so on… Through the eyes of the children, she saw the place where the flower grew. If it wasn't too far away, they would help her walk there to see it herself.

Even on the day she died, she had gone out into the woods, "To be with my flowers," she had said.

It was the children who had found her in a clearing in the woods, not far from home.

Sarah lay on the grass, curled up like a little girl sleeping. She looked peaceful in death, having lain down just to rest for a moment… and fallen asleep forever.

She was buried in the spot where she lay. Soon, small yellow and white flowers had sprung up over her grave.

The tribe would miss her greatly, but just thinking about her, and her flowers, made them smile. She had lived a long and beautiful life, learning and teaching about the beauty of all the things that grew around them: flowers and plants, herbs and shrubs, trees and fruits.

Her flower stories would be passed on from generation to generation.

As would the story of the Fengwidditch Scouts.

The Vikings

One

Vikings M.C. Clubhouse, Stockholm

"Hey, Fats. Gotta job for you."

"What?" The biker nicknamed 'Fats' shifted his gaze from the TV to where Jay stood by the clubhouse door.

"Come over here," Jay said.

"I'm in the middle of a show," Fats protested.

Jake rolled his eyes. "Fuck the TV," he said.

Jay was the president of The Vikings Motorcycle Club's Stockholm chapter. Their brother gang, The Angels, ruled Sweden's underworld: a world of drugs, prostitution, and violence. Up until a year ago, the Angels' main rivals had been Sweden's only other major motorbike gang, the Scandinavian Demons.

A vicious gang war had broken out between the two clubs. For the short duration of the war, the Vikings had joined with the Angels against their common enemy. Jay was chosen to lead their combined forces, partly so there would be no bad feelings between the other Angels presidents but mostly because everyone knew that he would be the perfect commander.

Angels versus Demons. It sounded almost silly, but there had been nothing silly about the shootings, bombings, and murders.

The war had been ended in one brutal action. On Jay's orders, a group of Angels had stolen a bulldozer from a construction site. The next day, they had packed its rear loader with military grade explosives stolen from Army depots.

Sweden's national defense was traditionally based on both a standing army and a civilian reserve force. Weapons, explosives, and other equipment were stored in depots deep in the forests so that the reserve force could quickly be armed if Sweden was invaded. Breaking into the depots was often just a case of cutting through heavy padlocks with power grinders—Easy pickings for professional criminals. Sometimes the Swedish really were naïve.

Crazy Andy had volunteered to drive the bulldozer into the Demons clubhouse and blow it up. The attack was planned for a Saturday night when lots of Demons and their hang-arounds would be partying there.

Stoked up on amphetamine, Crazy Andy lived up to his name.

Whooping and yelling in sheer delight, he drove the bulldozer at full speed through the clubhouse's reinforced gates. Hardly losing speed, he crushed through the line of parked motorbikes and slammed the brakes on, skidding the bulldozer sideways into the clubhouse wall. Crunching the gears, he drove forward and pulled hard on the steering wheel, then reversed, ramming the bulldozer's rear end through the wall and into the room full of partying bikers.

He hit the detonation button.

He had just ten seconds to get clear. In theory that would have given him enough time to open the bulldozer's door and run to safety—but theory doesn't always hold up. One door was blocked by part of the wall, and the handle of the other one had been bent in the crash and was jammed.

"*Shit, shit, shit!*" Crazy Andy shouted as he kicked the door again and again.

It swung open.

In the last three seconds before the explosion, he managed to throw himself to the ground and roll between the bulldozer's huge wheels.

The blast was massive. The bulldozer lifted a clear meter off the ground before crashing back down. Amazingly—miraculously— it didn't crush him. Crazy Andy lay curled up, hugging his head with his arms as the bulldozer tottered and bounced a couple of times before coming to rest. He couldn't hear anything. The explosion had temporarily deafened him.

He crawled out from underneath the bulldozer, then scrambled to his feet and ran out into the street, screaming maniacally and waving his arms for no other reason than for the sheer hell of it. Digging his hand into his jacket pocket, he found his bike keys and leaped onto his Hog, stomped on the kick-start, and roared away.

Twenty-nine people were killed by the blast. Another fifteen were seriously injured.

A couple of weeks later, Crazy Andy drove his bike straight into the path of an oncoming truck on the freeway. He died instantly.

No one knew why he had done it, but there again, he was crazy, wasn't he…

"Get one of the Jeeps," Jay said. "I want you to nick twelve good bikes. Take the angle grinder and a bolt cutter.

"Twelve bikes? No one's got their bike parked on the street this time of year…" Fats said.

Jay sighed. "Not motorbikes. Mountain bikes."

"Huh?"

"You know, push bikes. But good ones. Mountain bikes…"

"Yeah, okay,"

Fats weighed about twice as much as Jay, but that made no difference. He knew that in a fight that Jay was one of the few men he wouldn't stand a chance against. He was quick, vicious, deadly… That was another reason he was their leader: No one dared stand up to him. Not even Fats—although the thought of doing so had never crossed his mind.

Jay was forty years old. Twelve of those years had been spent in the Swedish Army. He had risen quickly in rank in the paratroop regiment in northern Sweden. A natural soldier, Jay not only had the uncanny ability to assess difficult situations and make split second decisions, but he combined it with a ruthless attitude to any task he was given.

Soldiers are trained to high levels of fitness, but only a few have the inherent ability to keep going no matter how exhausted they are and turn pain, fear, and doubt into determination. Jay was one of these men. His ruthlessness and single mindedness were uncommon. He could torture his body beyond its natural limits—never accepting defeat.

At the age of twenty-five he'd been hand-picked to join the Swedish elite special operations force, SOG.

The Swedish elite soldiers regularly cross-trained with other special forces—the best of the best—the British SAS, German KSK, American Delta Force, and Israeli Sayaret. The soldiers from the different international forces had the greatest of respect for each other. In training, competition between them was fierce.

They were trained to kill—and they were trained well. Their missions included the assassination of known terrorists, sometimes even of politicians and religious leaders, as well as the sabotage of industrial factories used for making chemical and biological weapons. Most of their missions were in the hostile areas of Afghanistan, Pakistan, Syria, and Iraq. Very rarely did any hints of their clandestine activities find their way into the world's newspapers and media outlets.

It was after a mission in Afghanistan that it had all gone sideways for Jay.

His small unit of four men had been searching one of the many maze-like cave systems in the mountainous area bordering Pakistan. The Taliban used the caves as fortresses and hideouts. This one seemed to be deserted though; all they'd found were the remains of old fires and some trash. Jay started to relax.

Turning a corner, he surprised two Afghan men sitting at a small table. They were playing cards by candlelight.

Jay instinctively raised his state-of-the-art SCAR-M rifle, and in a single automatic burst, killed them before they even managed to get to their feet—let alone return fire.

The dead Afghans looked like peasants but were armed with Kalashnikovs. They must have been here for a reason, Jay thought. Guarding something?

Jay and his men moved deeper into the cave: rifles at the ready.

Except for a row of wooden crates stacked along one of the cave walls, it was empty. Probably ammunition or explosives, Jay thought.

Ted Gustafson, Jay's second-in-command, counted the crates while Jay prized the lid off one of them to see what was inside.

It was packed with white powder pressed into hard bricks and wrapped in plastic: Heroin.

About a kilo, Jay reckoned, hefting one of the bricks in his hand. No, probably *exactly* one kilo, he thought. Each brick would have been worth about 100,000 dollars in the USA or Europe. Much more if it was cut to street quality. The crate was packed with twelve bricks.

"Twenty crates, Jay," Ted Gustafson said.

Jay whistled softly under his breath as he calculated the value of almost a quarter ton of pure heroin.

The four Swedish soldiers huddled together.

"What are we going to do?" Gustafson asked.

"Well, we aren't going to report it, are we?" Jay said. His question was more like a challenge.

He glared at each of his men in turn. None of them looked away.

"No," Gustafson said. "But we can't move all this without someone finding out, can we?"

"No, we'll just have to take as much as we can in our packs. No one says a word about this…"

"No," they all agreed.

Each man took six bricks of heroin.

"Shall we burn the rest?" Gustafson asked.

"No," Jay said. "We don't want to attract any attention, do we? When the Taliban discover what's happened, they'll move the rest of it to another hiding place. Nobody'll know who took it as long as we keep our mouths shut, right?"

"Got it," Gustafson said.

The other two men nodded in silent agreement.

"Now let's get the hell out of here," Jay said.

Two days later, Jay's unit was back on patrol in the same area. They checked the cave, just in case, but there was no trace of the crates or the dead Afghans. They weren't surprised.

A month later, Jay flew back to Sweden for a week's leave. The German military plane he'd hitched a ride on landed at Frankfurt, where he had a two-hour wait in transit before boarding a commercial flight to Stockholm. The heroin was packed in the bottom of his military rucksack along with all his other gear. On arriving at Arlanda, Stockholm's main civilian airport, he picked his rucksack up from the baggage conveyor belt and hoisted it onto his back.

He went through passport control and customs without even having to show his passport—probably because he was still in uniform. Automatic doors to the arrival area opened in front of him.

Home free, he thought… just as a dog started barking behind him.

If it hadn't been for that fucking dog, Jay had thought many times during the two long years he'd spent in the military prison in central Sweden.

The court martial had been a quick affair—Two years in prison and a dishonorable discharge. It would have been longer, but Jay's outstanding military record and his twelve years of service were taken into account as well as the fact that he'd pleaded guilty and declined the lawyer he was otherwise entitled to. He'd also agreed to sign a document stating that he would never mention his crime to the media. Neither the Swedish military—SOG in particular—nor the Swedish government wanted to answer the questions that would undoubtedly be asked if the story got out. Any breach of that agreement would put Jay behind bars for another five years.

Two years later, Jay found himself in a drab hotel room near Stockholm's main railway station. He had just enough money for a train ticket back to Wilhelmina, his hometown in the north of Sweden.

"Whatchya want bicycles for?" Fats asked.

"Christmas presents for my grandchildren, what do you think!" Jay laughed. "Can't you just do what I say and get the bikes? Take Rat with you. Don't waste time cutting the locks if the bikes aren't chained to something—just throw them in the Jeep. We can take care of them later."

"They won't all fit in a Jeep."

"Jesus! Just come back, dump off a load, and go back for more."

Fats decided it would be best to shut up and get to work.

Just over an hour later, they had the mountain bikes lined up in the back of the garage. A slap on the back told him that Jay was satisfied.

Later that evening, Fats fell asleep on the sofa watching a documentary about penguins.

Two

Jay felt trapped. He always did. Always had done.

He stared out of the clubhouse window and dragged his fingers through his long blond hair, letting the memory of the dream he'd woken from fade away. All that was left was the fog of last night's way too much vodka and beer—and the feeling of being trapped.

From his room in the loft, he could see all the way down the long driveway to the heavy gate and the high fence that encircled the clubhouse. No one came in uninvited.

Jay and Fats had moved into the clubhouse four years ago.

Four years, Jay thought. Getting old. Big forty now, he laughed to himself.

What a birthday party that had been! Members from all the Nordic Chapters had come. Even Big Jim all the way from San Francisco.

Not often the old guys in California think about us, Jay thought, but Big Jim had flown over just for Jay's fortieth. Even given him a present: the solid silver key which now hung around his neck. The key was engraved with the Angels' wings emblem. Jay knew exactly what it was, although he'd only ever seen one once before. Keep it safe, Big Jim had said. There was no need for him to say 'don't flash it around'.

The Viking colors and honorary Angels patches sewn onto Jay's leather jacket opened most doors, but the near mythical silver key was an even more potent symbol to anyone affiliated with the biker gang. It was recognition of the way he had upheld the honor of their organization and the bikers' code

Jay honored the code not out of fear of what happened to those who broke it—like many of the new generation of bikers did—

No, for him it was all about something else: Freedom.

For as far back as he could remember he'd had this feeling of being trapped—First in kindergarten by the wannabe mothers, then in school by endless days of boredom. They never got it, did they? he thought. Teachers are idiots. Strict ones, kind ones, they're all the same in the end. Telling you what to do and keeping you sitting behind your desk just like the office morons most of the kids would grow up to be. All they wanted was for you to 'be good'—be quiet and do your homework. Couldn't they just have left me alone? Day after day, year after year, stuffing you full of their stupid lessons. What were they thinking? That they'd make a model citizen out of me? A pillar of society? Yeah, right!

He had rebelled, of course. Not that it did much good. Getting mad at them didn't help, and being rude and making fun of them just made things worse. They had punished the unruly boy by giving him detention, trapping him in school for even longer.

That was the problem, you idiots, Jay had thought back then—not the solution.

As a teenager, he grew his hair long, wore Death Metal T-shirts, and more or less refused to talk to the teachers. That just made things worse, of course.

Sports had been the one thing that made sense. It was only when he was playing football or hockey, swimming laps at the local swimming pool, or skiing and running in cross country races that he felt any sense of freedom.

He loved the feeling of running harder and harder—breathless and drenched in sweat—until he could run no further… or in the water, of being weightless and powerful—like flying—not knowing if it was the sky he was staring at or the blue tiles on the bottom of the swimming pool. Here there was no rebel, just the youth he ought to have been.

Mr. Pearce, one of the PE teachers, had seen this in the boy. They never talked about it, but occasionally, after Jay had scored a goal or won or lost a race, they would give each other a wry smile—not much more than the creasing of a cheek. It said it all though: doesn't matter if you win or lose if you've done your best. Give it all you've got, and whatever happens, good or bad, you can laugh at it.

And that was the way Jay had lived. Head-on. Not caring about winning or losing. It didn't even matter if the odds were against him. You get kicked down, you just get to your feet and with a crooked smile get right back into it.

Living like that had given him scars and broken bones, but also respect and loyalty: first from his comrades in the army and now from his club mates. These were the only friends or family he had—or cared about.

Strange, he thought, I've never forgotten Mr. Pearce—even remember something he'd once said about enthusiasm being the best word in the dictionary… Funny how that had stuck.

At fifteen, when he looked old enough not to be turned away from the liquor store, it seemed like alcohol was a way out. Unlike his classmates who drank to party and have fun, alcohol gave Jay a short sense of freedom. But it was never enough. Once the rush of being drunk wore off, he just felt even more trapped.

"Freedom," Jay mumbled to himself and pulled his motorbike boots on.

It wasn't society that made him feel trapped anymore. He was an outlaw, living outside most of the dictates of normal life, breaking whatever laws he needed to but smart enough not to get caught and sent to prison.

Except for that one time. It had happened two years ago. The husband of a woman he'd been screwing had attacked him. He hadn't known that she was married. Not as if that would have made a difference.

Erik, as Jay found out later he was called, jumped him at the clubhouse gate. Jay had just rolled his bike to a stop, so he could tap in the code, when he was grabbed by the shoulders and pulled down from behind.

He hadn't seen the guy hiding behind a parked car on the other side of the street or heard him sneaking up, thanks to the noise of his motorbike.

Jay rolled with the fall. Coming to his feet, he let fly with a vicious kick. Erik ran straight into it. Jay's boot smashed into his gut, just below the ribs.

He crumpled to his knees, his face turning a sudden sickly

white. He was hardly breathing, just panting in shallow gasps.

He just sat there, his gaze focused on a void in front of him.

Fuck! Jay thought. He knew what had happened. His spleen has burst. He'll die.

He quickly pulled his cell phone out and dialed 112. Getting an ambulance there was more important than any first-aid. He calmly gave the emergency call-center details of Erik's injury and the address.

Jay stuffed his phone back into his pocket just in time to stop Erik from keeling over. He lay him gently down on his side.

"You'll be okay, an ambulance is on its way," he repeated again and again, not even knowing if the guy could hear him. "Hang on in there, they'll be here soon. You'll be okay…"

Erik was lucky. The ambulance arrived in less than ten minutes.

The paramedics pumped plasma into him, replacing the massive amount of blood that had flooded his abdominal cavity. They managed to keep him alive long enough to get him to the hospital where his spleen was operated on. Had they got there a couple of minutes later, the heavy internal bleeding would have killed him.

Jay wasn't so lucky. A police car had followed the ambulance.

He pleaded self-defense. The paramedics testified as to how Jay's 112 call had saved Erik's life, and later in court, Erik even admitted that he had started the fight. All to no avail. The judge wasn't going to miss the chance to put one of those motorbike gangsters behind bars.

"Three months in prison will serve as an example," he had said.

Could have been worse, Jay thought, and gave the judge a crooked smile.

Jay hated being back in prison. Never again, he swore to himself on the day he walked out through the prison gates.

His mates and his Harley were there waiting for him.

"Shit," he'd said later that evening. "She wasn't even a good lay."

Three

Things were going to change. You would have to be stupid—No, deaf, dumb, blind, *and* stupid not to pick up on that, Jay thought.

The war in Africa was getting worse. The so-called superpowers were getting more and more involved as they tried desperately to preserve their 'way of life': mindless consumption of luxury goods and a perverse level of comfort. To afford it, they had to keep the poor countries poor, strip them of their natural resources, and turn them into huge sweatshops that produced the never ending junk they measured their status and wealth by: Cars, smartphones, clothes… all just toys they discarded as soon as new and better ones came along.

People had gotten fat on junk food, lazy in front of their TV's, and addicted to their idea of pleasure and fun. All they had to do to earn this way of life was to loyally waste their meaningless lives away in mind-numbing jobs. They're even proud of their careers and toys, Jay thought. How stupid can you get? — Yeah, a change is coming. Soon. I can feel it. Everyone carries on as if it's going to stay this way forever. Doesn't matter if we've fucked up the environment, polluted the air, killed the fish, torn down the forests, nah, just keep making babies—exactly what the world needs—more workers and consumers. Slaves. All of them. But they don't even realize it. Unbelievable!

What's got me into this mood? Jay thought as he poured himself another mug of coffee. Must be hung-over. No, he decided, it's something else as well.

If and when everything crashed—and he didn't reckon there was any *if* about it, just a *when*—then it was easy to see what would happen. The Internet would go down, which would bring everything else crashing down along with it.

No computers meant no electricity. People would panic and hoard gas and food. When they realized there was no new stuff being brought into the cities, they'd go on a rampage—looting supermarkets and killing each other just to grab whatever food, fresh water, and fuel they could. If it happened in the winter, most people would freeze to death once they'd burnt all their furniture to keep warm. Those that managed to stay alive a bit longer would eventually starve to death—if diseases spread by all the dead bodies didn't get them first.

Cities and towns were not the places to be, he thought. People will try to get out, but in the panic they'll all just end up killing each other. Only the most violent would survive when society collapsed, he reckoned. So be it.

Jay had a plan. He'd been thinking about it for years but had only started serious preparations a year ago after the gang war.

Using his contacts in Stockholm's underworld, he'd steadily built up an arsenal of automatic and semi-automatic assault rifles, pistols, and ammunition. Nothing strange about that—just bikers preparing for another gang war. No one raised so much as an eyebrow.

But you had to have cash. Lots of it. Armed robbery was the easiest way to get it.

Jay, Fats, and Rat had held up an armored security van just before Christmas. It had been really easy. The security guards had surrendered immediately when they saw the three masked men carrying powerful assault rifles.

They got away with more money than they could count. At least ten times more than the bank whose money it was had admitted on the evening news. All of it was in unmarked used notes. They'd had an insider at the security company, but not even he had known just how big a heist it would be. Money wasn't a problem.

Ammunition would run out eventually, though. Jay thought— As would the fuel their vehicles ran on. Sure, there would be abandoned trucks they could siphon diesel from, but they wouldn't be the only ones doing that. It would probably run out quickly. Low tech was the way to go. That's what the bicycles were for. Bicycles didn't need fuel and were easy to repair. New bicycles would be easy to find as well, Jay reckoned.

Then there was the question of low-tech weapons. Jay had bought twelve high quality Japanese Samurai swords from an Internet supplier of martial arts equipment. From another website, he'd bought the same number of K-Bar knives: the American military grade knife that had been tried and proven in action around the world ever since World War Two. Even in unskilled hands, these two weapons—sword and knife—were deadly in close combat.

He'd even bought tents and sleeping bags—the best Swedish quality, of course. We can afford it, Jay had said to himself. All this gear had hardly made a dent in the stash from the transporter heist. Probably should have bought the mountain bikes as well, he thought, but heck, they were just lying around waiting to be stolen anyway...

The other bikers sort of knew about Jay's plans but mostly just shook their heads and let him get on with it. Jay was the best leader they could have ever wished for. He was brutally fair. All the bikers in Jay's chapter had been given a huge lump of cash from the robbery. They needed the money, too. The Vikings were nowhere near as criminal as the Angels, preferring to just hang out and work on their bikes. Unlike the Angels, they weren't into drug dealing or running prostitutes and protection rackets. Like all bikers, though, they were notoriously bad at hanging on to money. Partying, women, motorbikes... Sometimes it seemed like money was being sucked into a huge black hole. They'd learned not to be greedy though. Stay loyal and do whatever he said—that was all Jay asked. His rules were simple, and the rewards were high.

The Angels were stronger than ever now. They'd crushed the Demons, but Jay realized it would be dangerous to have what was left of them as enemies. Instead, he had let them join the Vikings or Angels as prospects. In time they'd be able to earn their colors and become full members. Only towards the Demons president, Matti Olsson, had Jay been less merciful.

Two days after the bombing of their clubhouse, Jay had received a text message telling him what he already knew—that the Demons wanted to surrender. A meeting had been set up. Matti and two other high-ranking Demons were invited to the Angels clubhouse.

The Demons president was a monster of a guy. Everything about him was big: from his clean-shaven head and nicotine-stained beard, down to his huge beer gut and size 52 motorcycle boots. At the gate, the Demons were frisked for weapons. They had none, of course. They weren't *that* stupid.

Jay saw that they still wore their club colors on the back of their jackets. He respected that. It showed that even in defeat they weren't cowards.

Fats and the two Angels who had frisked them escorted the Demons to the main clubroom. The large hall had a long wooden bar, a jukebox, and tables and chairs. In one corner there was even a sofa and armchairs. The main hall was where the Angels partied and hung out most of the time. The shelves behind the bar were stocked with vodka and whiskey.

When the group of bikers came in, Jay was standing at the bar with his back turned to the door. As they came closer, he slowly turned around, still holding a half-finished bottle of beer in his hand.

Jay's cold eyes locked on Matti's. It was as if the other bikers weren't even there.

Fats motioned for them to stop. All eyes were on Jay. No one uttered a word. Respect would be shown.

Jay turned back to the bar and took another swig of beer.

He gently put the bottle down, wiped his mouth with the back of his arm, and turned around again. As if by a conjuring trick, he now held two K-Bar knives: one in his right hand by its handle, the other by its blade in his left hand.

Jay took a few steps forwards.

Strange, Matti thought, I can't hear his footsteps—or hear him moving at all.

Jay stopped a meter from the Demons president and stretched his left hand out, offering him the knife.

Matti reached out slowly.

The moment he got a grip on the knife, he sprung into action, slashing the blade at Jay's chest, hoping to end the fight before it began.

He was too slow. Jay had read the intent in his eyes.

As the knife arched towards him, he took a small step forward with his right foot. Twisting his body slightly to the left, he grabbed Matti's knife hand and plunged his own knife into the side of the biker's head.

There was a loud cracking sound as the sharp steel broke through his skull and straight into his brain. The Demons leader was dead before he even realized that his own attack had failed. He crumpled to the floor.

Jay turned around and silently went back to the bar.

He lifted his beer—and drank deeply.

Four

Jay walked down the stairs to the clubroom with a mug of steaming coffee in his hand.

Here and there, bikers were still crashed out, strewn over sofas and armchairs. Fats lay in the middle of the bare wooden floor with his arms and legs spread out and his chest rising and falling slowly as he snored loud enough to wake the dead.

The dead, Jay thought, but not the Vikings. What a state!

Treading carefully around him, he went to the front door and opened it. Outside, fresh snow lay white and pure on the ground.

Taking a deep breath of the cold, crisp air, Jay surveyed his domain.

Fifteen Harley-Davidsons were parked in a perfect row. Gotta respect the Hogs, he thought to himself. Only fifteen, though… Must have been quite a few drunk motorbike riders on the streets last night.

Jay and Fats were the only ones living at the clubhouse. All the other Vikings had flats or houses in or around Stockholm. Some lived with their old ladies or girlfriends. Some even had kids.

Talk about being trapped! Jay thought. A nagging wife and kids—No way. *Never!*

None of his on-and-off girlfriends had ever tried to trap him into straight family life. Most of the girls who hung out with bikers weren't into that either. Well, not when they were young, at least. But something weird happened to the ones who didn't get hooked on booze or drugs. When they hit thirty, it was as if they changed overnight. All they seemed to want to do then was to settle down, buy a house, and make babies.

Same with a lot of the guys, Jay thought, just not so suddenly.

After long enough with the same girlfriend, and the dulling of their rebel spirit, many of them quit the gang and went straight. No hard feelings, though. Any old Angel or Viking could turn up at a party for old times' sake and would be welcomed and given the respect they'd earned.

Then there are those like me, Jay thought—those who would stay rebels until the day they died. The girls seemed to know that Jay would never be caught. He was like a wild bird of prey, flying higher than anyone else, surveying all that lay below, and sometimes swooping down to be with others—but never to be trapped by them.

Even so, girls and women still fell in love with him. Surprisingly, they found him to be a gentle lover, more interested in their pleasure than his own. Some part of him was never present, though, never quite there, even when making love.

The row of Harleys glistened in the morning sunlight reflecting off the fresh snow. End of the riding season, Jay thought. The snow had come early that year. Time to hibernate—that's how it felt anyway.

Bikers lived for the summer months—cruising to gatherings, festivals, and parties like a pack of wolves on the roam and meeting up with others like themselves. Jay loved the long summer nights, sitting around a campfire, drinking beer and sharing stories with old friends, reliving past adventures and laughing together about old shit that they couldn't remember too well—but which got crazier and crazier with each telling—and remembering those brothers who weren't with them anymore. The list is getting pretty long, Jay thought. Traffic accidents, drugs, gang wars… Living the life takes its toll.

That old Steppenwolf song 'Born to be Wild' ran through his mind. Yeah, Wild and Free.

"You okay, Jay?" Fats said. He knew better than to surprise Jay by coming up on him too quickly. Damn, he's fast, Fats thought, thinking back to the way he'd wasted Matti Olsson. He'd seen how vicious Jay was in other fights in the past too. Jay would never start a fight, but hell, could he finish them!

The two men had known each a long time—been through a lot

together. Fats always had Jay's back. Not that it was necessary for the most part though.

Fats knew he wasn't the smartest guy on the planet, although he was smart enough to have realized that. The really stupid ones always thought they were the smartest, he reckoned. That's why he left the thinking and planning to Jay.

Big as Fats was, one thing he wasn't, was soft. He'd inherited his natural strength from his parents: farmers from the north of Sweden. Helping his father in the fields had developed his strength from an early age. He'd always been the strongest boy in his class at school.

When he was nine years old, his mother had taken him to the wrestling club in Wilhelmina, the town closest to their farm. Back then Fats was called by his real name, Frederik.

He took to wrestling like a fish to water. His natural strength helped, of course, but even at that young age he'd realized that his greatest talent lay in being able to listen. He listened to everything his coach, Lars Hanson, said, and obeyed him to the letter.

Lars was an ex-national team member. He was tough but fair on the boys, always pushing them to their limits and encouraging them to surpass themselves.

Frederik worked harder than any of the other boys, spending all his free time practicing wrestling techniques and building up his strength, stamina, and flexibility. With stubborn single-mindedness, he repeated the exercises again and again until he'd mastered them.

At the age of eleven, he won the regional championship. At fourteen, he was the national under 16's champion, and then at eighteen, he became eligible to compete for the national senior team.

In two years time the Olympic Games were to be held in Paris. The leaders of the Swedish Wrestling Federation had kept their eye on the young Frederik's development. The big, quiet youngster might well cause an upset, they thought.

Two months before the Olympic Games, Lars had suddenly died of a massive heart attack. He'd only been fifty-one years old.

They found him slumped over his desk in the wrestling club.

After the autopsy, the doctors had said that he'd had a congenital heart defect. It had gone unnoticed all his life and hadn't caused him any problems, even when he'd been at the height of his wrestling career. It had been a ticking bomb, though—one which had finally exploded.

Frederik quit wrestling. That same evening he went to his bedroom, took down his wrestling medals and trophies from his trophy shelf, and put all of them except his most recent national championship medal in a cardboard box. After fetching a spade from the tool shed, he dug a shallow hole between the roots of the old oak tree that stood close to the barn and put the cardboard box into it. With his bare hands, he carefully packed the earth back into the hole until no trace of it could be seen.

His mother and father watched him silently from the kitchen window. Frederik's father put his arm around his wife's shoulders—something he hadn't done for many years now—as they shared their boy's grief.

When he was done, Frederik sat down with his legs crossed the way he'd always sat on the wrestling mat listening to his coach. He watched the sun go down behind the pine forest in the distance.

When it was time for them to go to bed, Frederik's mother came out and gave him a glass of milk and two of her home-baked rye biscuits.

Later, much later, Frederik stood up and nodded his head the way he'd always done when saying goodbye to Lars on the way out from the wrestling club. He walked backed to the farmhouse and went to bed.

The next day, he wrote a short letter to the Swedish Wrestling Federation to tell them he was quitting and to thank them for all their support. He put the letter and his medal into an envelope, sealed it with sellotape, and gave it to his mother to post in Wilhelmina.

It had never been about the medals or even about winning. It wasn't about the sport itself either, although he loved wrestling and would always have great memories. No, it was about having a leader and being loyal.

He finished school with above average grades thanks to his

ability to doggedly work through the various assignments his teachers gave him. He hadn't thought about the future too much. One day his father would be too old to manage the farm, and he had always thought he would just take over from him. The farm wasn't doing too well though. For years, big corporate farms had been pushing consumer prices down, making it harder and harder for small family farms like theirs to compete. Many independent farmers found themselves forced into selling their land to the corporations.

One evening at dinner table, Frederik's father told his wife and son that he had come to a decision. They were going to sell off most of their farmland except for the farmhouse and the small piece of land that stretched to where the old oak tree stood. They could turn it into a garden and a vegetable patch, he'd said. That way, they could keep their home in their old age and live comfortably from the sale of the rest of the land. There'd be no farming future for Frederik at home though, his father had explained—he'd have to find work in Wilhelmina or go to work for one of the corporate farms. He could stay and live with them for as long as he wanted to, of course.

It was the only sensible thing to do really—sell the farmland for a good price while they still could, rather than wait until they were desperate and maybe lose the farmhouse as well.

So be it then, Frederik thought.

The next day, he took the early bus into Wilhelmina. Best to start looking for a job straight away, he reckoned.

He jumped off the bus at the gas station on the edge of town. It was owned by the father of one of his old classmates.

"Hi, Frederik!" Bo Persson called when he saw his son's friend come through the door. He'd just opened for business.

"Morning, Mr. Persson. I'm looking for a job," Frederik said. No point beating about the bush. "We're selling the farm," he added. "Got to…"

"Ah, I see. Well, I don't need anyone at the moment, but I know you and your folks, so I'll be sure to let you know if I get a vacancy."

Frederik's heart sank a bit. "Oh, okay. Thanks anyway, Mr.

Persson," he said, and turned to walk towards the door.

"Hang on a second, Frederik. You're good with engines aren't you?"

"I know about tractors and farm machines," Frederik said. "And cars and bikes, a bit… How so?"

"Well, you know Brantström's Garage?"

"Of course. I bought my first moped there."

"I heard one of their mechanics was fired last week. Drunk on the job—almost dropped an engine on a customer. Not good for business that sort of thing. I heard Roy Brantström gave him a right old lecture and sent him home. Said he'd give him one more chance. Not sure if I'd have done that, but Roy's a nicer chap than me," Bo Persson said, and laughed. "Anyway, the idiot turned up drunk the next day—and that was that."

Frederik's hopes soared once again.

"Thanks, Mr. Persson. I'll go down there straight away!"

Brantström's was only a short walk towards town.

Frederik presented himself to the owner with much the same words as he had at the gas station.

"Hi, Mr. Brantström, I'm looking for a job. Mr. Persson said you might have an opening for a new mechanic?"

"Well, yes, we do. You're Johansson's son aren't you?"

"Yes."

"Good people," Brantström said with a nod. The people of north Sweden didn't waste words.

"Learned any mechanics?"

"Only what my father has taught me… and what I've picked up on my own," Frederik answered.

Brantström laughed. "Probably more than they teach at those fancy schools nowadays!"

Roy's grandfather had founded the Brantström Company back in the fifties. Roy had never been to mechanics school either, but there wasn't an engine made that he couldn't take to pieces and put back together again.

"Jay!" Brantström called out to the back of the workshop. "Come out here, will you?"

"Just a sec!" a voice called back.

A minute later, a gangly man with a mane of blond hair and strange pale blue eyes appeared. He was holding a mug of coffee.

"Jay, this is Frederik," Brantström said. "Think you can show him the ropes for a few days? See if he's any good?"

Jay looked at Frederik for a moment.

"Sure."

"That okay with you, Frederik? Give it a few days. If it doesn't work out—then no hard feelings?"

"Sure thing. I'll work hard," Frederik said. His heart jumped with joy. He'd got a job!

"Come on then," Jay said. "Get you a coffee and some overalls."

They headed off into the workshop.

"Into bikes?" Jay asked.

"Motorbikes?"

"Of course."

"I've got a Yamaha 250 off-road."

"Nice," Jay said. "Nifty."

"You?"

"Yeah, got a new ride last week. It's over here." He pointed towards the far end of the workshop by the door to the backyard. Gleaming in the morning light was a brand new, shiny black Harley-Davidson Dyna Glide.

"Like it?" Jay asked.

"Uh… It's, it's…" He was hardly able to speak. The Harley was the most beautiful machine he'd ever seen.

"Wanna hear her?" Jay asked, not waiting for a reply as he straddled the bike and kick-started it. The roar of the Harley exploded in the workshop.

"*Jay!*" Another roar—this time from the front office.

With a wink, Jay turned the engine off.

Brantström didn't really mind. A mechanic who truly loved engines was hard to find these days. Not only that, but Jay was honest and loyal. When the old mechanic, Anders, had dropped an engine from the crane and almost killed a customer, Jay had pulled him into the backyard and set about beating the living daylights out of him. Roy had only just got there in to time to save the drunken mechanic from being seriously hurt.

Roy Brantström had told Anders that if he agreed not to file charges against Jay, then they'd forget about the accident. He'd even given him a second chance, but as Frederik had been told, Anders had blown that straight away. You can't buy loyalty like that, Roy Brantström had thought.

Frederik learned quickly. He listened to Jay and did whatever he told him to. He had a new leader to follow now.

With money he'd borrowed from his parents, he bought a second hand Triumph Bonneville. In their spare time, the two mechanics worked on their own bikes: Frederik continually repairing the Bonneville, while Jay customized his Harley, slowly turning it into a unique 'chopper'.

It would take two years of hard work and many hours of overtime before Frederik had repaid his parents for the Bonneville and could make a down payment on a Harley of his own—a Softail Fat Boy.

"More my size," he'd joked when it was delivered.

"Yeah, *Fats!*" Jay had laughed.

The nickname stuck. Not many people knew how he had got it. They usually thought it was because of his size, although Frederik was all muscle and no fat.

One morning three years later, Jay dropped the bombshell over coffee.

"I'm off to Stockholm on Friday," he said.

"Yeah? What you doing there?" Frederik asked.

"No, I mean, I'm off. I'm not coming back."

"Huh!" Frederik couldn't believe his ears. His best friend was leaving? "For real?" he asked, though he knew Jay wouldn't joke about something like that.

"Yeah, time to get out of here," Jay said simply.

Frederik didn't say anything. There was nothing to say. No point in arguing, anyhow. Somehow he'd known this day would come. Jay was like a wild animal locked in a cage, looking for a way out.

"Okay," he said at last. "Got everything you need? I mean, anything I can do, just say. Fix things here, or whatever…" He trailed off. He wanted to add 'until you come back' but knew that was never going to happen.

"Nah, I'm all set. Thanks anyway, Fats. Be seeing you..."

"Yeah, be seeing you," Frederik said. He was unable to keep the glumness out of his voice.

"Oh, just one thing," Jay said. "I've got a present for you. Hang on..."

He walked over to where their two Hogs stood and lifted up a soft packet from behind them.

"Here you go," he said.

The package was wrapped in plain brown paper. It had the words *U.S. Postal Service* stamped on it in bold letters.

"From the USA?" Frederik said, turning it over in his hands.

"Yeah, Einstein. Aren't you going to open it?"

"Sure. Yeah, of course."

He carefully pulled the wrapping off. Inside were two leather motorbike satchels with the Harley-Davidson Motor Company emblem branded on them.

He didn't say a word, just held the satchels out to inspect them. The leatherwork was hand-stitched and pre-aged to look worn. Leather straps with sturdy brass buckles held the flaps closed.

"Like 'em?" Jay asked.

"Shit, they're gorgeous."

"Wanna pack them and come with me on Friday?"

"Of course I do." The words just seemed to pop out of his mouth. In the same moment that he uttered them, he knew they were true. Truer than anything he'd ever said before.

"Friday, after work, we're out of here," Jay said with a big smile.

"What about the boss?" Frederik asked, finally looking up from the satchels.

"I told him a month ago."

"What! How'd you know I'd want to come along?"

Jay laughed. "Yeah, well, I asked him not to say anything to you. Thought you'd like the surprise. He's cool with it—either way."

"But you were sure weren't you?"

"Course I was."

That same evening Frederik told his parents that he was leaving home. His mother cried. Well, she's a mother isn't she? Frederik thought. After she'd settled down, they ate dinner. As was their custom, they ate in silence.

When the plates had been cleared, Frederik's father put his hands on the table and took a deep breath.

"Frederik, there's something I'd like to say."

Frederik glanced at his mother.

"You've been a good son," his father went on. "Worked hard on the farm. I'm proud of you…" His voice caught. He wasn't used to making speeches, or even talking much at all, for that matter. "Anyhow, your mother and I have been putting away a little money each month. It's yours now. See it as a part of your inheritance, if you like."

Frederik didn't know what to say, so he just kept quiet.

"Well, like I said, it's yours, so you can spend it how you will, but think hard before you do. We'd like to think you used it when you really knew something was worth spending it on. Maybe put it towards a new motorbike when yours gets old. Just don't waste it on whiskey and women…"

"I understand," Frederik said. "Thank you. Both of you."

His mother rose from the table. "I'll make coffee," she said.

"I think a glass of something stronger would be in order too," his father said, looking warmly at her.

She went into the kitchen to put the coffee pot on the stove and fetch the vodka. She took three small glasses down from a cupboard. It wasn't often she drank alcohol—but I'll have a glass with the men, she thought, trying hard to hold back her tears. *With the men!* My baby's grown into a man!

Fredrik's father leaned closer, so his wife wouldn't hear. "One more thing," he said.

Frederik nodded.

"Give your mother a call on her birthday," he said. "Don't worry about cards, or presents, or anything. Just let her know you're well. Hearing your voice will be the best birthday present she can get."

Frederik nodded again. "Okay dad, I will."

"Thanks, son."

Five

It would be a fantastic summer.

They were in no rush to get to Stockholm. In fact, it would take them all summer long. The two friends toured the country on their Harleys—sleeping in their tents wherever they happened to be. If it hadn't been for the mosquitoes, Jay would have preferred to sleep in just his sleeping bag under the night sky as he had on military missions around the world.

They roamed from town to town, often heading towards one of the many open-air music festivals held in Sweden that summer.

There was always at least one group of bikers to be found at the festivals. With their customized Harley-Davidsons, leather jackets, and long hair, Jay and Fats fit right in, although unlike most of the other bikers, they didn't have any emblems or a club name sewn onto the back of their jackets.

June, July, August. The summer months passed in a haze of rock, beer, girls, and parties. As the summer went on, Jay and Fats found themselves hanging out more and more with a group of Angels and Vikings that they kept meeting at the festivals.

They got on especially well with the Vikings. It was because of the old guys, Jay had realized: the ones that had lived their lives for their Hogs and the biker code. Life as a biker had formed and hardened them. Age had brought with it the wisdom of experience as well—even humility. Not to be confused with softness, though, as some of the brash younger bikers had painfully found out over the years. Tough guys, Jay thought. So tough they don't have to prove it to anyone—not even to themselves.

The old bikers often sat together at festivals, usually a bit to one side where they could share old stories and a bottle of whiskey.

Jay and Fats liked to sit with them. It took no more than a glance to tell if they were welcome or not.

Jay and Fats listened, and learned.

The old guys had fought hard for their freedom—learning from their mistakes along the way.

Things had changed since the early days of biker gangs in the fifties and sixties. The criminal underworld had become globally organized. Chinese, and lately even African and Asian mafias, had pushed the Italians and East Europeans aside. In a world of international drug smuggling, human trafficking, and corporate corruption, only the most brutal and merciless were successful. Seeing huge advantages to be gained from belonging to an organized gang, many violent criminals joined the bikers' ranks.

Many clubs, including the Angels, found themselves split into two factions. On the one hand were those who had joined because of their passion for motorcycles and the brotherhood of a gang, and on the other, those who saw the organizations as a means of gaining profits from extortion, violent crime, drugs, and prostitution.

Eventually the Angels officially split into two separate clubs. Led by a number of the old-timers who wanted to get back to their roots, a minority split away from the Angels and formed the Vikings Motorcycle Club.

The leaders of the two groups saw no point in being rivals, so they came to a mutual understanding that Angels and Vikings would respect each other's sovereignty.

For the most part, the Vikings kept away from serious crime, preferring to ride, party, and work on their Hogs. In the recent biker war in Stockholm, though, they'd had no choice but to side with their former comrades and take up arms against the Demons. It wasn't that the Vikings had wanted to get mixed up in a gang war, but if they'd just stood to one side and the Angels had lost, they would have been crushed as well.

Summer was drawing to an end. The evenings were getting noticeably shorter. One evening late in August, Danny, one of the elder Vikings, came over to the campfire where Jay was sitting on his own.

He was well into his sixties—maybe even older. He had a long mane of white hair and a full salt-and-pepper beard.

"Hey," he said, and crouched down beside Jay.

"Hey," Jay replied. He offered the old Viking his beer.

"Nah, thanks. At my age you have to pace yourself so you can still get up the next day," Danny said with a gruff laugh. "You young'uns just shake it off. Damn, I miss those days."

"Yeah, that's what I hear," Jay laughed.

"Better believe it, kid. Hey, let me have a swig of that anyway. I ain't in the grave yet, yer know."

Jay passed him the bottle, and was thanked with a wink.

"Hear you're heading south," Danny said.

"You hear a lot of things, old man."

"Ain't nothing wrong with my ears—yet," Danny said with a grin.

"Yeah," Jay said. "Thought we'd look for work in Stockholm, me and Fats... We're from a small place up north."

Danny's gaze roamed over the open field to the river and the forest beyond. "Tell you something, son. Best thing about a city is getting out of it. Makes you appreciate this..."

Jay nodded. "Sure is beautiful country."

"Everything a man could want," Danny said. "Still unspoiled forests, and lakes where you can fish. You hunt, Jay?"

"I'm from the north."

"Hah! Yeah, got me there!" Danny laughed. "Course you do."

"Why do you live in the city then?" Jay asked.

"The old lady, you know," Danny said. "She never wanted to leave. Got three kids. All grown up now, but they're all still in Stockholm. Four grandkids too... Damn I'm getting old! Anyhow, she lets me off the leash in the summer for the most part—so I can do this..." He lifted his jaw slightly to make his point. "Guess she knows I'd go crazy if I couldn't get on my bike and hit the open road. Anyhow, that's not why I came over."

Jay didn't say anything—giving the older man time to gather his thoughts.

"Heard you're both good mechanics," Danny said at last.

Jay nodded, not sure what to say.

"I know a place in Stockholm I think you'd fit in," Danny said. "If you're interested that is?"

Jay nodded again. "What kind of place?"

"Bike repair. Mostly Harleys, but you might have to work on some of those Japanese pieces of crap as well," Danny said with another grin.

Jay turned his head to look at him. "Guess we could put up with that," he said, returning the grin. "What's the boss like?"

"Not bad. Old biker…"

"Sure. Sounds good. How do we get in touch with him?"

"Here's the number."

He handed Jay a business card.

Jay read it carefully by the light of the campfire.

"But that's you!" he said.

"Well, yeah, so it is!" Danny laughed in mock astonishment. "I've been running that place for forty years. Think it's time to bring in some new blood. What do you say?"

"We'd be honored," Jay said, and reached out to shake Danny's hand. "I'll have to check if Fats is in," he said—though he knew he would be.

Danny raised himself from the ground.

"One other thing," he said.

Jay looked up at him.

"There's a room or two vacant in the clubhouse next to the bike shop. If you want to crash there that is?"

Jay's nod and smile were answer enough.

"Call me when you get there," Danny said. "I'll be back day after tomorrow."

"Thanks, Danny."

"No sweat."

It took Jay and Fats another week to get to Stockholm. They stopped and visited some people along the way but were more eager than ever to get to Stockholm now that they had work and a place to stay. What a summer it had been!

Danny's bike shop was right next to the Vikings clubhouse. The Angels had bought the house fifteen years ago, but Danny had done most of the renovating and upkeep on it, so when they split into two clubs, it was natural for Danny and the Vikings to keep it. The Angels bought a new clubhouse on the other side of Stockholm instead.

Danny had pulled down most of the interior walls on the ground floor to make the clubroom as big as possible. He'd even built a room with a row of extra toilets out front. When there were a hundred partying bikers at the place, you didn't want them pissing all over the front driveway!

No one was living there at the moment. It wouldn't have been a problem, anyway, as Jay and Fats had got to know most of the Stockholm Vikings over the summer.

Jay and Fats were paid a fair wage. In return they worked hard, and although he would never have admitted it, Danny was glad to leave the heavier work to them. It also gave him time to do the paperwork and take care of customers without having to work every waking hour of the day. It was good to have the lads around too.

Jay still felt trapped, though. Working for Danny and living at the Vikings clubhouse was a great set up. Even so… Won't be forever, he thought to himself.

Still, the years rolled on.

In his quiet way, Fats was the happier of the two. Jay thought he'd probably stay there for the rest of his life. Working on bikes, hanging out with other bikers—it was all he wanted.

Even after Danny had officially retired, he still spent most of his time pottering around the workshop. Jay had free rein to run the shop as he felt best, but for the most part, he just kept things rolling the way Danny had. If it ain't bust, don't fix it, he reckoned.

Danny had passed on the title of Club President to him as well. In most respects, though, Jay had filled that role ever since he'd been there.

Six

I'll go check the Jeeps, Jay thought as he walked over the snow-covered driveway towards the garage.

The four second-hand Jeeps were his pet World War Zombie project, as he jokingly called it. Working on them was a hobby. His own Harley needed nothing more than regular tune-ups, so it was nice to work on something he could hang on to. He could modify and adapt the Jeeps as much as he wanted to. They looked like they'd somehow just managed to survive the Second World War, but their looks were deceptive. Under the hoods the engines were immaculately refurbished and tuned to perfection.

Jay had scavenged junkyards for suitable roof racks, then customized them to hold three mountain bikes each. He'd also welded racks to the sides and rear of the Jeeps so they could each carry four 20-liter jerry cans of diesel fuel and four spare wheels.

Each Jeep was fitted out for three people. All available spare space was filled with gear: a three-man tent, sleeping bags and mats, a multi-fuel cooking stove, and a first aid kit as well as tools, an axe, a spade, and climbing rope. Sealed food boxes were filled with instant oats, rice, dried beans, coffee, and bags of nuts and raisins.

Jay reckoned there was enough to keep three men alive for at least a month without even having to do any hunting or fishing.

Fishing rods lay neatly packed with the swords and knives. The assault rifles, pistols, and ammunition were hidden in the storage space under the benches in the back.

Apart from the modern weapons, everything else was decidedly low tech. Jay had often thought that the Boy Scouts had the right idea with their motto: 'Be Prepared'.

Society wasn't going to last. Just a matter of time before it all came crashing down. All his instincts and reasoning told him that. When it happened, only the strong would survive—the ones that were prepared that is—maybe not even them. If the human race wiped itself out, well, so what? he thought. Good riddance. As if the earth would care! It would just keep on turning as if nothing had happened. More like nature having a spring clean and getting rid of the vermin…

Whenever he thought about how fucked up people were, it reminded him of Janni. A couple of years ago, they'd been together for about six months. It was the longest he'd ever been in a relationship.

Unlike the girls that usually hung out with bikers, Janni was into her career as well. She was majoring in psychology at Stockholm University. She was the only person Jay had ever really talked about all that stuff with. He'd really enjoyed their long discussions, even if they could never agree with one another. Janni thought people could be helped and cured of their self-destructive behavior, whereas Jay reckoned it was too late— that they were too far gone down that path already and there was no turning back.

She couldn't help analyzing him, of course. Too many animal instincts had been her conclusion—Fight, survive, and lead the pack… Lot of truth there, Jay had to admit.

In the end, Janni had tired of the biker way of life. Realizing there was no point in trying to get Jay to change, she just moved on with her life.

About a year later, Jay had bumped into her in downtown Stockholm. They went for a coffee. It was all good, no hard feelings. Janni had asked if he still felt trapped—something they'd often talked about during their time together. Jay had grinned at her over the top of his espresso. No, he'd said. I'm the freest person you'll ever meet…

I know, Janni had said… I know.

Me too, Jay thought. He just wished it felt that way.

He turned away from the Jeeps.

A sudden flash of light made him squeeze his eyes shut. Pain drove through his head.

He let the agony wash over him, not daring to open his eyes.
What the fuck was that!
He opened his eyes carefully. At first he thought he was blind, seeing nothing but white.
Gradually his vision returned.
Another flash.
He dove to the ground, covering his head with his arms as white light filled the sky. Not quite as bad this time, but his eyes still hurt. Tears ran down his face.
A stroke? Could be…
Then the sound hit. A huge crackling like a thunderstorm, but one that never seemed to stop.
"Nukes!" he shouted.
The rumbling noise seemed to come from the east.
Finland? No. Russia, of course… Far enough away for the flashes to be seen but not to have blinded him instantly.
Another flash. Or was it two?
Unreal! Jay thought. No, it isn't, this *is* real!
He ran back to the clubhouse and flung the front door open. All the bikers were wide-awake now. They'd slept through Fat's snoring, but the unnatural booming and crackling had woken them with a start.
Rat was the first to speak. "What's going on?" he said.
"Dunno. I think Russia just got nuked," Jay said.
"Time to go?" Fats asked.
The other bikers didn't know Jay well enough to know what Fats meant.
"Yeah," Jay said simply. "Shut up and listen all of you. I've got four Jeeps. Anyone who wants to get out of the city with me and Fats can join us."
"That's nuts!" one of the bikers said.
"Look. If you don't want to come, *don't fucking come!*" Jay said, turning to glare at the guy who'd spoken.
Everyone was talking now. Everyone except Fats. He was putting his boots on.
"Ten minutes," Jay said. "Who's coming with us?"
Apart from Fats, seven of the bikers raised their hands. The

other six either shook their heads or just looked at the floor.

"Good... You others can keep the clubhouse. It's yours. Oh, and our bikes as well."

Fats stood by the open door, letting Jay lead the way to the garage.

By the time the other bikers came out of the clubhouse, they'd driven all four of the Jeeps onto the driveway, and the motors were running.

Two in each Jeep, except one with three. Good enough, Jay thought. Not surprisingly, the bikers who had chosen to leave with him were the unattached ones: the ones who had nothing much to leave behind except their motorbikes. The others, those that chose to stay, mostly had families and decent jobs in the city. They thought they'd be giving too much up, Jay reckoned.

"Nothing left to leave," was all he said as he gunned the Jeep through the open gates and turned right to lead the small convoy north.

He knew that together they'd have a much better chance of surviving than if they'd been on their own. A few more would have been better, he reckoned, though nine wasn't bad. No one wanted to mess with a gang of bikers. There was power in numbers. Didn't matter if it was when you walked into a bar together or just riding along the road. Kind of gave you a sense of freedom, Jay had often thought. Even the pigs were cautious around bikers. Strength is power, he reckoned. Even if it's sometimes just the power to be left alone.

Going north was the obvious thing to do. Jay had hardly thought about alternatives. The further north you went, the less people there were. Not only that, but northern Scandinavia was one of the few places where you could live off the land. North was the land Jay and Fats knew. They had equipment, weapons, and a gang.

They were lucky too. Had they gone south, they would have been killed by the nano-virus.

Half an hour down the road, Jay turned off at a gas station. He pulled two pistols out of the Jeep's glove compartment and handed one of them to Fats. They put the guns in their jacket pockets.

"Food," he said simply.

There was no point in using their supplies when food could still be found.

Jay opened the door to the gas station's mini-shop and led the way in. It was empty apart from a woman behind the counter.

"Hi," Jay said.

The woman didn't reply. She looked as if she had been so shocked by the flashes of light and the thundering noise that she'd forgotten how to speak.

Jay walked along the shelves of food and household items until he found what he was looking for: big black plastic trash bags. Opening one of the rolls, he tore a bag off and held it wide open. Fats started pulling stuff off the shelves and throwing it into the bag.

"Hey! You can't do that!" the woman at the counter said, finding her voice at last.

"Don't worry," Jay said. "We'll pay."

The woman stared open-mouthed at them, not knowing what to say. Jay and Fats filled two of the plastic sacks and carried them to the door. As they passed the counter, Jay pulled a handful of bills out of his wallet and slapped them on the counter without even bothering to count them. It was a lot. Much more than all the stuff they'd taken could possibly have cost.

"Enough?" he asked.

The woman nodded dumbfoundedly.

"Good," Jay said.

They put the sacks of food into the back of the Jeep.

"She'll probably call the pigs anyway," Jay said as he got in. "Probably say we're bank robbers or something." He laughed. "There's an intersection just a few kilometers down the road. They won't know which way we went… Keep your eyes peeled anyway, Fats, yeah?"

"Yeah."

Jay doubted whether the police would respond even if the woman from the gas station called them. They probably had a lot of other things to worry about.

Fats drove straight on at the intersection.

Twenty minutes later they stopped at a roadside cafe. The nine bikers went in and filled their trays with hot food and coffee.

They sat at a window-side table where they could keep an eye on the Jeeps. Jay paid for the food with cash. The girl behind the till said the machine for credit cards wasn't working. No shit, Jay thought. Soon nothing would be working…

The coffee was good, though.

Talking in a soft voice, just loud enough so as not to be overheard by anyone else, Jay told the other bikers what they were going to do.

"If I'm wrong, and this isn't the end of the world, we can always go back to Stockholm and take our bikes back. But if I'm right, we've got to get as far north as possible, as quick as possible."

They all ate in silence.

When they were done, Jay looked at each of them in turn.

"So, anyone out?"

None of them were.

Seven

As they drove further north, Jay let his mind wander. He realized that he'd concentrated too much on the first inevitable period of anarchy that would follow the collapse of society and not enough about the other people who would survive it—people who could be a threat to him and his gang.

There would be a fair number of tough and resourceful folk in the north of Sweden. Like everybody else, they had enjoyed the comforts of modern society, but there were still many who knew the forest, could hunt and fish, and endure the harsh winter climate. They would be armed, too, but mostly with hunting rifles and shotguns, Jay reckoned. No match for the Vikings' automatic rifles in a firefight, but still, a danger not to be taken lightly. Our advantage is that we're a gang, he thought. They'll either have families or be loners living in the forest. Unless they get properly organized, that is. That would change things. We'll see…

That night the bikers stayed in a campground by the edge of a lake. The entrance was blocked by a barrier and locked with a simple padlock. Fats cut through it with a pair of bolt cutters and raised the barrier. When all the Jeeps were in, he lowered the barrier again and replaced the broken padlock to hold it in place. To any casual passer-by, the campsite would look empty and closed. At the far end there was a row of holiday cabins. Perfect, Jay thought.

The cabin doors were easily forced open. Electric heaters had been left on to keep the cabins from rotting in winter. Each cabin had beds for four people, so they only had to break into three of them. There was no bedding, but they had their sleeping bags.

Yes, perfect, Jay thought as he slowly drifted into sleep. For the first time in his life, he didn't feel trapped.

He slept dreamlessly and woke up at six o'clock. Looking out of the cabin window, he saw that the night sky had a strange red shimmer, as if the aurora borealis—the northern lights—had changed hue and spread across the whole sky.

He put his leather jacket on and gently opened the cabin door.

The surrounding forest was quiet. Jay took a deep breath of the cold, clear air. I will never be trapped again, he swore to himself.

A hint of amber moonlight behind the dark trees reflected in his strange blue eyes. If anyone had looked into them, they would have seen a subtle shift of emotion—a ripple gone before it became clear. Maybe they would have called it determination—or something much more dangerous.

"Got a plan?" Fats asked as he put the Jeep into gear.

Jay was fiddling with the radio. There was mostly only static, but every now and again he'd get a signal. No one was playing music anymore. There was only the news—and only one story.

Jay had been right. There had been a nuclear war.

Nothing was being broadcast from anywhere except Norway and Sweden either. At first, people wouldn't know what this meant, but they would work it out soon enough, Jay thought. Even the radio buffs who had diesel driven generators weren't broadcasting from anywhere south of Stockholm. Not even from Gothenburg or Malmö, Sweden's two other cities. Jay knew it probably meant they were all dead, along with everybody else.

"Dunno, Fats. Seems like Stockholm and everything further north has survived. Weird. Guess no one thought we were worth bombing. Things are going to be pretty fucked up for a while. Best thing for us is to hide up for a while away from towns. See what happens."

But where? He pulled a roadmap out of the Jeep's door pocket and began studying it.

"Just keep heading north-west," he said after a while. "Towards Åre."

"Okay," Fats said.

Åre was nestled in the Swedish mountains which ran from

north to south and created a natural border with Norway. In winter, it was a popular ski resort and in summer, a center for hiking, kayaking, and other outdoor sports. The mountains were one of the country's most uninhabited regions.

For over an hour, Jay pored over the maps. What am I looking for? he kept asking himself.

Fats drove on in silence.

The longer he studied the maps, the more he kept coming back to one place: a small village in the northern mountains, Tärnaby. Like Åre, it was a ski resort but much smaller and much further north.

Tärnaby sat beside Lake Gäuta and near the source of two rivers: the Blue River and the Vindel River. Fed by countless tributaries, the rivers wound their way eastwards across the country until they converged near the university town of Umeå and ran into the Baltic Sea.

Jay tapped his finger slowly on the map. Tärnaby. It felt right.

"Yeah, Fats," he said at last. "I think I've got a plan…"

"Good," was all Fats said. He didn't ask Jay to explain. It didn't matter. He would have followed him to Hell and back without even asking why they had to go there in the first place. Just the way he was.

There wasn't much traffic on the road, and there would be even less the further north they drove. That was normal. Still, it seemed as if there were even fewer cars and trucks than there ought to have been.

Everyone's seeking shelter, I guess, Jay thought… Stay at home, keep your head down, and pray that everything will get back to normal.

He checked the map again.

"There's a wilderness hotel just before we get to Åre. We'll check it out. Should be about another hour."

Fats nodded, then checked his back mirror.

"What now!" he said. Behind the fourth Jeep, he'd seen the flashing lights of a police car.

Jay looked out of the back window.

"Slow down," he said.

"Stop?"

"Yeah, I'll handle this."

Fats braked slowly, giving the Jeeps behind him time to follow his lead. They all pulled over to the hard shoulder and stopped.

"Quick, slide over," Jay said, and raised himself up to let Fats move over to the passenger seat.

Keeping his eyes on the rear mirror, Jay shifted himself into the driver's seat, then rolled the window down.

The police car had pulled up behind the last Jeep. Two women police officers got out. Both of them had their hands resting on the holsters of their service pistols. They hadn't drawn them yet, though.

Idiots, Jay thought.

He leaned his head out of the window and waved his arm to motion the two policewomen over to him.

"Hi! Morning girls. What's going on?" he called out.

"Put your hands where I can see them!" Anna Terngren, the more experienced policewoman of the two, called back.

"Sure," Jay said in a friendly tone. "I've got my driver's license here…"

He pretended to fumble in the inside pocket of his leather jacket with his left hand.

"Put your hands out where I can see them!" Anna shouted again.

"Oh, okay, sorry…" Jay said with an embarrassed grin. He pulled his hand out from inside his jacket. In the same moment, he swung his other hand up and out of the window. In it was a black pistol.

Anna and her colleague had only a split second to wonder where the gun had come from before they were both dead.

"Idiots," Jay whispered softly to himself.

He closed the window and stared emotionlessly out of the front windscreen. Fats didn't say a word.

Eight

A thin layer of fresh snow covered the narrow driveway that led to the wilderness hotel. There were no car tracks on it.

Good sign, Jay thought. If we're lucky, nobody will be there.

The hotel looked as if it was empty.

"We'll check the whole place out, anyway," he said. Best to be sure, he reckoned. "Rat, take three guys and search everywhere. I don't think anyone's here, but even so… yeah?"

"Yeah, no problem," Rat said.

"Every room. Don't miss a thing," Jay added, the slightest hint of a threat in his voice.

"Got it."

"You others, check outside. Garages, outhouses, garden sheds, everything, right? If you see any footprints in the snow, or anything else, I want to know. Me and Fats will start making some grub."

There was no one there. All the fifteen guest rooms were empty and immaculately clean.

The driveway was the only way to get from the main road to the hotel. We'll block that, Jay thought, although there seemed to be no reason for anyone else to come there at all.

Two weeks, he reckoned. Give it two weeks, and things will have changed. People will have used up most of their fuel, and there won't be anything left worth looting in the towns. They'll head out to the farms where there's food.

Two weeks to plan the future.

The lounge in the wilderness hotel was strangely reminiscent of the Vikings clubhouse in Stockholm. It was a bit smaller but had a fully stocked bar as well as sofas and armchairs arranged in small groups. The far end of the room was taken up by a pool table. There was even a dartboard in one corner.

"Right," Jay said when all the Vikings were done searching the hotel and its grounds. "We're going to hole up here for a couple of weeks. I want a guard watching the driveway night and day. Take that duty very seriously, okay?" He didn't wait for an answer. "The rest of the time you can do what the hell you want… Play pool, get drunk, jack off!" He laughed. "But no one leaves the grounds. Do that, and you don't come back."

He gazed at the guys one at a time, searching for something in their eyes. Satisfied that they'd all got the message and were committed, he nodded.

"We'll do four hours guard duty at a time. I'll make a list. Eight hours before your guard duty, you don't drink. Anyone drunk or who falls asleep on guard duty…" He made a slight cutting motion with his hand. "Got it?"

They understood precisely and had no doubt that Jay would waste anyone who disobeyed him. They'd seen what he'd done to the policewomen.

"Oh, one last thing," Jay said. "No fighting. Those are the rules, and the game has changed. This isn't a club for rebels anymore. Okay?"

They all nodded.

Jay grinned. "Good. Do what I say, and we can rule here… Be kings!" He laughed. "Yeah, Kings! Drink to that?"

"Hell yeah!" Rat said. He fetched a bottle of whiskey from the bar and handed it to Jay.

Fats drew himself up from his chair. "I'll do guard duty," he said.

"Then me," Rat said. "Just save me some whiskey for later. Anyone got a Coca-Cola?"

The tension broke. They all cracked up.

They'll do, Jay thought. A hint of a smile creased his cheek, though it never reached his eyes.

The two weeks passed in a daze of alcohol, sleep, and endless games of pool and darts. Now and again they checked the radio, sweeping through all the frequencies. There was only static. Nothing. Even the radio buffs were silent or gone.

No one came to the lodge. It had been the perfect spot, Jay thought. But now we've got to get things together. The guys are getting restless. That's good.

That evening he told them it was time to leave.

"Day after tomorrow, daybreak at eight o'clock, we're out of here," he said. "Tomorrow we get our stuff together and pack the Jeeps. No more drinking. We've got to stay sharp."

They were all partied out anyway, so that was no big deal.

Nine

It felt good to be back on the road.

Tärnaby was just over four hundred kilometers away. That far north it would be dark by about five o'clock in the afternoon. Jay wanted to get there before nightfall, so they could find somewhere to sleep not too far from the village.

The road was deserted. They didn't meet a single car all day.

Wow, Jay thought. Just two weeks. They're all dead or holed up like scared rabbits.

Daylight was waning by the time they got close.

Just past a signpost that read 'Tärnaby 20 km', Jay saw an unpaved path that led to a solitary homestead a hundred meters or so from the main road. They'd been passing fewer and fewer farms the closer to the mountains they got. There'd been signs of life in some of them, though: smoking chimneys, and faces peering out of windows as the small convoy of Jeeps rolled by… Scared, you could tell, Jay thought. Their pathetic, secure way of life had come crashing down around them. Still, these were the lucky ones who had potatoes in their cellars and firewood stocked for the winter.

"Over there, Fats. See it?" Jay said.

Fats had seen the farmhouse, too, and nodded. He signaled to let the others know he was going to turn, then drove slowly up the farmyard path.

Jay kept his eyes peeled. They'll have weapons, he reminded himself. He'd discussed this kind of situation with his gang before they'd left the wilderness hotel. They all knew what to do.

Fats touched his brake pedal three times, flashing the brake lights. The other Jeeps spread out in a wide semicircle in front of the farmhouse.

They all got out, rifles at the ready.

They had left the Jeeps' headlights and fog lights fully on and directed at the farmhouse as Jay had told them to. It wasn't so dark yet, but the lights would be a distraction to anyone opening the door or looking out the windows.

Jay saw a man's face at one of the downstairs windows. Probably got his family gathered together inside, he thought. Must be shitting himself…

"Thirty seconds to come out and throw your weapons down!" he called out.

Nothing happened.

The silence exploded as Jay fired a short burst of automatic gunfire, splaying the front of the house with bullets. He wasn't aiming at anything in particular, but he wasn't going to repeat his order.

Ten seconds later the front door opened. A fat, pale-faced farmer threw out his shotgun.

"Come out. Hands on your head," Jay ordered.

The man obeyed.

"Now, on your knees and down on your stomach. Keep your hands on your head."

The man did exactly as Jay said.

Fats walked towards the farmer, careful not to block Jay's line of fire.

"Hi," he said in a friendly tone and wrapped his hand around one of the farmer's arms, guiding it firmly behind his back. He tightened a thick zip-tie around the man's wrist, before slipping a second one through the loop and around his other wrist—handcuffing them together.

Grabbing the man under his armpits, Fats lifted him with ease onto his feet, even though the farmer must have weighed well over a hundred kilos. He turned the man towards the farmhouse door.

"Put the Jeeps round the back," Jay said to the others.

Through the open front door, they could see past the hallway into a large kitchen. The farmer's wife and two daughters sat at a wooden table. Two oil lamps and the flames from a wood stove lit the room. They'd been eating their evening meal. It looked cozy.

Fats opened the door to the toilet in the hallway. He gave the farmer a gentle nudge.

"In," he said. "Sit on the toilet."

The man sat down.

"You'll be okay in here," Fats said. "Stay put and don't make a sound. We aren't going to hurt your family, but if you open the door or make a sound, we'll kill you all. Understand?"

The terrified farmer could only nod his head.

Fats closed the toilet door, then joined Jay, Sammy and Ola in the kitchen.

"What do you want?" Greta, the farmer's wife, asked.

She was trying hard to keep her voice calm, not wanting to scare her daughters. She clutched Avril, their youngest daughter, tightly to her with one arm around the girl's small body and the other around her head as if to shield her. Freja, their sixteen-year-old daughter, stared defiantly at the bikers who had invaded their home.

"Food," Jay said simply. "Just cook us a meal."

Greta nodded. Her husband was still alive. That was a good sign. Just do what these men want, and they might go away, she thought to herself. Just don't hurt my babies, she prayed silently.

"Freja, get bacon, eggs, and potatoes from the larder."

"Yes, mum."

"Avril, can you help mummy lay the table?" she asked the six-year-old on her lap. The young girl looked up at her mother and nodded. Greta lowered her to the floor.

"I'll get the plates down for you," she said, reaching up to open the cupboard above the sink. "How many? she asked.

"Nine," Jay said. "And you…"

Greta turned back to the stove. She bit her lip and was trying desperately not to cry. "We've already eaten," she said.

Greta and her daughters sat at the far end of the kitchen table while the men ate. She couldn't help noticing the way they looked at Freja.

At sixteen, her daughter hardly looked like a little girl anymore.

Her hair was long and dyed fashionably blonde with darker streaks. She wore tight jeans and a top which did nothing to hide her mature body. Greta had been beautiful once, herself. Two children and all the years of hard work on the farm had left their mark.

Rat wiped the back of his hand over his mouth and glanced at Jay.

He got the slightest of nods. Never forget who the boss is, he reminded himself.

He pushed his chair back and got up.

"Come on," he said to Freja, and held his out his hand.

"No, please don't!" Greta cried, not able to hold her tears back anymore.

Rat didn't even look at her.

"It's okay, mum," Freja said. "I want to."

"No, Freja! *Don't!*" Greta stared wide-eyed at her daughter. What did she mean? *She wanted to?*

"You don't get it, do you, mum?" Freja said gently. "This is the future. These guys can protect me… You can't."

The teenager took Rat's hand in hers. Greta watched, lost for words as her daughter led Rat out of the kitchen towards the stairs.

Two hours later, Rat came back down, alone.

"She's sleeping," he said.

"You want to keep her?" Jay asked.

"Yeah."

Jay nodded. Freja was off limits to the others now. She belonged to Rat.

At sunrise the next morning, the nine bikers and one teenage girl left the farm. They drove on towards Tärnaby.

When they got there, the village was deserted.

"They all headed for the farms when food ran out," Freja said. "We had to shoot at cars to scare people off. Didn't keep you away," she added with a grin. "What are we going to do here?" she asked, turning to Jay.

"Have a look round," he replied. "See if it'll do…"

"Do for what?"

"Oh, rule a kingdom."

He wandered off across the village square. To the west were the mountains and ski slopes. Below the village lay Lake Gäuta. The forest around the lake stretched out as far as the eye could see. Here and there he could see wisps of smoke rising gently into the cold morning sky. Farmhouses, he thought.

A church dominated the square. Built in 1850, it was a simple rectangular building with a tall spire.

Jay studied the church for a long while from where he stood.

"Fats, come on over here," he called out at last. "Bring me a sword."

Fats rummaged in the back of one of the Jeeps and pulled out a Samurai sword.

"Me and Fats'll go check the church," Jay told the others. "Stay here. Keep your eyes and ears open. There could still be some people around."

One, at least, he thought. The reflected light of the morning sun in one of the church spire's windows had fleetingly revealed a silhouette. Someone had been peeking out of the window before disappearing back into the darkness behind them.

Jay tied the sword to his leather belt, so it hung naturally on his left side.

They walked all the way around the outside of the church. There were no signs of life in any of the shops or apartments on the other side of the village square. The windows in most of the shops had been smashed. The Co-op supermarket had been completely looted. Even the small sports shop had been emptied.

Coming back around to the church's main entrance, Jay pulled his sword out of its scabbard. He banged the end of its hilt three times on the solid oak door.

They waited… Nothing. Not a sound.

He hammered another three times.

At last, the grating sound of a heavy bolt being pulled back came from the other side of the door—then the sound of a turning key.

The door opened a tiny crack, then, hesitantly, a bit more.

"Begone demons! In the name of the Father, the Son, and the Holy Spirit, I command you! Return to the underworld from whence you came!"…

Fats grabbed the edge of the door and pulled it open. An old man in the robes of a priest glared out at them. Sharp cheekbones and wide staring eyes dominated his painfully thin face. In front of him, the priest clutched a massive crucifix with both hands. His grip was so tight that his knuckles had turned white. Dirty and broken fingernails dug deep into the emancipated flesh of his hands.

The priest screamed, "… *et proiectus est draco ille magnus serpens antiquus qui vocatur Diabolus et Satanas qui seducit universum orbem proiectus est in terram et angeli eius cum illo missi sunt!* … and the huge dragon was cast down and out, that age-old serpent, who is called the Devil and Satan, he who is the deceiver of all humanity the world over, he was forced out and down to the earth, and his angels were flung out along with him!"

Madness shone in his eyes. Fear, rapture, desperation… The horrors he had witnessed had broken his mind. Voices of avenging angels echoed in his church. The end of days was upon them.

He had retreated into the sanctity of the church and barred the door, surviving on the small amount of food in the church pantry and drinking sacramental wine to quench his thirst.

He had prayed for the Lord's angels to come, but now the minions of the Devil stood before him!

"Begone! You are the Angels of Hell!"

Jay laughed, "Well, yeah, guess you could say that."

The priest's ramblings became incoherent. He was convinced that his last moments on earth had come, and that he would spend the rest of eternity in the fiery pits of hell.

He raised the crucifix high above his head. The sinews of his arms quivered as he gathered his mad strength to smite at the devil before him.

"… *in nomine Patris, et Filii, et Spiritus Sancti!* …"

Jay brought his sword up. Its gleaming tip pressed against the priest's chest.

"Put it down, old man," he ordered.

Like a shadow across the moon, the priest's fervor vanished. He lowered the crucifix.

"... *Pater dimitte mihi quoniam peccavi!* ... Father forgive me for I have sinned!" he mumbled—and let go of the crucifix.

Even as it fell, his bony hands snatched at Jay's sword.

Its razor sharp edges sliced into the flesh of his palms. Blood welled from the cuts.

Jay tried to pull the sword away, but it was too late.

With a last maniacal scream, the priest pushed his body against the tip of the sword.

There was no resistance. The blade was perfectly honed. It sliced almost gently through his flesh. Missing his ribs, it cut straight through his heart.

Crimson red with blood, the sword emerged from the priest's back as he fell further forward. The sword's hilt and Jay's fists stopped his fall.

Jay stared into the dying priest's eyes just a hand's breadth from his own. A froth of blood and spittle bubbled from the old man's mouth and ran down his unshaven chin.

Jay kept his eyes locked onto the priest's until he saw the last glint of life—and madness—fade into blackness.

With one arm wrapped around his back, he gently lowered him to the ground and pulled his sword out. He wiped it clean on the dead priest's robes before putting it back in its scabbard.

"Vaya con Dios," Jay said softly.

Fats hadn't a clue what that meant. He laid his hand on Jay's shoulder and gently pulled him away from the dead body, then gathered the front of the priest's robes in one hand and half lifted, half dragged him to the church door.

"Thanks, Fats," Jay said. "Put him in the cemetery behind the church, yeah?"

"Yeah, no problem, Jay."

Fats carried the priest's body down the church steps, leaving a trail of blood in the snow. He dumped the body unceremoniously under a yew tree in the far corner of the cemetery.

Behind the cemetery was a white wooden fence that marked

the boundary between the church and the village school. In front of the schoolhouse was a small playground.

A sign above the school's entrance read: 'Tärnaby Skola 1927'.

Fats went back to the church. All the gang had gathered outside with Jay.

"The school looks like a good place," Fats said.

Jay raised his face slightly—as if to catch the breeze. Like an animal scenting the air for danger, Fats thought.

"Yeah," he said, as if satisfied.

The door to the school's main entrance was slightly ajar.

Strange, Jay thought. They would have locked the door wouldn't they? Or maybe not, if they knew they'd never be coming back.

"We'll search it," Jay said. "Fats, you and Rat stay with the Jeeps. Won't take long."

The school *felt* empty, but best to be sure.

He placed his hand on the hilt of his sword. Somehow, the sword felt right, even though he still had an Uzi machine gun slung over his back.

The difference in killing power between the two weapons was enormous, but the sword seemed to imbue him with a sense of power that modern weaponry couldn't match—an ancient symbol of strength wielded by warriors and kings—one that everyone understood.

A gun was still basically a device for throwing stones, albeit the stones were made of metal and traveled faster than the eye could see, but a sword was the extension of a man's arm, able to strike down an enemy in one blow. Wielding the power over life and death, the bearer of a sword became more than human—a god.

Three of the Vikings followed Jay into the school. They all had automatic rifles slung over their shoulders and shotguns held nonchalantly by their sides.

"Me and Jon will go left. You two go right," Jay said. "Search every room on the bottom floor. When we're done, we'll meet back here and go upstairs together. Got it?"

The three other Vikings nodded.

"No rush," Jay added. "Be certain."

It only took a few minutes. All the classrooms, as well as the cafeteria and kitchen, were empty.

They met back at the spiral staircase that led to the upper floor.

This is where it might get tricky, Jay thought.

Staircases invariably wound anti-clockwise on the way up. It was a design that dated back to medieval times. Anyone going up the stairs with a sword in their right hand would be at a great disadvantage against an armed defender above them.

"I'll go first," Jay said. "Jon, Ola, give me your shotguns. Sammy, go last. Keep checking behind you, yeah?"

"Got it," the youngest of the bikers answered.

The barrels of their shotguns had been sawn off. This made them inaccurate at long distances—useless for hunting—but lethal as close-combat weapons. You didn't even have to aim properly.

Jay held two shotguns, one in each hand. A hail of lead would meet anyone coming down the stairs.

Slowly, he started to climb the stairs. The others followed, guns at the ready. Sammy kept checking over his shoulder—just in case.

The school's upper floor had a long corridor with doors on both sides. From the signs on the doors, Jay saw that they were administrative offices, a small library, toilets, and even an extra kitchen.

Perfect, he thought.

He handed the shotguns back to Jon and Ola, then motioned with his fingers for them to search the rooms in the same way they had downstairs.

All the rooms were empty.

There was an emergency exit at the end of the corridor, which could only be opened from the inside. A metal staircase led down from it to the school's car park.

"Let's go back down," Jay said when they were done. "Oh, and welcome home, lads!" he added with a laugh.

The staffroom was the biggest room on the upper floor. It had large windows that looked out over the playground. A big, round table dominated the room. Twelve wooden chairs were evenly placed around it. There were even a few comfy chairs and a sofa. A huge fireplace stood in the far corner. Back in 1927 when the school had been built, there would have been no other way of heating it.

Rat peered up the chimney.

"Dirty. But I think it'll be okay," he said. "I can see daylight at least. We'll give it a try." He grinned. "Let's get some wooden chairs from downstairs. We can start a fire. I'll go get an axe."

The fire was smoky at first. They had to open all of the windows, but once the wood was burning steadily, most of the smoke went up the chimney.

They'll know we're here now, Jay thought, meaning anyone who saw the smoke drifting up from the village.

"Be back soon," he said, and left the room.

A couple of minutes later, he came back with two bottles of whiskey, one in each hand. Ceremoniously, he put one of them in the middle of the round table and opened the other one.

"Home," he said simply, and took a deep swig of whiskey before handing it to Fats.

The bottle was passed between them until it was empty. Even Freja took a small sip, but the look on her face told the others what she thought of it.

"Sit," Jay said.

They all pulled up chairs and sat down around the table.

Jay opened the second bottle. Then without drinking from it, he put it back in the middle of the table.

"Fats…"

Frederik stood up. Without saying a word, he reached out for the whiskey and drank.

He put the bottle back, and sat down.

One by one, the men stood and drank. A silent oath of fealty was being sworn.

The bottle was still half full when they'd all drunk from it.

Jay stood up and drank deeply before passing it to Fats. Then he started to speak.

He spoke in a soft voice—like a storyteller. But his was a story not of the past, but of the future.

Jay spoke until the sun had set and the only light came from the cinders in the fireplace. A magical sense of mystery and adventure encompassed them.

Ten

The four Jeeps formed a defensive line in front of the church.

Jay had a clear view across the village square and of Lake Gäuta from the passenger seat of one of them. He was studying a map—and thinking.

Tärnaby was his fortress. Protected by the mountains, it would be his base, but power came from controlling a larger area, and that meant spreading out via the roads and riverways.

The main road from Tärnaby ran east across the breadth of Sweden, connecting the mountains with the Baltic Sea. Control the road and the two rivers, Jay thought, and you controlled a vast area of forests and farmlands: A kingdom.

They'd been in Tärnaby for a week now. No one else was there. The priest had been the only person not to have left the village.

They had built a large bonfire surrounded by a ring of stones in front of the church. Originally, it was so that whoever was on guard could keep warm, but it had become a natural gathering place where everyone hung out when there was nothing else to do.

Jay had been in two minds about what to do with all the religious stuff in the church: the Bibles, hymn books, and the large wooden cross, which hung at the front of the church below the stained glass windows.

At first, he thought that they should just burn it all. Something held him back, though, and eventually he realized it was because of the power those things symbolized: the power and authority that religion had given to priests and kings throughout history… Remember that, he told himself.

The private room where the priest had kept his robes and other church belongings, the sacristy, had been turned into an armory. Fats had reinforced the door with metal plates and hung a huge padlock on it. All their spare weapons were kept there.

There were only two keys. Whoever was on guard duty hung one of them around their neck. Jay kept the other one with him at all times unless he left the village. Then he gave it to one of his knights.

Knights—that was how he was beginning to see his men. They had a castle. He was the king. So they were his knights. Made sense.

Inside the church, a central aisle divided the two rows of pews. The side aisles were blocked by rolls of barbed wire so that anyone who breached the front door had to come down the narrow center aisle to get to the armory: a killing field. It was the barbed wire more than anything else that had transformed the church into something quite different than a place of worship.

Soon the whole village center had been turned into a stronghold. Abandoned cars and pick-up trucks were moved so that they blocked the side streets leading to the square. The only way to get there now was from the main road, which could be blocked off in minutes as well.

The church was their second line of defense. Anyone who got past it and wanted to attack the school would have to cross the open playground. Machine gun fire from the school's upper windows would cut them down before they got very far.

It was a start, Jay thought. They were prepared to defend themselves.

His plans stretched much further than to just having control of a simple mountain village though. The next stage would be more complicated. He reckoned the biggest danger would come from the people who were managing to survive on the outlying farms. For now they were probably mostly concerned with their personal survival, but sooner or later they would start organizing themselves. People are only brave in groups or when they're desperate, he thought. As long as they feel alone and vulnerable, or have something to lose, will they be fearful… We will make them fear.

Jay knew how to use fear both as a tool and as a weapon. First through threats and intimidation, then with violence and retribution, until finally their reputation alone would be enough to control people and keep them harmless.

Later that day, Jay gathered them all together in a classroom. He'd hung a large map in front of the blackboard. Jon was on guard duty, but all the rest of the bikers and Freja were sitting at the classroom desks.

Jay had to laugh. "Look at you! he said. "Bet the school's never seen a class like you before!"

"Yeah, School's Out Forever!" Rat said.

That cracked everyone up.

"Pay attention, now," Jay said at last, trying not to laugh, but not doing so well.

When the class had finally quietened down, he pointed out the village, the main road, and the two rivers on the map.

"No rush," he said. "We'll go from farm to farm towards the rivers. Take food from them—meat, milk, vegetables… They'll refuse at first. Our job is to make them realize that they have no choice. There'll be some who think they'll be able to stand up to us, and maybe some leaders… Kill them."

He gazed at the Vikings one at a time. "Anybody got a problem with that?"

No one said anything.

Jay nodded. "No, didn't think so."

"How'll we know who the leaders are?" Rat asked.

"That's easy," Jay said, fixing his cold stare on him. "They're the ones that don't turn their eyes away."

Seconds passed. Something electric hung in the air.

At last Rat looked down. Jay knew it wasn't because he wanted to, but because he chose to.

"What about the women?" Sammy asked.

"Leave the children alone," Jay said. "The women…" He shrugged his shoulders. "Just remember—don't take everything away from the children. Do that, and they'll grow up not just fearing us but hating us as well." And with nothing to lose, he added to himself. Those are the dangerous ones.

Eleven

Jay woke with a start. It was the middle of the night. He was sweating even though the air was cold. He sat upright on his mattress and listened.

Nothing. Not a sound.

What was I dreaming about? he asked himself. What could have woken me up like that? He tried hard to remember... Horses! Yes, something about horses. Galloping. A herd of horses. Trampling everything. Killing everyone.

Horses! Of course! Why hadn't I thought of that? We've got to get horses!

Jay could have kicked himself. It was so obvious. He should have thought about it earlier... In medieval times, it was the horses that gave power to kings and their knight warriors. The power to move quickly and dominate battles. Mountain bikes were fine for getting around. But horses! Yes, horses!

Jay pulled his jeans and jacket on. Careful not to wake the others, he crept down the stairs and out into the cold night.

He was wide-awake now. Part of his plan had been a bit vague—as if he knew it would be hard to put into practice. They'd been so busy strengthening their defenses that he'd been able to push it to the back of his mind. Now everything fell into place. They would be unstoppable. Strong. Free. He walked across the playground and the cemetery.

Fats was sitting alone at the fire.

"Hey," Jay called softly, not wanting to alarm him.

"Hey, what'ya doing up this early?"

"Dunno, woke up and realized something important."

He pulled up a wooden chair and sat down. "Know how to ride a horse, Fats?"

"No, you?"

"Sort of," Jay said. "But we're going to learn…"

Fats thought about this for a while as they both stared out across the moonlit lake. Jay let him take his time.

"Yeah, makes sense," Fats said at last. "I don't know anything about horses, though…" He grinned at Jay. "No motor."

Jay grinned back. "Doubt any of the other guys do either."

"Freja?"

"Maybe. We can ask her in the morning. Good thinking, Fats. She grew up on a farm. I'll bet she knows how to take care of horses and can teach us to ride."

"I grew up on a farm as well, but we didn't have any horses." Fats said. "Just as long as I don't have to wear one of those silly hats. Bad enough with motorbike helmets."

Jay laughed out loud. "I can see you in horse riding gear, Fats! Tights, boots and a hat! What are those things called? Jodhpurs or something?"

They both cracked up.

"No, second thoughts," Jay said. "Maybe that's *not* something I want to see!"

"Of course I can ride," Freja said. "I grew up with horses. We've got two on our farm."

"Good. I thought you might." Jay said. "Rat, take Freja and one of the other guys and drive to the farm. She can ride back on one of the horses and lead the other one. Stay with her though, yeah?" He paused and thought for a moment. "Where are we going to keep them? They can't be outside. They'd freeze to death, wouldn't they?"

Freja laughed. "No, of course they wouldn't! You don't know much about horses, do you? They'll be fine as long as they've got enough hay and somewhere out of the wind. There's a trailer at our farm we can fill with hay and bring here. I'll look after them really well, Jay." Her face lit up at the thought of being reunited with her beloved horses.

The next day, Rat, Ola, and Freja drove to the farm.

Her parents were delighted to see their daughter. Her mother couldn't stop crying and hugging her. She was overwhelmed with relief when she saw that Freja was healthy—and even happy. She had been so worried…

Even her father seemed to have accepted the way things were. He surprised Rat by shaking his hand before mumbling something about getting the horses and the trailer ready.

He went out through the back door and walked to the barn. With Freja no longer there, they didn't have time to look after the horses anyway, he thought. He started to heave hay onto the trailer.

The thought of killing the two bikers and rescuing his daughter crossed his mind. His pitchfork would make a good weapon, he thought… He shook his head. No, he said to himself. It would be foolish. Would only get us all killed in the end. Better to give them what they want. Life is going to be hard enough as it is now. Better to live in peace.

Twelve

Jay had found a map in Tärnaby's small library that showed where all the farms were. He had taped it to the wall at the back of the church and had studied it for a long time. It was twenty years old, but he didn't think much would have changed in twenty years—not around these parts, anyway.

He traced his finger slowly from one farm to the next. Most of them lay in the fertile valleys where rivers and streams flowed.

One by one, Jay thought. One by one... Tomorrow we'll start. Everything hung on this. Would they be able to control them?

We'll see... He rested his hand on his sword. We'll see.

The message the Vikings brought to the farmers and the villagers who had fled to the farms was twofold: Hope, and fear.

They were told to bring their farm produce, and anything else they had to barter, to the village square in Tärnaby on Saturdays. If they were honest and fair, there would be enough food for them all to live well. Dishonesty and swindle would be punished by whipping; theft, by hanging; and other crimes, by the sword.

Work hard, and life will go on peacefully, the Vikings said. Disobey, and you and your sons will die.

As Jay had expected, some of the men protested. But they had too much to lose: their homes, their wives and children... It was often the womenfolk who calmed them down, begging them not to endanger all their livelihoods.

A few decided to fight anyway. They were chanceless against the well organized, better armed, and brutal Viking warriors.

Freja went along on the first trips to the outlying farms to find good horses. The strongest and healthiest were taken back to Tärnaby.

She also had a knack of finding those girls, like herself, who wanted to get away from their parents. These girls quickly paired up with Jay's men, instinctively looking for protection and the status that came from belonging to one of the Vikings. The price they had to pay was obedience and total fidelity. There were no marriage ceremonies, no promises made. Still, everyone knew who was protected. In time, these women became known as their ladies.

Young men and teenage boys were also brought into the inner circle. They were most often the ones who would have become rebels or bikers in the old world. When they had proven their loyalty and worth, they became Viking warriors themselves.

Jay was surprised at how quickly people accepted their new rulers. After just a matter of weeks—when the market in Tärnaby was running well—people would even defend their new way of life against any hotheads who wanted to challenge the Vikings.

People had grown up thoroughly protected by a governing state: one they unthinkingly supported and trusted. It had formed the basis of their self-identities. Being part of a benign society had made them weak. Most had little or no self-resilience. Even those who liked to think of themselves as hardy Northerners had been mollycoddled from birth. Their self-image as tough guys was mostly a show put on for their peers and to impress girls. Deep down, though, most of them were cowards. When faced with true violence—the sharp edge of a knife or sword—their veneer of toughness crumbled. Those that were truly tough either died fighting or became Viking warriors.

Jay knew that leaders would always emerge and wield power over the masses. This is the way it has been since the dawn of civilization. Rule and protect… At times he wondered what they were protecting the people from—there didn't seem to be an enemy. Deep inside, though, he knew that sooner or later one would appear, either from outside of the society they were building or from within. Somewhere there were others who had survived. They were probably organizing themselves and growing in number. One day they would come looking for land, food, or women.

When that day arrived, he would be prepared… First to defeat them, then to invade their lands and conquer them.

Through the winter and spring months, the Vikings gradually extended their control. They set up a fortified outpost in the town of Storuman where the East-West and North-South roads crossed.

The market in Tärnaby had grown too. At first, people had grumbled about the share they had to give to the Vikings, but in time, they saw it as no more than a fee to be paid for a spot in the marketplace. No worse than paying taxes in the old days, they joked.

Anyhow, they said, we're surviving, and things are getting better. Summer was coming, and with it long days of hard work in the fields and the promise of new harvests.

Epilogue

Three years later.

Jay raised his hand. "Hold up!" he ordered, and reined in his horse.

The thirty men on horseback came to a halt. Ahead of them lay the town of Umeå. It was an hour after dawn. Smoke from a few chimneys rose into the morning air.

"Lock and load!" Jay called out.

All his men were armed with either AK-5's, the Swedish Army's assault rifle or Uzi machine guns. Jay and the three Viking lords wore swords by their sides—symbols of their nobility.

The Vikings rode on towards the town center. In the distance, a few people scurried between burnt out buildings before disappearing from sight.

"They know we're here," Jay said.

The Vikings constantly checked the rooftops, windows, and doorways for any signs of ambush.

"How many?" Rat asked.

"I don't know, but we're getting close, and not many of the buildings look lived in."

The road was blocked two hundred meters ahead by cars and buses that had been parked raggedly across it.

At least fifty men stood in front of the barricade.

The Vikings rode slowly towards them.

Jay could see that the townsmen were armed. Most of them had what looked like homemade spears or pitchforks. Only a few looked as if they were carrying firearms.

Good, he thought. They must be almost out of ammunition,

otherwise more of them would have rifles and guns. It's probably most of the town's men as well.

Jay raised his arm. The Vikings drew to a halt.

In his lap he cradled his Uzi. Deliberately, he thumbed the safety to 'off'. His trigger finger rested along the side of the gun.

Six of the townsmen took a few steps forward. They were all armed with hunting rifles or shotguns.

The leaders, Jay thought. Good.

A huge man with a bald head and a thick beard took another step forward. He held a shotgun across his broad chest.

His deep voice rang out, "What do you want!"

Jay climbed off his horse. With his Uzi dangling by his side, he walked towards the man. At a sign from Rat, the other Vikings raised their weapons and took aim.

The townsmen's leader lifted his shotgun and pointed it straight at Jay. "Get out of here!" he shouted, and tensed to fire.

In that same moment Jay brought his Uzi up, firing on automatic. A hail of bullets cut into the big man and those standing beside him. They fell—dead or screaming.

"Wait!" Rat ordered the Vikings.

As Jay's Uzi came to the end of its arc, he grabbed hold of it with his other hand and swept it back in the other direction. Another volley of bullets sprayed the street in front of the townsmen.

It had happened so quickly. Even the men who had rifles hadn't had time to react. They reeled in shock from the sudden onslaught.

There was a strange moment when time seemed to stand still as both sides judged the strength of their opponents.

The sight of the armed horsemen in front of them was too much for the townsmen. They knew they didn't stand a chance. If they retaliated, they would be slaughtered.

There was only one course of action.

Heads bowed, they lay their weapons on the ground and put their hands up. Defeated, they kept their eyes down. It was behavior as old as mankind when men are beaten into submission.

Only one of them kept staring at Jay.

He was young. Maybe still a teenager.

Brave, or a fool? Jay thought as he walked towards him.

The lad's eyes glowed with hate.

Jay stopped an arm's length from him. His cold blue eyes showed no emotion.

Seeing his chance, the lad swung his fist at Jay's head.

The blow didn't land.

Jay smashed his forehead into his nose. Blood seemed to explode from his face as he crumpled to the ground.

Jay's boot slammed into his stomach. Gasping for air and crying in pain, he curled up, covering his bloody and tear-streaked face with his hands.

Jay raised his gun and pointed it at his head.

"No, please... He's my son!"

Jay shifted his gaze to look at the man who had spoken, then raised his gun so it pointed straight between his eyes.

"Please," the lad's father begged again. "Kill me instead..."

Jay didn't move for a couple of seconds. Then with the slightest of nods, he let the Uzi drop to his side.

"Rat! Gather up their weapons..."

Jay shifted his attention to the townsmen.

"You. Help the injured. Get rid of the dead. If we see anyone carrying a weapon, we'll kill you all—even the women and children. Understood?"

The men's downcast eyes told him it was.

From the mountains to the sea, the North of Sweden belonged to the Vikings.

End of Book One

Printed in Great Britain
by Amazon